The Golf Course Mystery

Chester K. Steele

Contents

THE GOLF COURSE
MYSTERY

BY

Chester K. Steele

CHAPTER I. PUTTING OUT

There was nothing in that clear, calm day, with its blue sky and its flooding sunshine, to suggest in the slightest degree the awful tragedy so close at hand--that tragedy which so puzzled the authorities and which came so close to wrecking the happiness of several innocent people.

The waters of the inlet sparkled like silver, and over those waters poised the osprey, his rapidly moving wings and fan-spread tail suspending him almost stationary in one spot, while, with eager and far-seeing eyes, he peered into the depths below. The bird was a dark blotch against the perfect blue sky for several seconds, and then, suddenly folding his pinions and closing his tail, he darted downward like a bomb dropped from an aeroplane.

There was a splash in the water, a shower of sparkling drops as the osprey arose, a fish vainly struggling in its talons, and from a dusty gray roadster, which had halted along the highway while the occupant watched the hawk, there came an exclamation of satisfaction.

"Did you see that, Harry?" called the occupant of the gray car to a slightly built, bronzed companion in a machine of vivid yellow, christened by some who had ridden in it the "Spanish Omelet." "Did you see that kill? As clean as a hound's tooth, and not a lost motion of a feather. Some sport-that fish-hawk! Gad!"

"Yes, it was a neat bit of work, Gerry. But rather out of keeping with the day."

"Out of keeping? What do you mean?"

"Well, out of tune, if you like that better. It's altogether too perfect a day for a killing of any sort, seems to me."

"Oh, you're getting sentimental all at once, aren't you, Harry?" asked Captain Gerry Poland, with just the trace of a covert sneer in his voice. "I suppose you wouldn't have even a fish-hawk get a much needed meal on a bright, sunshiny day, when, if ever, he must have a whale of an appetite. You'd have him wait until it was dark and gloomy and rainy, with a north-east wind blowing, and all that sort of thing. Now for me, a kill is a kill, no matter what the weather."

"The better the day the worse the deed, I suppose," and Harry Bartlett smiled as he leaned forward preparatory to throwing the switch of his machine's self-starter, for both automobiles had come to a stop to watch the osprey.

"Oh, well, I don't know that the day has anything to do with it," said the captain--a courtesy title, bestowed because he was president of the Maraposa Yacht Club. "I was just interested in the clean way the beggar dived after that fish. Flounder, wasn't it?"

"Yes, though usually the birds are glad enough to get a moss-bunker. Well, the fish will soon be a dead one, I suppose."

"Yes, food for the little ospreys, I imagine. Well, it's a good death to die--serving some useful purpose, even if it's only to be eaten. Gad! I didn't expect to get on such a gruesome subject when we started out. By the way, speaking of killings, I expect to make a neat one to-day on this cup-winners' match."

"How? I didn't know there was much betting."

"Oh, but there is; and I've picked up some tidy odds against our friend Carwell. I'm taking his end, and I think he's going to win."

"Better be careful, Gerry. Golf is an uncertain game, especially when there's a match on among the old boys like Horace Carwell and the crowd of past-performers and cup-winners he trails along with. He's just as likely to pull or slice as the veriest novice, and once he starts to slide he's a goner. No reserve comeback, you know."

"Oh, I've not so sure about that. He'll be all right if he'll let the champagne alone before he starts to play. I'm banking on him. At the same time I haven't bet all my money. I've a ten spot left that says I can beat you to the clubhouse, even if one of my cylinders has been missing the last two miles. How about it?"

"You're on!" said Harry Bartlett shortly.

There was a throb from each machine as the electric motors started the engines, and then they shot down the wide road in clouds of dust--the sinister gray car and the more showy yellow--while above them, driving its talons deeper into the sides of the fish it had caught, the osprey circled off toward its nest of rough sticks in a dead pine tree on the edge of the forest.

And on the white of the flounder appeared bright red spots of blood, some of which dripped to the ground as the cruel talons closed until they met inside.

It was only a little tragedy, such as went on every day in the inlet and adjacent ocean, and yet, somehow, Harry Bartlett, as he drove on with ever-increasing speed in an endeavor to gain a length on his opponent, could not help thinking of it in contrast to the perfect blue of the sky, in which there was not a cloud. Was it prophetic?

Ruddy-faced men, bronze-faced men, pale-faced men; young women, girls, matrons and "flappers"; caddies burdened with bags of golf clubs and pockets bulging with cunningly found balls; skillful waiters hurrying here and there with trays on which glasses of various shapes, sizes, and of diversified contents tinkled musically-such was the scene at the Maraposa Club on this June morning when Captain Gerry Poland and Harry Bartlett were racing their cars toward it.

It was the chief day of the year for the Maraposa Golf Club, for on it were to be played several matches, not the least in importance being that of the cup-winners, open only to such members as had won prizes in hotly contested contests on the home links.

In spite of the fact that on this day there were to be played several matches, in which visiting and local champions were to try their skill against one another, to the delight of a large gallery, interest centered in the cup-winners' battle. For it was rumored, and not without semblance of truth, that large sums of money would change hands on the result.

Not that it was gambling-oh, my no! In fact any laying of wagers was strictly prohibited by the club's constitution. But there are ways and means of getting cattle through a fence without taking down the bars, and there was talk that Horace Carwell had made a pretty stiff bet with Major Turpin Wardell as to the outcome of the match, the major and Mr. Carwell being rivals of long standing in the matter of drives and putts.

"Beastly fine day, eh, what?" exclaimed Bruce Garrigan, as he set down on a tray a waiter held out to him a glass he had just emptied with every indication of delight in its contents. "If it had been made to order couldn't be improved on," and he flicked from the lapel of Tom Sharwell's coat some ashes which had blown there from the cigarette which Garrigan had lighted.

"You're right for once, Bruce, old man," was the laughing response. "Never mind the ashes now, you'll make a spot if you rub any harder."

"Right for once? 'm always right!" cried Garrigan "And it may interest you to know that the total precipitation, including rain and melted snow in Yuma, Arizona, for the calendar year 1917, was three and one tenth inches, being the smallest in the United States."

"It doesn't interest me a bit, Bruce!" laughed Sharwell. "And to prevent you getting any more of those statistics out of your system, come on over and we'll do a little precipitating on our own account. I can stand another Bronx cocktail."

"I'm with you! But, speaking of statistics, did you know that from the national forests of the United States in the last year there was cut 840,612,030 board feet of lumber? What the thirty feet were for I don't know, but--"

"And I don't care to know," interrupted Tom. "If you spring any more of those beastly dry figures--Say, there comes something that does interest me, though!" he broke in with. "Look at those cars take that turn!"

"Some speed," murmured Garrigan. "It's Bartlett and Poland," he went on, as a shift of wind blew the dust to one side and revealed the gray roadster and the Spanish Omelet. "The rivals are at it again."

Bruce Garrigan, who had a name among the golf club members as a human encyclopaedia, and who, at times, would inform his companions on almost any subject that chanced to come uppermost, tossed away his cigarette and, with Tom Sharwell, watched the oncoming automobile racers.

"They're rivals in more ways than one," remarked Sharwell. "And it looks, now, as though the captain rather had the edge on Harry, in spite of the fast color of Harry's car."

"That's right," admitted Garrigan. "Is it true what I've heard about both of them-that each hopes to place the diamond hoop of proprietorship on the fair Viola?"

"I guess if you've heard that they're both trying for her, it's true enough," answered Sharwell. "And it also happens, if that old lady, Mrs. G. 0. 5. Sipp, is to be believed, that there, also, the captain has the advantage."

"How's that? I thought Harry had made a tidy sum on that ship-building project he put through."

"He did, but it seems that he and his family have a penchant for doing that sort of thing, and, some years ago, in one of the big mergers in which his family took a prominent part, they, or some one connected with them, pinched the Honorable Horace Carwell so that he squealed for mercy like a lamb led to the Wall street slaughter house."

"So that's the game, is it?"

"Yes. And ever since then, though Viola Carwell has been just as nice to Harry as she has to Gerry--as far as any one can tell-there has been talk that Harry is persona non grata as far as her father goes. He never forgives any business beat, I understand."

"Was it anything serious?" asked Garrigan, as they watched the racing automobiles swing around the turn of the road that led to the clubhouse.

"I don't know the particulars. It was before my time--I mean before I paid much attention to business."

"Rot! You don't now. You only think you do. But I'm interested. I expect to have some business dealing with Carwell myself, and if I could get a line--"

"Sorry, but I can't help you out, old man. Better see Harry. He knows the whole story, and he insists that it was all straight on his relatives' part. But it's like shaking a mince pie at a Thanksgiving turkey to mention the matter to Carwell. He hasn't gone so far as to forbid Harry the house, but there's a bit of coldness just the same."

"I see. And that's why the captain has the inside edge on the love game. Well, Miss Carwell has a mind of her own, I fancy."

"Indeed she has! She's more like her mother used to be. I remember Mrs. Carwell when I was a boy. She was a dear, somewhat conventional lady. How she ever came to take up with the sporty Horace, or he with her, was a seven-days' wonder. But they lived happily, I believe."

"Then Mrs. Carwell is dead?"

"Oh, yes-some years. Mr. Carwell's sister, Miss Mary, keeps The Haven up to date for him. You've been there?"

"Once, at a reception. I'm not on the regular calling list, though Miss Viola is pretty enough to--"

"Look out!" suddenly cried Sharwell, as though appealing to the two automobilists, far off as they were. For the yellow car made a sudden swerve and seemed about to turn turtle.

But Bartlett skillfully brought the Spanish Omelet back on the road again, and swung up alongside his rival for the home stretch-the broad highway that ran in front of the clubhouse.

The players who were soon to start out on the links; the guests, the gallery, and the servants gathered to see the finish of the impromptu race, murmurs arising as it was seen how close it was likely to be. And close it was, for when the two machines, with doleful whinings of brakes, came to a stop in front of the house, the front wheels were in such perfect alignment that there was scarcely an inch of difference.

"A dead heat!" exclaimed Bartlett, as he leaped out and motioned for one of the servants to take the car around to the garage.

"Yes, you win!" agreed Captain Poland, as he pushed his goggles back on his cap. He held out a bill.

"What's it for?" asked Bartlett, drawing back.

"Why, I put up a ten spot that I'd beat you. I didn't, and you win."

"Buy drinks with your money!" laughed Bartlett. "The race was to be for a finish, not a dead heat. We'll try it again, sometime."

"All right-any time you like!" said the captain crisply, as he sat down at a table after greeting some friends. "But you won't refuse to split a quart with me?"

"No. My throat is as dusty as a vacuum cleaner. Have any of the matches started yet, Bruce?" he asked, turning to the Human Encyclopedia.

"Only some of the novices. And, speaking of novices, do you know that in Scotland there are fourteen thousand, seven hundred--"

"Cut it, Bruce! Cut it!" begged the captain. "Sit in--you and Tom--and we'll make it two bottles. Anything to choke off your flow of useless statistics!" and he laughed good-naturedly.

"When does the cup-winners' match start?" asked Bartlett, as the four young men sat about the table under the veranda. "That's the one I'm interested in."

"In about an hour," announced Sharwell, as he consulted a card. "Hardly any of the veterans are here yet."

"Has Mr. Carwell arrived?" asked Captain Poland, as he raised his glass and seemed to be studying the bubbles that spiraled upward from the hollow stem.

"You'll know when he gets here," answered Bruce Garrigan.

"How so?" asked the captain. "Does he have an official announcer?"

"No, but you'll hear his car before you see it."

"New horn?"

"No, new car-new color-new everything!" said Garrigan. "He's just bought a new ten thousand dollar French car, and it's painted red, white and blue, and-"

"Red, white and blue?" chorused the other three men.

"Yes. Very patriotic. His friends don't know whether he's honoring Uncle Sam or the French Republic. However, it's all the same. His car is a wonder."

"I must have a brush with him!" murmured Captain Poland.

"Don't. You'll lose out," advised Garrigan. "It can do eighty on fourth speed, and Carwell is sporty enough to slip it into that gear if he needed to."

"Um! Guess I'll wait until I get my new machine, then," decided the captain.

There was more talk, but Bartlett gradually dropped out of the conversation and went to walk about the club grounds.

Maraposa was a social, as well as a golfing, club, and the scene of many dances and other affairs. It lay a few miles back from the shore near Lakeside, in New Jersey. The clubhouse was large and elaborate, and the grounds around it were spacious and well laid out.

Not far away was Loch Harbor, where the yachts of the club of which Captain Gerry Poland was president anchored, and a mile or so in the opposite direction was Lake Tacoma, on the shore of which was Lakeside. A rather exclusive colony summered there, the hotel numbering many wealthy persons among its patrons.

Harry Bartlett, rather wishing he had gone in for golf more devotedly, was wandering about, casually greeting friends and acquaintances, when he heard his name called from the cool and shady depths of a summer-house on the edge of the golf links.

"Oh, Minnie! How are you?" he cordially greeted a rather tall and dark girl who extended her slim hand to him. "I didn't expect to see you today."

"Oh, I take in all the big matches, though I don't play much myself," answered Minnie Webb. "I'm surprised to find you without a caddy, though, Harry."

"Too lazy, I'm afraid. I'm going to join the gallery to-day. Meanwhile, if you don't mind, I'll sit in here and help you keep cool."

"It isn't very hard to do that to-day," and she moved over to make room for him. "Isn't it just perfect weather!"

At one time Minnie Webb and Harry Bartlett had been very close friends--engaged some rumors had it. But now they were jolly good companions, that was all.

"Seen the Carwells' new machine?" asked Bartlett.

"No, but I've heard about it. I presume they'll drive up in it to-day."

"Does Viola run it?"

"I haven't heard. It's a powerful machine, some one said-more of a racer than a touring car, Mr. Blossom was remarking."

"Well, he ought to know. I understand he's soon to be taken into partnership with Mr. Carwell."

"I don't know," murmured Minnie, and she seemed suddenly very much interested in the vein structure of a leaf she pulled from a vine that covered the summer-house.

Bartlett smiled. Gossip had it that Minnie Webb and Le Grand Blossom, Mr. Carwell's private secretary, were engaged. But there had been no formal announcement, though the two had been seen together more frequently of late than mere friendship would warrant.

There was a stir in front of the clubhouse, followed by a murmur of voices, and Minnie, peering through a space in the vines, announced:

"There's the big car now. Oh, I don't like that color at all! I'm as patriotic as any one, but to daub a perfectly good car up like that--well, it's--"

"Sporty, I suppose Carwell thinks," finished Bartlett. He had risen as though to leave the summerhouse, but as he saw Captain Poland step up and offer his hand to Viola Carwell, he drew back and again sat down beside Minnie.

A group gathered about the big French car, obviously to the delight of Mr. Carwell, who was proud of the furor created by his latest purchase.

Though he kept up his talk with Minnie in the summer-house, Harry Bartlett's attention was very plainly not on his present companion nor the conversation. At any other time Minnie Webb would have noticed it and taxed him with it, but now, she, too, had her attention centered elsewhere. She watched eagerly the group about the big machine, and her eyes followed the figure of a man who descended from the rear seat and made his way out along a path that led to a quiet spot.

"I think I'll go in now," murmured Minnie Webb. "I have to see--" Bartlett was not listening. In fact he was glad of the diversion, for he saw Viola Carwell turn with what he thought was impatience aside from Captain Poland, and that was the very chance the other young man had been waiting for.

He followed Minnie Webb from the little pavilion, paying no attention to where she drifted. But he made his way through the press of persons to where Viola stood, and he saw her eyes light up as he approached. His, too, seemed brighter.

"I was wondering if you would come to see dad win," she murmured to him, as he took her hand, and Captain Poland, with a little bow, stepped back.

"You knew I'd come, didn't you?" Bartlett asked in a low voice.

"I hoped so," she murmured. "Now, Harry," she went on in a low voice, as they moved aside, "this will be a good time for you to smooth things over with father. If he wins, as he feels sure he will, you must congratulate him very heartily--exceptionally so. Make a fuss over him, so to speak. He'll be club champion, and it will seem natural for you to bubble over about it."

"But why should I, Viola? I haven't done anything to merit his displeasure."

"I know. But you remember what a touch-fire he is. He's always held that business matter against you, though I'm sure you had nothing to do with it. Now, if he wins, and I hope he will, you can take advantage of it to get on better terms with him, and--"

"Well, I'm willing to be friends, you know that, Viola. But I can't pretend--I never could!"

"You're stubborn, Harry!" and Viola pouted.

"Well, perhaps I am. When I know I'm right--"

"Couldn't you forget it just once?"

"I don't see how!"

"Oh, you provoke me! But if you won't you won't, I suppose. Only it would be such a good chance--"

"Well, I'll see him after the match, Viola. I'll do my best to be decent."

"You must go a little farther than that, Harry. Dad will be all worked up if he wins, and he'll want a fuss made over him. It will be the very chance for you."

"All right-I'll do my best," murmured Bartlett. And then a servant came up to summon him to the telephone.

Viola was not left long alone, for Captain Poland was watching her from the tail of his eye, and he was at her side before Harry Bartlett was out of sight.

"Perhaps you'd like to come for a little spin with me, Miss Carwell," said the captain. "I just heard that they've postponed the cup-winners' match an hour; and unless you want to sit around here--"

"Come on!" cried Viola, impulsively. "It's too perfect a day to sit around, and I'm only interested in my father's match."

There was another reason why Viola Carwell was glad of the chance to go riding with Captain Poland just then. She really was a little provoked with Bartlett's stubbornness, or what she called that, and she thought it might "wake him up," as she termed it, to see her with the only man who might be classed as his rival.

As for herself, Viola was not sure whether or not she would admit Captain Poland to that class. There was time enough yet.

And so, as Bartlett went in to the telephone, to answer a call that had come most inopportunely for him, Viola Carwell and Captain Poland swept off along the pleasantly shaded country road.

Left to herself, for which just then she was thankful, Minnie Webb drifted around until she met LeGrand Blossom.

"What's the matter, Lee?" she asked him in a low voice, and he smiled with his eyes at her, though his face showed no great amount of jollity. "You're as solemn as though every railroad stock listed had dropped ten points just after you bought it."

"No, it isn't quite as bad as that," he said, as he fell into step beside her, and they strolled off on one of the less-frequented walks.

"I thought everything was going so well with you. Has there been any hitch in the partnership arrangement?" asked Minnie.

"No, not exactly."

"Have you lost money?"

"No, I can't say that I have."

"Then for goodness' sake what is it? Do I have to pump you like a newspaper reporter?" and Minnie Webb laughed, showing a perfect set of teeth that contrasted well against the dark red and tan of her cheeks.

"Oh, I don't know that it's anything much," replied LeGrand Blossom.

"It's something!" insisted Minnie.

"Well, yes, it is. And as it'll come out, sooner or later, I might as well tell you now," he said, with rather an air of desperation, and as though driven to it. "Have you heard any rumors that Mr. Carwell is in financial difficulties?"

"Why, no! The idea! I always thought he had plenty of money. Not a multi-millionaire, of course, but better off financially than any one else in Lakeside."

"He was once; but he won't be soon, if he keeps up the pace he's set of late," went on LeGrand Blossom, and his voice was gloomy.

"What do you mean?"

"Well, things don't look so well as they did. He was very foolish to buy that ten-thousand-dollar yacht so soon after spending even more than that on this red, white and blue monstrosity of his!"

"You don't mean to tell me he's bought a yacht, too?"

"Yes, the Osprey that Colonel Blakeson used to sport up and down the coast in. Paid a cool ten thousand for it, though if he had left it to me I could have got it for eight, I'm sure."

"Well, twenty thousand dollars oughtn't to worry Mr. Carwell, I should think," returned Minnie.

"It wouldn't have, a year ago," answered LeGrand. "But he's been on the wrong side of the market for some time. Then, too, something new has cropped up about that old Bartlett deal."

"You mean the one over which Harry's uncle and Mr. Carwell had such a fuss?"

"Yes. Mr. Carwell's never got over that. And there are rumors that he lost quite a sum in a business transaction with Captain Poland."

"Oh, dear!" sighed the girl. "Isn't business horrid! I'm glad I'm not a man. But what is this about Captain Poland?"

"I don't know? haven't heard it all yet, as Mr. Carwell doesn't tell me everything, even if he has planned to take me into partnership with him. But now I'm not so keen on it."

"Keen on what, Lee?" and Minnie Webb leaned just the least bit nearer to his side.

"On going into partnership with a man who spends money so lavishly when he needs all the ready cash he can lay his hands on. But don't mention this to any one, Minnie. If it got out it might precipitate matters, and then the whole business would tumble down like a house of cards. As it is, I may be able to pull him out. But I've put the soft pedal on the partnership talk."

"Has Mr. Carwell mentioned it of late?"

"No. All he seems to be interested in is this golf game that may make him club champion. But keep secret what I have told you."

Minnie Webb nodded assent, and they turned back toward the clubhouse, for they had reached a too secluded part of the grounds.

Meanwhile, Viola Carwell was not enjoying her ride with Captain Poland as much as she had expected she would. As a matter of fact it had been undertaken largely to cause Bartlett a little uneasiness; and as the Seeing this, the latter changed his mind concerning something he had fully expected to speak to Viola about that day, if he got the chance.

Captain Poland was genuinely in love with Viola, and he had reason to feel that she cared for him, though whether enough to warrant a declaration of love on his part was hard to understand.

"But I won't take a chance now," mused the captain, rather moodily; and the talk descended to mere monosyllables on the part of both of them. "I must see Carwell and have it out with him about that insurance deal. Maybe he holds that against me, though the last time I talked with him he gave me to understand that I'd stand a better show than Harry. I must see him after the game. If he wins he'll be in a mellow humor, particularly after a bottle or so. That's what I'll do."

The captain spun his car up in front of the clubhouse and helped Viola out. "I think we are in plenty of time for your father's match," he remarked.

"Yes," she assented. "I don't see any of the veterans on the field yet," and she looked across the perfect course. "I'll go to look for dad and wish him luck. He always wants me to do that before he starts his medal play. See you again, Captain;" and with a friendly nod she left the somewhat chagrined yachtsman.

When Captain Poland had parked his car he took a short cut along a path that led through a little clump of bushes. Midway he heard voices. In an instant he recognized them as those of Horace Carwell and Harry Bartlett. He heard Bartlett say:

"But don't you see how much better it would be to drop it all--to have nothing more to do with her?"

"Look here, young man, you mind your own business!" snapped Mr. Carwell. "I know what I'm doing!"

"I haven't any doubt of it, Mr. Carwell; but I ventured to suggest?" went on Bartlett.

"Keep your suggestions to yourself, if you please. I've had about all I want from you and your family. And if I hear any more of your impudent talk--"

Then Captain Poland moved away, for he did not want to hear any more.

In the meantime Viola hurried back to the clubhouse, and forced herself to be gay. But, somehow, a cloud seemed to have come over her day.

The throng had increased, and she caught sight, among the press, of Jean Forette, their chauffeur.

"Have you seen my father since he arrived, Jean?" asked Viola.

"Oh, he is somewhere about, I suppose," was the answer, and it was given in such a surly tone with such a churlish manner that Viola flushed with anger and bit her lips to keep back a sharp retort.

At that moment Minnie Webb strolled past. She had heard the question and the answer.

"I just saw your father going out with the other contestants, Viola," said Minnie Webb, "for they were friends of some years' standing. I think they are going to start to play. I wonder why they say the French are such a polite race," she went on, speaking lightly to cover Viola's confusion caused by the chauffeur's manner. "He was positively insulting."

"He was," agreed Viola. "But I shouldn't mind him, I suppose. He does not like the new machine, and father has told him to find another place by the end of the month. I suppose that has piqued him."

While there were many matches to be played at the Maraposa Club that day, interest, as far as the older members and their friends were concerned, was centered in that for cup-winners. These constituted the best players--the veterans of the game--and the contest was sure to be interesting and close.

Horace Carwell was a "sport," in every meaning of the term. Though a man well along in his forties, he was as lithe and active as one ten years younger. He motored, fished, played golf, hunted, and of late had added yachting to his amusements. He was wealthy, as his father had been before him, and owned a fine home in New York, but he spent a large part of every year at Lakeside, where he might enjoy the two sports he loved best-golfing and yachting.

Viola was an only child, her mother having died when she was about sixteen, and since then Mr. Carwell's maiden sister had kept watch and ward over the handsome home, The Haven. Viola, though loving her father with the natural affection of a daughter and some of the love she had lavished on her mother, was not altogether in sympathy with the sporting proclivities of Mr. Carwell.

True, she accompanied him to his golf games and sailed with him or rode in his big car almost as often as he asked her. And she thoroughly enjoyed these things. But what she did not enjoy was the rather too jovial comradeship that followed on the part of the men and women her father associated with. He was a good liver and a good spender, and he liked to have about him such persons-men "sleek and fat," who if they did not "sleep o' nights," at least had the happy faculty of turning night into day for their own amusement.

So, in a measure, Viola and her father were out of sympathy, as had been husband and wife before her; though there had never been a whisper of real incompatibility; nor was there now, between father and daughter.

"Fore!"

It was the warning cry from the first tee to clear the course for the start of the cup-winners' match. In anticipation of some remarkable playing, an unusually large gallery would follow the contestants around. The best caddies had been selected, clubs had been looked to with care and tested, new balls were got out, and there was much subdued excitement, as befitted the occasion.

Mr. Carwell, his always flushed face perhaps a trifle more like a mild sunset than ever, strolled to the first tee. He swung his driver with freedom and ease to make sure it was the one that best suited him, and then turned to Major Wardell, his chief rival. "Do you want to take any more?" he asked meaningly.

"No, thank you," was the laughing response. "I've got all I can carry. Not that I'm going to let you beat me, but I'm always a stroke or two off in my play when the sun's too bright, as it is now. However, I'm not crawling."

"You'd better not!" declared his rival. "As for me, the brighter the sun the better I like it. Well, are we all ready?"

The officials held a last consultation and announced that play might start. Mr. Carwell was to lead.

The first hole was not the longest in the course, but to place one's ball on fair ground meant driving very surely, and for a longer distance than most players liked to think about. Also a short distance from the tee was a deep ravine, and unless one cleared that it was a handicap hard to overcome.

Mr. Carwell made his little tee of sand with care, and placed the ball on the apex. Then he took his place and glanced back for a moment to where Viola stood between Captain Poland and Harry Bartlett. Something like a little frown gathered on the face of Horace Carwell as he noted the presence of Bartlett, but it passed almost at once.

"Well, here goes, ladies and gentlemen!" exclaimed Mr. Carwell in rather loud tones and with a free and easy manner he did not often assume. "Here's where I bring home the bacon and make my friend, the major, eat humble pie."

Viola flushed. It was not like her father to thus boast. On the contrary he was usually what the Scotch call a "canny" player. He never predicted that he was going to win, except, perhaps, to his close friends. But he was now boasting like the veriest schoolboy.

"Here I go!" he exclaimed again, and then he swung at the ball with his well-known skill.

It was a marvelous drive, and the murmurs of approbation that greeted it seemed to please Mr. Carwell.

"Let's see anybody beat that!" he cried as he stepped off the tee to give place to Major Wardell.

Mr. Carwell's white ball had sailed well up on the putting green of the first hole, a shot seldom made at Maraposa.

"A few more strokes like that and he'll win the match," murmured Bartlett.

"And when he does, don't forget what I told you," whispered Viola to him.

He found her hand, hidden at her side in the folds of her dress, and pressed it. She smiled up at him, and then they watched the major swing at his ball.

"It's going to be a corking match," murmured more than one member of the gallery, as they followed the players down the field.

"If any one asked me, I should say that Carwell had taken just a little too much champagne to make his strokes true toward the last hole," said Tom Sharwell to Bruce Garrigan.

"Perhaps," was the admission. "But I'd like to see him win. And, for the sake of saying something, let me inform you that in Africa last year there were used in nose rings alone for the natives seventeen thousand four hundred and twenty-one pounds of copper wire. While for anklets--"

"I'll buy you a drink if you chop it off short!" offered Sharwell.

"Taken!" exclaimed Garrigan, with a grin.

The cup play went on, the four contestants being well matched, and the shots duly applauded from hole to hole.

The turn was made and the homeward course began, with the excitement increasing as it was seen that there would be the closest possible finish, between the major and Mr. Carwell at least.

"What's the row over there?" asked Bartlett suddenly, as he walked along with Viola and Captain Poland.

"Where?" inquired the captain.

"Among those autos. Looks as if one was on fire."

"It does," agreed Viola. "But I can see our patriotic palfrey, so I guess it's all right. There are enough people over there, anyhow. But it is something!"

There was a dense cloud of smoke hovering over the place where some of the many automobiles were parked at one corner of the course. Still it might be some one starting his machine, with too much oil being burned in the cylinders.

"Now for the last hole!" exulted Mr. Carwell, as they approached the eighteenth. "I've got you two strokes now, Major, and I'll have you fourby the end of the match."

"I'm not so sure of that," was the laughing and good-natured reply.

There was silence in the gallery while the players made ready for the last hole.

There was a sharp impact as Mr. Carwell's driver struck the little white ball and sent it sailing in a graceful curve well toward the last hole.

"A marvelous shot!" exclaimed Captain Poland. "On the green again! Another like that and he'll win the game!"

"And I can do it, too!" boasted Carwell, who overheard what was said.

The others drove off in turn, and the play reached the final stage of putting. Viola turned as though to go over and see what the trouble was among the automobiles. She looked back as she saw her father stoop to send the ball into the little depressed cup. She felt sure that he would win, for she had kept a record of his strokes and those of his opponents. The game was all but over.

"I wonder if there can be anything the matter with our car?" mused Viola, as she saw the smoke growing denser. "Dad's won, so I'm going over to see. Perhaps that chauffeur--"

She did not finish the sentence. She turned to look back at her father once more, and saw him make the putt that won the game at the last hole. Then, to her horror she saw him reel, throw up his hands, and fall heavily in a heap, while startled cries reached her ears.

"Oh! Oh! What has happened?" she exclaimed, and deadly fear clutched at her heart--and not without good cause.

CHAPTER II. THE NINETEENTH HOLE

For several seconds after Mr. Carwell fell so heavily on the putting green, having completed the last stroke that sent the white ball into the cup and made him club champion, there was not a stir among the other players grouped about him; nor did the gallery, grouped some distance back, rush up. The most natural thought, and one that was in the minds of the majority, was that the clubman had overbalanced himself in making his stance for the putt shot, and had fallen. There was even a little thoughtless laughter from some in the gallery. But it was almost instantly hushed, for it needed but a second glance to tell that something more serious than a simple fall had occurred.

Or if it was a fall caused by an unsteady position, taken when he made his last shot, it had been such a heavy one that Mr. Carwell was overlong in recovering from it. He remained in a huddled heap on the short-cropped, velvety turf of the putting green.

Then the murmurs of wonder came, surging from many throats, and the friends of Mr. Carwell closed around to help him to his feet-to render what aid was needed. Among them were Captain Poland and Harry Bartlett, and as the latter stepped forward he glanced up, for an instant, at the blue sky.

Far above the Maraposa golf links circled a lone osprey on its way to the inlet or ocean. Rather idly Bartlett wondered if it was the same one he and Captain Poland had seen dart down and kill the fish just before the beginning of the big match.

"What's the matter, Horace? Sun too much for you?" asked Major Wardell, as he leaned over his friend and rival. "It is a bit hot; I feel it myself. But I didn't think it would knock you out. Or are you done up because you beat me? Come--"

He ceased his rather railing talk, and a look came over his face that told those near him something serious had happened. There was a rush toward the prostrate man.

"Keep back, please!" exclaimed the major. "He seems to have fainted. He needs air. Is Dr. Rowland here? I thought I saw him at the clubhouse a while ago. Some one get him, please. If not--"

"I'll get him!" some one offered

"Here, give him a sip of this--it's brandy!" and an automobilist, who had come across the links from the nearest point to the highway, offered his flask.

The major unscrewed the silver top, which formed a tiny cup, and tried to let some of the potent liquor trickle between the purplish lips of the unconscious victor in the cup-winners' match. But more of the liquid was spilled on his face and neck than went into his mouth. The air reeked with the odor of it.

"What has happened? Is he hurt?" gasped Viola, who made her way through the press of people, which opened for her, till she stood close beside her father. "What is it? Oh, is he--?"

"He fell," some one said.

"Just as he made his winning stroke," added another.

"Oh!" and Viola herself reeled unsteadily.

"It's all right," a voice said in her ear, and though it was in the ordinary tones of Captain Poland, to the alarmed girl it seemed as though it came from the distant peaks of the hills. "He'll be all right presently," went on the captain, as he supported Viola and led her out of the throng.

"It's just a touch of the sun, I fancy. They've gone for a doctor."

"Oh, but, Captain Poland--father was never like this before--he was always so strong and well--I never knew him to complain of the heat. And as for fainting-- why I believe I almost did it myself, just now, didn't I?"

"Almost, yes."

"But father never did. Oh, I must go to him!"

She struggled a little and moved away from his half encircling arm, for he had seen that her strength was failing her and had supported her as he led her away. "I must go to him!"

"Better not just now," said Captain Poland gently. "Harry is there with him, the major and other friends. They will look after him. You had better come with me to the clubhouse and lie down. I will get you a cup of tea."

"No! I must be with my father!" she insisted. "He will need me when he--when he revives. Please let me go to him!"

The captain saw that it was of little use to oppose her so he led her back toward the throng that was still about the prostrate player. A clubman was hurrying back with a young man who carried a small black bag.

"They've got a doctor, I think," said Gerry. "Not Dr. Rowland, though. However, I dare say it will be all right."

A fit of trembling seized Viola, and it was so violent that, for a moment, Captain Poland thought she would fall. He had to hold her close, and he wished there was some place near at hand to which he might take her. But the clubhouse was some distance away, and there were no conveyances within call.

However, Viola soon recovered her composure, or at least seemed to, and smiled up at him, though there was no mirth in it.

"I'll be all right now," she said. "Please take me to him. He will ask for me as soon as he recovers."

The young doctor had made his way through the throng and now knelt beside the prostrate man. The examination was brief--a raising of the eyelids, an ear pressed over the heart, supplemented by the use of the stethoscope, and then the young medical man looked up, searching the ring of faces about him as though seeking for some one in authority to whom information might be imparted. Then he announced, generally:

"He is dead."

"Dead!" exclaimed several.

"Hush!" cautioned Harry Bartlett "She'll hear you!"

He looked in the direction whence Viola and Captain Poland were approaching the scene.

"Are you sure, Dr. Baird?" he asked.

"Positive. The heart action has entirely stopped."

"But might that not be from some cause--some temporary cause?"

"Yes, but not in this case. Mr. Carwell is dead. I can do nothing for him."

It sounded brutal, but it was only a medical man's plain statement of the case.

"Some one must tell her," murmured Minnie Webb, who had been attracted to the crowd, though she was not much of a golf enthusiast. "Poor Viola! Some one must tell her."

"I will," offered Bartlett, and he made his way through a living lane that opened for him. Then it closed again, hiding the body from sight. Some one placed a sweater over the face that had been so ruddy, and was now so pale.

Captain Poland, still supporting Viola on his arm, saw Bartlett approaching. Somehow he surmised what his fellow clubman was going to say.

"Oh, Harry!" exclaimed Viola, impulsively holding out her hands to him. "Is he all right? Is he better?"

"I am sorry," began Harry, and then she seemed to sense what he was going to add.

"He isn't--Oh, don't tell me he is--"

"The doctor says he is dead, Viola," answered Bartlett gently. "He passed away without pain or suffering. It must have been heart disease."

But Viola Carwell never heard the last words, for she really fainted this time, and Captain Poland laid her gently down on the soft, green grass.

"Better get the doctor for her," he advised Bartlett. "She'll need him, if her father doesn't." As Harry Bartlett turned aside, waving back the curiosity seekers that were already leaving the former scene of excitement for the latest, LeGrand Blossom came up. He seemed very cool and not at all excited, considering what had happened.

"I will look after Miss Carwell," he said.

"Perhaps you had better see to Mr. Carwell--Mr. Carwell's remains, Blossom," suggested Captain Poland. "Miss Carwell will be herself very soon. She has only fainted. Her father is dead."

"Dead? Are you sure?" asked LeGrand Blossom, and his manner seemed a trifle more naturally excited.

"Dr. Baird says so. You'd better go to him. He may want to ask some questions, and you were more closely associated with Carwell than any of the rest of us."

"Very well, I'll look after the body," said the secretary. "Did the doctor say what killed him?"

"No. That will be gone into later, I dare say. Probably heart disease; though I never knew he had it," said Bartlett.

"Nor I," added Blossom. "I'd be more inclined to suspect apoplexy. But are you sure Miss Carwell will be all right?"

"Yes," answered Captain Poland, who had raised her head after sprinkling in her face some water a caddy brought in his cap. "She is reviving."

Dr. Baird came up just then and gave her some aromatic spirits of ammonia.

Viola opened her eyes. There was no comprehension in them, and she looked about in wonder. Then, as her benumbed brain again took up its work, she exclaimed:

"Oh, it isn't true! It can't be true! Tell me it isn't!"

"I am sorry, but it seems to be but too true," said Captain Poland gently. "Did he ever speak of trouble with his heart, Viola?"

"Never, Gerry. He was always so well and strong."

"You had better come to the clubhouse," suggested Bartlett, and she went with them both.

A little later the body of Horace Carwell was carried to the "nineteenth hole"--that place where all games are played over again in detail as the contestants put away their clubs.

A throng followed the silent figure, borne on the shoulders of some grounds workmen, but only club members were admitted to the house. And among them buzzed talk of the tragedy that had so suddenly ended the day of sports.

"He looked all right when he started to play," said one. "Never saw him in better form, and some of his shots were marvelous."

"He'd been drinking a little too much for a man to play his best, especially on a hot day," ventured another. "He must have been taken ill from that, and the excitement of trying to win over the major, and it affected his heart."

"Never knew him to have heart disease," declared Bruce Garrigan.

"Lots of us have it and don't know it," commented Tom Sharwell. "I suppose it will take an autopsy to decide."

"Rather tough on Miss Carwell," was another comment.

"That's true!" several agreed.

The body of Horace Carwell was placed in one of the small card rooms, and the door locked. Then followed some quick telephoning on the part of Dr. Baird, who had recently joined the golf club, and who had arrived at the clubhouse shortly before Mr. Carwell dropped dead.

It was at the suggestion of Harry Bartlett that Dr. Addison Lambert, the Car-well family physician, was sent for, and that rather aged practitioner arrived as soon as possible.

He was taken in to view the body, together with Dr. Baird, who was almost pathetically deferential to his senior colleague. The two medical men were together in the room with the body for some time, and when they came out Viola Carwell was there to meet them. Dr. Lambert put his arms about her. He had known her all her life--since she first ventured into this world, in fact--and his manner was most fatherly.

"Oh, Uncle Add!" she murmured to him--for she had long called him by this endearing title--Oh, Uncle Add! What is it? Is my father--is he really--"

"My dear little girl, your father is dead, I am sorry to say. You must be very brave, and bear up. Be the brave woman he would want you to be."

"I will, Uncle Add. But, oh, it is so hard! He was all I had! Oh, what made him die?"

She questioned almost as a little child might have done.

"That I don't know, my dear," answered Dr. Lambert gently. "We shall have to find that out later by--Well, we'll find out later, Dr. Baird and I. You had better go home now. I'll have your car brought around. Is that--that Frenchman here--your chauffeur?"

"Yes, he was here a little while ago. But I had rather not go home with him--at least, unless some one else comes with me. I don't like--I don't like that big, new car."

"If you will come with me, Viola--" began Bartlett.

"Yes, Harry, I'll go with you. Oh, poor Aunt Mary! This will be a terrible shock to her. I--"

"I'll telephone," offered Dr. Lambert. "She'll know when you arrive. And I'll be over to see you, Viola, as soon as I make some arrangements."

"And will you look after--after poor father?"

"Yes, you may leave it all to me."

And so, while the body of the dead clubman remained at the nineteenth hole, Viola Carwell was taken to 'The Haven' by Harry Bartlett, while Captain Poland, nodding farewell to LeGrand Blossom and some of his other friends, left the grounds in his gray car.

And as he rode down past the inlet where the tide was now running out to the sea, he saw an osprey dart down and strike at an unseen fish.

But the bird rose with dripping pinions, its talons empty.

"You didn't get any one that time!" murmured the captain.

CHAPTER III. "WHY?"

Through the silent house echoed the vibration of the electric bell, sounding unnecessarily loud, it seemed. The maid who answered took the caller's card to Miss Mary Carwell, Viola's aunt.

"He wants to see Miss Viola," the servant reported. "Shall I tell her?"

"You had better, yes. She went to lie down, but she will want to see Captain Poland. Wait, I'll tell her myself. Where is he?"

"In the library, ma am.

"Very well. I'll see him."

Mr. Carwell's sister literally swept down the stairs, her black silk dress rustling somberly and importantly. She was a large woman, and her bearing and air were in keeping. "It was very good of you to come," she murmured, as she sank, with more rustling and shimmerings, into a chair, while the captain waited for her to be settled, like a boat at anchor, before he again took his place. "Viola will be down presently. I gave her a powder the doctor left for her, and she slept, I hope, since we were both awake nearly all of last night."

"I should imagine so. The strain and shock must have been intense. But please don't disturb her if she is resting. I merely called to see if I could do anything."

"Thank you so much. We are waiting for the doctors' report. It was necessary to have an autopsy, I understand?" she questioned.

"Yes. The law requires it in all cases of sudden and mysterious death."

"Mysterious death, Captain Poland!"

Mary Carwell seemed to swell up like a fretful turkey.

"Well, by that I mean unexplained. Mr. Carwell dropped dead suddenly and from no apparent cause."

"But it was heart disease--or apoplexy--of course! What else could it be?"

"It must have been one or the other of those, Miss Carwell, I am sure," the captain murmured sympathetically. "But the law requires that such a fact be established to the satisfaction of the county physician."

"And who is he?"

"Dr. Rowland."

"Will there be a coroner's inquest, such as I have read about? I couldn't hear anything like that."

"It is not at all necessary, Miss Carwell," went on the captain. "The law of New Jersey does not demand that in cases of sudden and unexplained death, unless the county physician is not satisfied with his investigation. In that matter New Jersey differs from some of the other states. The county physician will make an autopsy to determine the cause of death. If he is satisfied that it was from natural causes he gives a certificate to that effect, and that ends the matter."

"Oh, then it will be very simple."

"Yes, I imagine so. Dr. Rowland will state that your brother came to his death from heart disease, or from apoplexy, or whatever it was, and then you may proceed with the funeral arrangements. I shall be glad to help you in any way I can."

"It is very kind of you. This has been so terrible--so sudden and unexpected. It has perfectly unnerved both poor Viola and myself, and we are the only ones to look after matters."

"Then, let me help," urged Captain Poland. "I shall only be too glad. The members of the golf club, too, will do all in their power. We had a meeting this morning and passed resolutions of sympathy. I have also called a meeting of our yacht club, of which your brother was a member. We will take suitable action."

"Thank you. And when do you think we may expect the certificate from Dr. Rowland?"

"Very soon. He is performing the autopsy now, at the club. Dr. Lambert and Dr. Baird are with him. It was thought best to have it there, rather than at the undertaking rooms."

"I shall be glad when matters can proceed as they ought to proceed. This publicity is very distasteful to me."

"I can readily believe that, Miss Carwell. And now, if you will ask Miss Viola if I may be of any service to her, I shall--"

"Before I call her, there is one matter I wish to ask you about," said Mr. Carwell's sister. "You are familiar with business, I know. I was going to ask Mr. Bartlett, as this seemed more in his line, but perhaps you can advise me."

"I shall do my best, Miss Carwell. What is it?"

"One of the clerks came from my brother's office this morning with a note from the bank. It seems that Horace borrowed a large sum for some business transaction, and put up as collateral certain bonds. He often does that, as I have heard him mention here time and again to Mr. Blossom, when they sat in consultation in the library.

"But now it appears, according to the note from the bank, that more securities are needed. There has been a depreciation, or something--I am not familiar with the terms. At any rate the bank sends word that it wants more bonds. I was wondering what I had better do. Of course I have securities in my own private box that I might send, but--"

"Why didn't Mr. Blossom attend to this?" asked Captain Poland, a bit sharply, it would have seemed to a casual listener. "That was his place. He knows all about Mr. Carwell's affairs."

"I asked the clerk from the office why Mr. Blossom--did you ever hear such an absurd name as he has?--LeGrand Blossom--I asked the clerk why the matter was not attended to," went on Miss Carwell, "and he said Mr. Blossom must have forgotten it."

"Rather odd," commented the captain. "However, I'll look after it for you. If necessary, I'll loan the bank enough additional securities as collateral to cover the loan. Don't let it disturb you, Miss Carwell. It is merely a small detail of business that often crops up. Securities in these days so often fluctuate that banks are forced to call for more, and different ones, to cover loans secured by them. I'll attend to the matter for you."

"Thank you so much. And now I believe I may safely call Viola. She would not forgive me if she knew you had been here and she had not seen you to thank you for your care of her yesterday."

"Oh, that was nothing. I was very glad--"

Captain Poland was interrupted by a ring at the door.

"Perhaps that is a message from the doctors now," suggested Miss Carwell.

"It is Dr. Lambert himself," announced the captain, looking from a window that gave a view of the front porch. "Dr. Baird is with him. They must have completed the autopsy. Shall I see them for you?"

"Please do. And please tell me at once that everything is all right, and that we may proceed with the funeral arrangements," begged the sister of the dead man.

"I will do so, Miss Carwell."

Captain Poland, anticipating the maid, went into the hall and himself opened the door for the medical men.

"Oh! I'm glad you're here!" exclaimed the rather gruff voice of Dr. Lambert. "Yes, I'm glad you're here." The captain was on the point of asking why, when Dr. Lambert motioned to him to step into a little reception room off the main hall. Somewhat wonderingly, Captain Poland obeyed, and when the door had closed, shutting him in with the two doctors, he turned to the older physician and asked:

"Is anything the matter?"

"Well, we have completed the autopsy," said Dr. Lambert.

"That's good. Then you are ready to sign a certificate, or at least get Dr. Rowland to, so that we can proceed with the arrangements. Miss Mary Carwell is anxious to have--"

"Well, I suppose the funeral will have to be held," said Dr. Lambert slowly. "That can't be held up very long, even if it was worse than it is."

"Worse than it is! What do you mean?" cried Captain Poland sharply. "Is there any suspicion--"

"There is more than suspicion, my dear sir," went on Dr. Lambert, as he sank into a chair as though very, very tired. "There is, I regret to say, certainty."

"Certainty of what?"

"Certainty that my old friend, Horace Carwell, committed suicide!"

"Suicide!"

"By poisoning," added Dr. Baird, who had been anxious to get in a word. "We found very plain evidences of it when we examined the stomach and viscera."

"Poison!" cried Captain Poland. "A suicide? I don't believe it! Why should Horace Carwell kill himself? He hadn't a reason in the world for it! There must be some mistake! Why did he do it? Why? Why?"

And then suddenly he became strangely thoughtful.

CHAPTER IV. VIOLA'S DECISION

That is the very question we have been asking ourselves, my dear Captain," said Dr. Lambert wearily. "And we are no nearer an answer now than, apparently, you are. Why did he do it?"

The three men, two gravely professional, one, the younger, more so than his elder colleague, and the third plainly upset over the surprising news, looked at one another behind the closed door of the little room off the imposing reception hall at The Haven. They were in the house of death, and they had to do with more than death, for there was, in the reputed action of Horace Carwell, the hint of disgrace which suicide always engenders.

"I suppose," began Captain Poland, rather weakly, "that there can be no chance of error He looked from one medical man to the other.

"Not the least in the world!" quickly exclaimed Baird. "We made a most careful examination of the deceased's organs. They plainly show traces of a violent poison, though whether it was irritant or one of the neurotics, we are not yet prepared to say."

"It couldn't have been an irritant," said Dr. Lambert gently. It was as though he had corrected a too zealous student reciting in class. Dr. Baird was painfully young, though much in earnest.

"Perhaps not an irritant," he agreed. "Though I know of no neurotic that would produce such effects as we saw.

"You are right there," said Dr. Lambert. "Whatever poison was used it was one the effects of which I have never seen before. But we have not yet finished our analysis. We have only reached a certain conclusion that may ultimately be changed."

"You mean as to whether or not it was suicide?" asked Captain Poland eagerly.

"No, I don't see how we can get away from that," said Dr. Lambert. "That fact remains. But if we establish the kind of poison used it may lead us to the motive. That is what we must find."

"And we will find the kind of poison!" declared Dr. Baird.

The older medical man shook his head.

"There are some animal and vegetable poisons for which there is no known test," he said gently. "It may turn out to be one of these."

"Then may it not develop that Mr. Carwell, assuming that he did take poison, did it by mistake?" asked the captain.

"I hope so," murmured Dr. Lambert.

"But from the action of the poison, as shown by the condition of the mucous coat of the alimentary canal, I hardly see how Mr. Carwell could not have known that he took poison," declared Dr. Baird.

"Yet he seemed all right except for a little pardonable exhilaration during the game of golf," remarked Captain Poland. "He was feeling 'pretty good' as we say. I don't see how he could have taken poison knowingly or unknowingly."

"There are some poisons which, taken in combination, might mix and form a comparatively harmless mixture," said Dr. Lambert. "Though I confess this is a very remote possibility. Some poisons are neutralized by an alcoholic condition. And some persons, who may have been habitual users of a drug, may take a dose of it that would kill several persons not so addicted."

"Do you mean that Mr. Carwell was a drug user?" demanded the captain.

"I would hesitate very long before saying so," answered Dr. Lambert, "and I have known him many years."

"Then what was it? What in the world does it all mean?" asked Captain Poland. "What's the answers in other words?"

"I wish I knew," replied Dr. Lambert, and he shook his head. Something more than the weight of years seemed bowing him down. Dr. Baird seemed duly impressed by the circumstances that had brought him--a young and as yet unestablished physician--to a connection with such a startling case in the well known and wealthy Carwell family.

As for Captain Gerry Poland, he was clearly startled by the news the physicians had brought. He looked toward the closed door as though seeking to see beyond it-

-into the room where Viola was waiting. To her, sooner or later, the tragic verdict must be told.

"Can't you say anything?" he asked, a bit sharply, looking from one physician to the other "Is this all you came to tell--that Mr. Carwell was a suicide? Isn't there any mitigating circumstance?"

"I believe he poisoned himself before he began his championship game," said Dr. Baird, with startling frankness--almost brutal it seemed.

"But why should he do such a thing?" demanded the captain, rather petulantly.

"He may have taken some dope, thinking would brace him up," went on the young medical man, "and it had the opposite effect--a depressing action on the heart. Or, he may have taken a overdose of his favorite drug. That is what shall have to find out by making suitable inquiries of members of the family."

"Oh, must we tell-them," exclaimed Captain Poland in startled tones. And it was easy to determine by his voice that by "them" he meant Viola. "Must we tell?" he repeated.

"I must do my duty as a physician both to the public and to the family," said Dr. Lambert, and he straightened up as though ready to assume the burden he knew would fall heavily on his shoulders. "I must also think of Viola. I feel like another father to her now. I have always, more or less, regarded her as my little girl, though she is a young lady now. But the facts must come out. Even if I were disposed to aid in a concealment--which I am far from doing--Dr. Rowland, the county physician, was present at the autopsy. He knows."

"Does he know the poison used?" asked Captain Poland quickly, and then, almost as soon as the words had left his lips, he seemed sorry he had uttered them.

"No, no more than we," said Dr. Baird. "It will require some nice work in medical jurisprudence, and also a very delicate analysis, to determine that. I am inclined to think--"

But what he thought no one heard or cared to hear at that moment, for, even as he spoke, the door of the little room was thrown hastily and somewhat violently open, and Viola Carwell confronted the three men. Her face showed traces of grief, but it had lost little of the beauty for which she was noted.

Tall and dark, with hair of that blue--black sheen so rarely observed, with violet eyes and a poise and grace that made her much observed, Viola Carwell was at the height of her beauty. In a sense she had the gentle grace of her mother and with that the verve and sprightliness of her father mingled perfectly. It was no wonder that Captain Poland and Harry Bartlett and many others, for that matter, were rivals for her favors.

"I thought you were here," she said quietly to Dr. Lambert. "Oh, Uncle Add, what is it? Tell me the truth!" she begged as she placed a hand on his arm, a hand that trembled in spite of her determination to remain calm. "Please tell me the truth!"

"The truth, Viola?" he questioned gently.

"Yes. I'm afraid you are trying to keep something back from me. This looks like it--you men in here talking--consulting as to what is best to do. Tell me. My father is dead. But that, I know, is not the worst that can happen. Tell me! Is there-is there any disgrace? I know--"

Viola stopped as though she herself feared the words she was about to utter. Dr. Lambert quickly spoke.

"There has been no disgrace, my dear Viola," he said, gently. "We have just come from the--from having made an investigation--Dr. Baird and myself and Dr. Rowland. We discovered that your father was poisoned, and--"

"Poisoned?" she gasped, and started back as though struck, while her rapid glances went from face to face, resting longest on the countenance of Captain Poland. It was as though, in this great emergency, she looked to him for comfort more than to the old doctor who had ushered her into the world.

"I am sorry to have to say it, Viola, but such is the case," went on the family physician. "Your father was poisoned. But the kind of poison we have not yet determined."

"But who gave it to him?" she cried. "Oh, it doesn't seem that any one would hate him so, not even his worst enemy. And he had so many friends-too many, perhaps."

"We don't know that any one gave him the poison, Viola," said Dr. Lambert, gently. "In fact, it does not seem that any one did, or your father would have known it. Certainly if any one had tried to make him take poison there would have been a struggle that he would have mentioned. But he died of poison, nevertheless."

"Then there can be but one other explanation," she murmured, and her voice was tense and strained. "He must have--"

"We fear he took it himself," blurted out Dr. Baird, in spite of the warning look cast at him by his colleague.

"Oh, I won't believe that! It can't be true!" cried Viola, and she burst into a storm of sobs. Dr. Lambert placed his arms about her.

"Tell me it isn't true, Uncle Add! Tell me it isn't true!" she sobbed.

The three men, looking at one another--Dr. Lambert's glance coming over the bowed head of Viola--said nothing for a few moments. Then as her sobs died away, and she became calmer, the old physician said:

"You must not take on so, Vi. I know it is hard, but you must meet the issue squarely. At the same time you must realize that even the most suspicious circumstances may be explained away. While it does look as though your father had deliberately taken the poison, it may easily be established by an investigation that it was an accident--an accident of which even your father was ignorant."

"There are so many poisons that do not manifest themselves for a long time-- often days--after they are taken, that there is every chance of proving this to have been an accident."

"Then there must be an investigation!" was Viola's quick decision. There were still tears in her eyes, but she looked through them now, as through a veil that must be torn aside. "I can not believe that my father was a--a suicide--" she halted at the awful word. "I will not believe it!" she went on more firmly. "It can not be true!"

Hardly had she uttered the last word than a figure passed through the hall, flitting past the half-opened door of the little room where Viola stood with the three men.

"Who is there?" she called sharply, for she had spoken rather loudly, and she did not want any of the servants to hear. "Who is there?"

"It is I--Minnie," was the answer. "Dear Viola, I have come to see if I could do anything. I rang and rang, but no one answered the bell, and, as the door was open, I walked in."

"I'm afraid I didn't close it when I let you in," said Captain Poland to Dr. Lambert.

"Dear Viola!" said Minnie Webb, as she placed cheek against that of her friend.

"Is there anything I can do in your terrible trouble? Please let me do something!"

"Thank you, Minnie. You are very kind. I don't know. We are in such distress. Tell me--" and Viola seemed to nerve herself for some effort. "Tell me! Did you hear what I said just now--as you passed the door?"

"Do you mean about not believing that your father was a suicide?" asked Minnie, in a low voice.

"Yes."

"I--I heard you."

"Then the only thing you can do is to help me prove otherwise," said Viola. "That would be the greatest help. It can't be true, and we want that made plain. Father never killed himself. He was not that kind of man. He did not fear death, but he would not go deliberately to meet it. It is not true that he killed himself!" and Viola's voice seemed to ring out.

A strange look came over the face of Minnie Webb. There was a great pity shining in her eyes as she said:

"I--I am sorry, Viola, but--but I am afraid it may be true."

"What! That my father committed suicide?"

"Yes," whispered Minnie. "I--I'm afraid it may be true!"

CHAPTER V. HARRY'S MISSION

Minnie Webb's announcement affected her four hearers in four different ways. It shocked Viola--shocked her greatly, for she had, naturally, expected kindly sympathy and agreement from her friend.

Dr. Baird, who had involuntarily begun to twist his small mustache at the entrance of Miss Webb, looked at her in admiration of her good looks and because she upheld a theory to which he felt himself committed--a theory that Mr. Carwell was a plain out-and-out suicide.

Dr. Lambert was plainly indignant at the bald manner in which Minnie Webb made her statement, and at the same time he had pity for the ignorance of the lay mind that will pronounce judgment against the more cautious opinions of science. And this was not the first poisoning case with which the aged practitioner had dealt.

As for Captain Poland, he gazed blankly at Miss Webb for a moment following her statement, and then he looked more keenly at the young woman, as though seeking to know whence her information came.

And when Viola had recovered from her first shock this was the thought that came to her:

"What did Minnie know?"

And Viola asked that very question--asked it sharply and with an air which told of her determination to know.

"Oh, please don't ask me!" stammered Minnie Webb. "But I have heard that your father's affairs are involved, Viola."

"His affairs? You mean anything in his--private life?" and the daughter of Horace Carwell--"Carwell the sport," as he was frequently called--seemed to feel this blow more than the shock of death.

"Oh, no, nothing like that!" exclaimed Minnie, as though abashed at the mere suggestion. "But I did hear--and I can not tell where I heard it--that he was involved financially, and that, perhaps--well, you know some men have a horror of facing the world poor and--"

"That can't be true!" declared Viola stoutly. "While I do not know anything about my father's financial affairs, I know he had no fear of failure--no fear of becoming poor."

"I do not believe he would have feared to face poverty if there was need. But there was not, I'm sure. Minnie, who told you this?"

"I--I can not tell!" said Minnie, with a memory of the insinuating manner in which LeGrand Blossom had spoken. Bearing in mind her promise to him not to mention the matter, she began to wish that she had not spoken.

"But you must tell!" insisted Dr. Lambert. "This amounts to an accusation against a dead man, and you owe it to Viola to give the source of your information."

"No, Doctor, I can not! Please don't ask me, Viola. Oh, I shouldn't have spoken, but I thought only to help you solve the problem."

"You have only made it harder, unless you tell us more," said Dr. Lambert gently. "Why can not you tell us, Miss Webb?"

"Because I--I promised not to. Oh, can't you find out for yourselves--in your own way, about his affairs? Surely an examination--"

"Yes, of course, that would be the proper way," said Dr. Lambert gravely. "And it must be done, I suppose."

"It will lead to nothing--it will prove nothing," insisted Viola. "I am sure my father's affairs were not involved. Wait, I'll call Aunt Mary. She was in close touch with all the money matters of our household. Father trusted her with many business matters. Call Aunt Mary!"

Her eyes red with weeping, but bearing up bravely withal, Miss Mary Carwell joined the conference. She, it seemed, had guessed something when Dr. Lambert and Dr. Baird were closeted so long with Captain Poland.

"We must face the facts, however unpleasant they are," said Dr. Lambert, in a low voice. "We must recognize that this will be public talk in a little while. A man--so well-known a character as was my old friend Horace Carwell--can not die suddenly in the midst of a championship golf game, and let the matter rest there."

"The papers will take it up," said Dr. Baird.

"The papers!" broke in Viola.

"Yes, even now I have been besieged by reporters demanding to know the cause of death. It will have to come out. The report of the county physician, on which only a burial certificate can be obtained, is public property. The bureau of vital statistics is open to the public and the reporters. There is bound to be an inquiry, and, as I have said, Dr. Rowland has already announced it as a suicide. We must face the issue bravely."

"But even if it should prove true, that he took the poison, I am sure it will turn out to be a mistake!" declared Viola. "As for my father's affairs being in danger financially--Aunt Mary, did you ever hear of such a thing?"

"Well, my dear, your father kept his affairs pretty much to himself," was the answer of her aunt. "He did tell me some things, and only to-day something came up that makes me think--Oh, I don't know what to think--now!"

"What is it?" asked Dr. Lambert, quietly but firmly. "It is best to know the worst at once."

"I can't say that it is the 'worst,'" replied Miss Carwell; "but there was something about a loan to the bank, and not enough collateral to cover--Mr. Blossom should have attended to it, but he did not, it seems, and--Won't you tell them?" she appealed to Captain Poland.

"Certainly," he responded. "It is a simple matter," he went on. "Mr. Carwell, as all of us do at times, borrowed money from his bank, giving certain securities as collateral for the loan.

"The bank, as all banks do, kept watch this security, and when it fell in market value below a certain point, where there was no longer sufficient margin to cover the loan safely, demanded more collateral.

"This, for some reason, Mr. Carwell did not put up, nor did his clerk, Mr. Blossom. I know nothing more in this respect than Miss Carwell told me," and he bowed to indicate the dead man's sister. "I offered to see to the matter for her, putting up some collateral of my own until Mr. Carwell's affairs could be straightened out. It is a mere technicality, I imagine, and can have nothing to do with--with the present matter, even though Miss Webb seems to think so."

"Oh, I am so sorry if I have made a mistake!" exclaimed Minnie, now very penitent. "But I only thought it would be helping--"

"It will be--to know the truth," said Dr. Lambert. "Is this all that you heard, Miss Webb?"

"No, it was nothing like that. It had nothing to do with a bank loan. Oh, please don't ask me. I promised not to tell."

"Very well, we won't force you to speak," said the family physician. "But this matter must be gone into. What one person knows others are sure to find out. We must see Blossom. He is the one who would have the most complete knowledge of your father's affairs, Viola. Did I hear something about his going into partnership with your father?"

"Yes, there was some such plan. Father decided that he needed help, and he spoke of taking in Mr. Blossom. I know no more than that," Viola answered.

"Then LeGrand Blossom is the person to throw more light on that subject," said Dr. Lambert.

To himself he added a mental reservation that he did not count much on what information might come from the head clerk. Blossom, in the mind of Dr. Lambert, was a person of not much strength of character. There had been certain episodes in his life, information as to which had come to the physician in a roundabout way, that did not reflect on him very well; though, in truth, he felt that the man was weak rather than bad.

"Then is it to be believed that my father was a suicide?" asked Viola, as though seeking to know the worst, that she might fight to make it better.

"On the bare facts in the case--yes," answered Dr. Lambert. "But that is only a starting point. We will make no hard and fast decision."

"Indeed we will not," declared Viola. "There must be a most rigid investigation."

And when the others had gone, Dr. Lambert to make funeral arrangements for his old friend, Captain Poland to see the bank officials, Dr. Baird to his office, taking Minnie Webb home in his car, and Miss Garwell to her room to lie down, Viola, left alone, gave herself up to grief. She felt utterly downcast and very much in need of a friend.

And perhaps this feeling made her welcome, more cordially than when she had last seen him, Harry Bartlett, who was announced soon after the others left.

"Oh, Harry, have you heard the terrible news?" faltered Viola.

"You mean about your father? Yes," he said gently. "But I do not believe it. I may as well speak plainly, Viola. Your father, for some reason best known to himself, did not care for me. But I respected him, and in spite of a feeling between us I admired him. I feel sure he did not commit suicide."

"But they say it looks very suspicious, Harry! Oh, tell me what to do!" and, impulsively, Viola held out her hands to him. Bartlett pressed them warmly.

"I'll serve you in any way I can," he said, gazing fondly into her eyes. "But I confess I am puzzled. I don't know what to do. Perhaps it would be better, as Dr. Lambert says, to look into your father's affairs."

"Yes. But I want more than that!" declared Viola. "I want his name cleared from any suspicion of suicide. And I want you to undertake it, Harry!"

"You want me?" he exclaimed, drawing back. "Me?"

"Yes. I feel that you will do better than any one else. Oh, you will help me, won't you?" she pleaded.

"Of course, Viola. But I don't know how."

"Then let me tell you," and she seemed to be in better control of herself than at any time that day. "This must be gone into systematically, and we can best do it through a detective."

"A detective!" cried Harry Bartlett, and he started from his chair. "Why, my dear Viola, a detective would be the worst possible person to call in on a case like this! Let me investigate, if you think it wise, but a detective--"

"I am not speaking of an ordinary detective, Harry. I have in mind an elderly man who was a friend of my father. He has an extraordinary reputation for solving mysteries."

"Well, of course, if you know the man it makes a difference." Bartlett eyed the girl curiously. "I didn't know you knew any detectives."

"The man I have in mind was in some business deal with my father once, and they became very well acquainted. I met him several times, and liked him immensely. He is well along in years, but I think sharper than many younger men. But there is one difficulty."

"What is that?"

"More than likely he will shy at having anything to do with the case. He told my father he was going to retire and devote his leisure time to fishing--that being his great pastime."

"Humph! he can't be much of a detective if he wants to spend most of his time fishing," was Bartlett's comment.

"You're mistaken, Harry. My father, and other men too, considered him one of the greatest detectives in the world, even though he sometimes works in a very peculiar and apparently uninterested manner." "All right then, Viola. If you say so, I'll look up this wonderful detective for you and get him to take hold of the case."

CHAPTER VI. BY A QUIET STREAM

Drooping willows dipped their pendant branches in the stream that foamed and rippled over green, mossy stones. In a meadow that stretched fair and wide on either side of the water, innumerable grasshoppers were singing their song of summer. On a verdant bank reclined a man, whose advanced age might be indicated in his whitening locks, but whose bright eyes, and the quick, nervous movements as he leafed the pages of a small, green-covered book, made negative the first analysis. A little distance from him, where the sun beat down warmly, unhindered by any shade, lolled a colored man whose look now and then strayed to the reading figure.

A glance over the shoulder of the reader, were one so impolite as to take that liberty, would have disclosed, among others, this passage on the printed page:

"But yet you are to note, that as you see some willows or palm trees bud and blossom sooner than others do, so some trouts be, in rivers, sooner in season; and as some hollies or oaks are longer before they cast their leaves, so are some trouts in rivers longer before they go out of season."

The gray-haired man closed the book, thereby revealing the title "Walton's Compleat Angler," and looked across the stream. The sunlight flickered over its rippling surface, and now and then there was a splash in the otherwise quiet waters--a splash that to the reader was illuminating indeed.

"Shag!" he suddenly exclaimed, thereby galvanizing into life the somnolent negro.

"Yes, sah, Colonel! Yes, sah!" came the response.

"Hum! Asleep, weren't you?"

"Well, no, sah. Not zactly asleep, Colonel. I were jest takin' the fust of mab forty winks, an'--"

"Well, postpone the rest for this evening. I think I'll make some casts here. I don't expect any trout, my friend Walton to the contrary. Besides they're out of season now. But I may get something. Get me the rod, Shag!"

"Yes, sah, Colonel! Yes, sah!"

And while the fishing paraphernalia was being put in readiness by his colored servant, Colonel Robert Lee Ashley once more opened the little green book, as though to draw inspiration therefrom. And he read:

"Only thus much is necessary for you to know, and to be   mindful and careful of, that if the pike or perch do breed   in that river, they will be sure to bite first and must   first be taken. And for the most part they are very large."

"Well, large or small, it doesn't much matter, so I catch some," observed the colonel.

Then he carefully baited the hook, after he had taken the rod and line from Shag, who handled it as though it was a rare object of art; which, indeed, it was to his master.

"I think we shall go back with a fine mess of perch, Shag," observed the fisherman.

"Yes, sah, Colonel, dat's what we will," was the cheerful answer.

"And this time we won't, under any consideration, let anything interfere with our vacation, Shag."

"No, sah, Colonel. No, sah!"

"If you see me buying a paper, Shag, mind, if you ever hear me asking if the last edition is out, stop me at once."

"I will, Colonel."

"And if any one tries to tell me of a murder mystery, of a big robbery, or of anything except where the fish are biting best, Shag, why, you just--"

"I'll jest natchully knock 'em down, Colonel! Dat's what I'll do!" exclaimed the colored man, as cheerfully as though he would relish such "Well, I can't advise that, of course," said the colonel with a smile, "but you may use your own judgment. I came here for a rest, and I don't want to run into another diamond cross mystery, or anything like it."

"No, sah, Colonel. But yo' suah did elucidate dat one most expeditious like. I nevah saw sech--"

"That will do now, Shag. I don't want to be reminded of it. I came here to fish, not to work, nor hold any post-mortems on past cases. Now for it!" and the elderly man cast in where a little eddy, under the grassy bank, indicated deep water, in which the perch or other fish might lurk this sunny day.

And yet, in spite of his determination not to recall the details of the diamond cross mystery to which Shag had alluded, Colonel Ashley could not help dwelling on one or two phases of what, with justifiable pride, he regarded as one of the most successful of his many cases.

Colonel Robert Lee Ashley was a detective by instinct and profession, though of late years he had endeavored, but with scant success, to turn the more routine matters of his profession over to his able assistants.

To those who have read of his masterly solution of the diamond cross mystery the colonel needs no introduction. He was a well known character in police and criminal circles, because of his success in catching many a slippery representative of the latter.

He had served in the secret service during the Spanish-American war, and later had become the head of the police department of a large Eastern city. From that he had built up a private business of his own that assumed large proportions, until advancing age and a desire to fish and reflect caused him virtually to retire from active work. And now, as he had so often done before, he had come to this quiet stream to angle.

And yet, even as he dropped his bait into the water, he could not keep his active mind from passing in rapid review over some of the events of his career--especially the late episode of the Darcy diamond cross.

"Well, I'm glad I helped out in that case," mused the colonel, as he sat up more alertly, for there came a tremor to his line that told much to his practiced and sensitive hands.

A moment later the reel clicked its song of a strike, and the colonel got first to his knees and then to his feet as he prepared to play his fish.

"I've hooked one, Shag!" he called in a low but tense voice. "I've hooked one, and I think it's a beauty!"

"Yes, sah, Colonel! Yes, sah! Dat's fine! I'll be ready as soon as yo' is!"

Shag caught up a landing net, for, though the colonel was not anticipating any gamy fish in this quiet, country stream, yet for such as he caught he used such light tackle that a net was needed to bring even a humble perch to shore.

"I've got him, Shag! I've got him!" the colonel cried, as the fish broke water, a shimmering shower of sparkling drops falling from his sides. "I've got him, and it's a bass, too! I didn't think there were any here! I've got him!"

"Yes, sah, Colonel! Yo' suah has!" exclaimed the delighted George Washington Shag. "You suah has got a beauty!"

And as Shag started forward with the landing net, while the colonel was playing with the skill of long years of practice the fish which had developed unexpected fighting powers, there was a movement among the bushes that lined the stream below the willows, and a young man, showing every evidence of eagerness, advanced toward the fisherman. Shag saw him and called:

"Keep back! Keep back, sah, if yo' please! De Colonel, he's done got a bite, an'--"

"Bite! You mean that something's bitten him?" asked the young man, for he could not see the figure of the colonel, who, just then, in allowing the bass to have a run, had followed him up stream.

"No, he's catchin' a fish--he's got a strike--a big one! Don't isturb him."

"But I must see him. I've come a long distance to--"

"Distance or closeness don't make no mattah of diffunce to de colonel when he's got a bite, sah! I'm sorry, but I can't let yo' go any closer, an' I'se got to go an' land de fish. Aftah dat, if you wants to hab a word wif de colonel, well, maybe he'll see yo', sah," and Shag, with a warning gesture, like that of a traffic policeman halting a line of automobiles, started toward the colonel, who was still playing his fish.

Harry Bartlett, for he it was who had thus somewhat rudely interrupted the detective's fishing, stopped in the shade of the willows, somewhat chagrined. He had come a long way for a talk, and now to be thus held back by a colored man who seemed to have no idea of the importance of the mission was provoking.

But there was something authoritative in Shag's manner, and, being a business man, Harry Bartlett knew better than to make an inauspicious approach. It would be as bad as slicing his golf ball on the drive.

So he waited beside the silent stream, not so silent as it had been, for it was disturbed by the movements, up and down, of Colonel Ashley, who was playing his fish with consummate skill.

Seeing a little green book on the grass where it had fallen, Harry Bartlett picked it up. Idly opening the pages, he read:

"There is also a fish called a sticklebag, a fish without   scales, but he hath his body fenced with several prickles.   I know not where he dwells in winter, nor what he is good   for in summer, but only to make sport for boys and women anglers, and to feed other fish that be fish of prey, as   trout in particular, who will bite at him as at a penk, and   better, if your hook be rightly baited with him; for he may   be so baited, as, his tail turning like a sail of a   windmill, will make him turn more quick than any penk or   minnow can."

"I guess I've got the right man," said Harry Bartlett with a smile.

CHAPTER VII. THE INQUEST

R eady, now, Shag! Ready!" called Colonel Ashley, in tense tones. "Ready
with the net!"

"Yes, sah! All ready!"

"I've got him about ready for you! And he's better than I thought!"

"Yes, sah, Colonel! I won't miss!"

"If you do you may look for another place!" At this dire threat Shag turned as
white as he would ever become, and took a firmer grip on the "Ready now, Shag!"
called the colonel, at the same time directing his helper to come down the bank
toward a little pool whither he was leading the now well-played fish. "Ready!"

Shag did not speak, but while the colonel slowly reeled in and the tip of the
slender pole bent like a bow, he slipped the net into the water, under the fish, and,
a moment later, had it out on the grass.

"There!" exclaimed the famous detective, with a sigh of relief. "There he is, and
as fine a fish as I've ever landed in these parts! Now, Shag--"

But there came an interruption. Reasoning that now was a most propitious
time to make his appeal, Harry Bartlett advanced to where the colonel and Shag
were bending over the panting bass. As the detective, with a smart blow back of its
head, put his catch out of misery, Bartlett spoke.

"Excuse me," he said, deferentially enough, for he saw the type of man with
whom he had to deal, "but are you not Colonel Ashley?"

"I am, sir!" and the colonel looked up as he slipped the fish into his grass-lined
creel.

"I am Mr. Bartlett. I followed you here from New York, and I wish to--"

"If it's anything about business, Mr. Bartlett, let me save your time and my
own--both valuable, I take it--by stating that I came here to fish, and not to talk

business. Excuse me for putting it thus bluntly, but I see no reason for many words. I can not consider any business. That is all attended to at my New York office, and I am surprised that they should even have given you my address. I told them not to."

"It was no easy matter to get it, Colonel, I assure you," and--Bartlett smiled genially. "And please don't blame any one in your office for disclosing your where-abouts. I did not get your address from them, I assure you."

"From whom, then, if I may ask?"

"From Spotty." And again Bartlett smiled.

"What? Spotty Morgan?"

"Yes."

"Are you--do you know him?" and the detective could not keep the interest out of his voice.

"Rather well. I saved him from drowning once some years ago, and he hasn't forgotten it. It was at a summer resort, and Spotty, though he is a good swimmer, didn't estimate the force of the undertow. I pulled him out just in time."

"Strange," murmured the colonel. "A strange coincidence."

"I beg pardon," said Harry politely.

"Oh, nothing," went on the detective. "Only, as it happens, Spotty saved my life some time ago. It's just a coincidence, that's all. So Spotty gave you my address, did he?"

"Yes. I had called at your New York office, and, as you say, your clerks had orders not to disclose your whereabouts. I used every cajolery and device of which I was master, but it was no avail. I urged the importance it was to myself and others to know where you were, but they were obdurate. I was coming out, much disap-pointed, when I saw Spotty emerging from an inner office. He knew me at once, though it is years since we met, and going down in the elevator I mentioned that I was looking for you. I told him something of the reason for wanting to find you and--Well, he told me you were here."

"And he is about the only person in New York outside of my most confidential man who could have done that," observed the colonel, as he slowly reeled up his line. "One reason why the clerks in my office could not give you my address was because they did not have it. So Spotty, who must just have finished his bit, told."

"But please don't hold that against him," urged Bartlett. "If he violated a confidence--"

"He did, in a way, yes," observed the disciple of Izaak Walton. "But I shall have to forgive him, I suppose. It must have been rather a strong reason that induced him to tell you where I had gone."

"It was, Colonel Ashley, the strongest reason in the world. It is to help clear up the mystery--"

"Stop!" fairly shouted the colonel. "If it's a detective case I don't want to hear it! Not a word! Shag, show this gentleman the door--I beg your pardon, I didn't mean to be rude," went on the colonel with his usual politeness. "But I really can not listen. I came here to rest and fish, not to take up new detective cases. You know where my office is. They will attend to you there. I have given up business for the time being."

"And yet, Colonel Ashley, the person who sent me will have no one but you. She says you are the only one who can get at the bottom of the puzzling case."

In spite of himself the colonel's face lighted up at the words "puzzling case," but as his eyes fell on the creel containing his fish he turned aside. "No," he said, "I am sorry, but I can not listen to you. Shag, kindly--"

Harry Bartlett was not a successful business man for nothing. He knew how to make an appeal. "I came to see you at the request of Miss Viola Carwell," he said slowly. "She sent me to find you--told me not to come back to her without you. A change came over the colonel's face at the mention of Viola's name.

"You came from her--from the daughter of Horace Carwell?" he asked quickly.

"I did," answered Bartlett.

"Well, of course, that might make a difference. I hope my old friend is not in trouble--nor his daughter," and there was a new quality in the voice.

"Mr. Carwell's troubles are all over--if he had any," returned Bartlett simply.

"You mean--"

"He is dead."

The colonel uttered an exclamation.

"Pardon my rather brusk reception of you," he apologized. "I did not know that. Was it recently--suddenly?"

"Both recently and suddenly."

"I did not know that I seldom read the papers, and have not looked at one lately. I had not heard that he was ill."

"'He wasn't, Colonel Ashley. Mr. Carwell died very suddenly on the Maraposa Golf Club links, after making a stroke that gave him the championship."

"Heart disease or apoplexy?"

"Neither one. It was poison."

"You amaze me, Mr.--er--Mr.--"

"Bartlett. Yes, Mr. Carwell died of poison, as the autopsy showed."

"'Was he--did he--"

"That is what we want to find out," interrupted the messenger eagerly. "The county physician says Mr. Carwell is a suicide. His daughter, Miss Viola, can not believe it. Nor can I. There has been some talk that his affairs are involved. As you may have known, he was somewhat of a--"

"His sporting proclivities were somewhat different from mine," said the old detective dryly. "You needn't explain. Every man must live his own life. But tell me more."

Thereupon Bartlett gave the details as he knew them, bearing on the death of the father of the girl he loved.

"And she sent you to find me?" asked the detective.

"Yes. Miss Viola said you were an old friend of her father's, and if any one could solve the mystery of his death you could. For that there is a mystery about it, many of us believe."

"There may be. Poison is always more or less of a mystery. But just what do you want me to do?"

"Come back with me if you will, Colonel Ashley. Miss Carwell wants you to aid her--aid all of us, for we are all at sea. Will you? She sent me to plead with you. I went to your New York office, and from Spotty Morgan learned you were here. I--"

"I suppose I shall have to forgive Spotty," murmured the fisherman.

"They told me at the hotel you had come here," went on Bartlett, "so I followed. I was lucky in finding you."

"I don't know about that," murmured the colonel, smiling. "It may be unfortunate. Well, I am deeply shocked at my old friend's death--and such a tragic taking off. Horace Carwell was my very good friend. He once did me a great service, when I needed money badly, by helping me make an investment in copper that turned out extremely well. I feel myself under obligations to him; and, since he is no more, I must transfer that obligation to his daughter."

"Then you'll come with me to see her, Colonel Ashley?"

"Yes. Shag, pack up! We're going back to civilization."

The colored man's face was a study. He looked at the quiet stream, at the drooping willows, at the fish rod in his master's hand, and at the creel. He opened his mouth and spoke:

"But, Colonel, yo' done tole me t'--"

"No matter what I told you, Shag, these are new orders. Pack up!" came the crisp command. "We're going back to town. I'll do what I can in this case," he went on to Bartlett. "I came here for some quiet fishing, and to get my mind off detective work. I was dragged into a diamond cross mystery not long since, sorely against my will, and now--"

"I am sorry--" began Bartlett.

"Oh, well, it can't be helped," the colonel said. "I'd give up more than a fishing trip for a daughter of Horace Carwell. You may let her know that I'll come, if it will give her any comfort. Though, mind you," the colonel's manner was impressive, "I promise nothing."

"That is understood," said Bartlett eagerly. "I'll wire her that you are coming. There's a train that leaves right after supper. We can get that--"

"I'll take it!" decided the colonel. Now that he had given up his cherished fishing he was all business again. "Shag!"

"Yes, sah, Colonel!"

"Pack up for the evening train. Give that fish to the cook and have it served for Mr. Bartlett and myself. You'll dine with me," he went on. It was an order, not an invitation, but Bartlett understood, and accepted with a bow.

A few hours later he and the colonel left the little town where the detective had gone for such a short vacation, and were on their way to Lakeside, which they reached early in the morning.

"Now if you'll tell me the best hotel to stop at here," said the colonel, as they alighted from the train, "I'll put up there and see Miss Carwell."

"She requested me to bring you at once to her home," said Bartlett. "You are to be her guest. She thought perhaps you would want to examine the-- to see Mr. Carwell's body--before--"

"Oh, yes. I suppose I had better. Then the funeral has not been held?"

"No, it was postponed at the request of the county physician."

"Has there been a coroner's inquest?"

"No. None was deemed necessary at the time I left, at the solicitation of Miss Carwell, to get you."

"I see. Inquests are less often held in New Jersey than in some of the other states. Well, then I suppose I may as well go to the Carwell home with you."

"Yes. I wired for my car to meet us. It's here I see. Right over here."

Bartlett led the way, the colonel following, and Shag bringing up the rear with the bags.

As the machine started from the station Bartlett looked up to the morning sky. There was a little speck in it, no larger than a man's hand. It grew larger, and became an osprey on its way to the sea in search of a fish.

As the car drew up in front of the Carwell mansion, from the bell of which fluttered a dismal length of crepe, a man stepped from the shadow of the gate posts and held out a paper to Harry Bartlett.

"What is it?" asked Bartlett.

"A subpoena," was the rather gruff answer.

"A subpoena? What for?"

"The coroner's inquest. You'll have to appear and give evidence. They're going to have an inquest to find out more about Mr. Carwell's death. That's all I know. I'm from police headquarters. I was told to wait around here, as you were expected, and to serve that on you. Don't forget to be there. It's a court order," and the man slunk away.

"An inquest," murmured Bartlett, as he looked at the paper in his hand. "I thought they weren't going to have any," and he glanced quickly at Colonel Ashley.

CHAPTER VIII. ON SUSPICION

Colonel Robert Lee Ashley was used to surprises. This was natural, considering his calling, and at some of the surprises he was a silent spectator, while at others he furnished the surprise. In this case he served in his former capacity, merely noting the rather startled look on the face of Harry Bartlett when handed the subpoena to the coroner's inquest.

"I thought they weren't going to have any," Bartlett repeated, but whether to himself in a sort of daze, to Colonel Ashley, or to the man from headquarters was not clear. At any rate Colonel Ashley answered him by saying:

"You never can tell what Jersey justice is going to do. Coroner's inquests are not usual in this state, but they are lawful."

"But why do they consider one necessary?" asked Bartlett, as they prepared to enter the house of death.

"That, my dear sir, I don't know. Perhaps the county physician may have requested it, or the prosecutor of the pleas. He may want to be backed up by the verdict of twelve men before taking any action."

"But if Mr. Carwell's death was due to suicide who can be held guilty but himself?"

"No one. But I thought you said there was a doubt as to its being suicide," commented the detective.

"Miss Carwell doubts," returned Bartlett; "and I admit that it does seem strange that a man of Mr. Carwell's character would do such a thing, particularly when he had shown no previous signs of being in trouble. But you can never tell."

"No, you can never tell," agreed Colonel Ashley, and none knew, better than himself, how true that was.

"But why should they subpoena me?" asked Bartlett.

"Don't fret over that," advised his companion, with a calm smile. "You probably aren't the only one. A coroner's inquest is, as some one has said, a sort of fishing excursion. They start out not expecting much, not knowing what they are going to get, and sometimes they catch nothing--or no one--and again, a big haul is made. It's merely a sort of clearing house, and I, for one, will be glad to listen to what is brought out at the hearing."

"Well, then I suppose it will be all right," assented the young man, but the manner in which he looked again at the legal document was distinctly nervous.

"Had we better tell--her?" and he motioned to the house, on the steps of which they stood, Shag having pressed the bell for his master.

"Miss Carwell probably knows all about it," said Colonel Ashley.

They found Viola waiting for them in the library, passing on their way the darkened and closed room which held all that was mortal of the late owner of The Haven--no, not quite all of him, for certain portions were, even then, being subjected to the minute and searching analysis of a number of chemists, under the direction of the county prosecutor.

"It was very good of you to come, Colonel Ashley," said Viola quietly. "I appreciate it more than I can express--at this time."

"I'm very glad to come," said the colonel as he held her hand in his warm, firm clasp. "I am only sorry that it was necessary to send for me on such an occasion. Believe me, I will do all I can for you, Miss Carwell. Your father was my very good friend."

"Thank you. What most I want is to clear my father's name from the imputation of having--of having killed himself," and she halted over the words.

"You mean that you suspect--" began Colonel Ashley.

"Oh, I don't know what to think, and certainly I don't dare suspect any one!" exclaimed Viola. "It is all so terrible! But one thing I would like all father's friends to know--that he did not take his own life. He would not do such a thing."

"Then," said Colonel Ashley, "we must show that it was either an accident--that he took the fatal dose by mistake or that some one gave it to him. Forgive me for thus brutally putting it, but that is what it simmers down to."

"Yes, I have thought of that," returned Viola, and her shrinking form and the haunted look in her eyes told what an ordeal it was for her. "I leave it all to you,

Colonel Ashley. Father often spoke of you, and he often said, if ever he had any mystery to clear up, that you were the only man he would trust. Now that I am alone I must trust you," and she smiled at the colonel. It was something of her former smile--a look that had turned many a man's head, some even as settled in life and years as Colonel Ashley.

"Well, I'll do my best for the sake of you and your father," replied the detective. "I don't mind saying that I hoped I was done with all mystery cases, but fate seems to be against me.

"Mind, I am not complaining!" he said quickly, as he saw Viola about to protest. "It's just my luck. And I can't promise you anything. From what Mr. Bartlett told me, there seem to be very few suspicious circumstances connected with the case."

"I realize that," answered Viola. "And that makes it all the stranger. But tell me, Colonel, haven't you often found that the cases which, at first, seemed perfectly plain and simple, afterward turned out to be the most mysterious?"

"Jove, but that's true!" exclaimed the former soldier. "You spoke the truth then, Miss Viola. My friend Izaak never put a statement more plainly. And that's the theory I always go on. Now then, let me have all the facts in your possession. And you too," he added, turning to Bartlett. "You might remain while Miss Carwell talks to me, and you can add anything she may forget, while she can do the same in your case. I suppose you know there is to be a coroner's inquest?" he added to the girl.

"Yes," she answered. "I have received a subpoena. I think it is well to have it, for it will show the public how mistaken a verdict arrived at when all the facts are not known may be. I shall attend."

"I just received a summons," said Bartlett, and he seemed to breathe more easily.

"Shag--Where's that black boy of mine?" exclaimed the colonel.

"I sent him to the servants' quarters," said Miss Mary Carwell, coming in just then. "How do you do, Colonel Ashley. I don't know whether you remember me, but--"

"Indeed I do. And I remember that the last time I dined with you we had chicken and waffles that--well, the taste lingers yet!" and the colonel bowed gallantly, which seemed to please Miss Carwell very much indeed. "So you have looked after Shag, have you?"

"Yes. We have plenty of spare rooms, and I thought you'd want him near you."

"I want him this moment," said the detective. "If you will be so good as to send him here I'll get him to open my bag and take out a note-book I wish to use."

A little later Colonel Ashley had thrown himself heart and soul into the "Golf Course Mystery," as he marked it on a page in his note-book.

On the preceding page were the last entries in a case, the beginning of which was inscribed "The Diamond Cross Mystery." It was thus that Colonel Ashley kept the salient facts of his problems before him as he worked.

Between them Viola Carwell and Harry Bartlett told the colonel such facts leading up to the death of Mr. Carwell as they knew. They spoke of the day of the big golf matches, and the exhilaration of Mr. Carwell as he anticipated winning the championship contest.

The scene at the links was portrayed, the little excitement among the parked cars, caused, as developed later, by a blaze in a machine standing next the big red, white, and blue car belonging to Mr. Carwell, and then the sudden collapse of Carwell as he make his winning stroke. The finding of some peculiar poison in the stomach and viscera of the dead man was spoken of, and then Viola made her appeal again for a disclosure of such truth as Colonel Ashley might reveal.

"I'll do my best," he promised. "But I believe it will be better to wait until after the inquest before I take an active part. And I think I can best work if I remain unknown--that is if it is not published broadcast that I am here in my official capacity."

To this Viola and Bartlett agreed. As neither of them had, as yet, spoken of bringing the colonel into the case, it was a comparatively easy matter to pass him off as an old friend of the family; which, in truth, he was.

So Colonel Ashley was given the guest chamber, Shag was provided with comfortable quarters, and then Viola seemed more content.

"I know," she said to her aunt, "that the truth will be found out now."

"But suppose the truth is more painful than uncertainty, Viola?"

"How can it be?" asked the girl, as tears filled her eyes.

"I don't know," answered Miss Carwell softly. "It is all so terrible, that I don't believe it can be any worse. But we must hope for the best. I trust business matters will go along all right. I confess I don't like the forgetting, on the part of LeGrand Blossom, of attending to the bank matter."

"It was probably only an oversight."

"Yes. But it has started a rumor that your poor father's affairs might not be in the best shape. Oh, dear, it's all so terrible!"

But there were other terrors to come.

Following his plan of acting merely as a guest and an old friend of the family who had journeyed from afar to attend the funeral, Colonel Ashley went about as silent as though on a fishing trip. He looked and listened, but said little. He was not yet ready for a cast. He was but inspecting the stream--several streams, in fact, to see where he could best toss in his baited hook.

And it was in this same spirit that he attended the coroner's inquest, which was held in the town hall. Over the deliberations, which were, at best, rather informal, Coroner Billy Teller presided.

The office of coroner was, in Lakeside, as in most New Jersey cities or towns, much of an empty title. At every election the names of certain men were put on the ticket to be voted for as coroners.

Few took the trouble to ballot for them, scarcely any one against them, and they were automatically inducted into office by reason of a few votes.

Just what their functions were few knew and less cared. There used to be a rumor, perhaps it is current yet in many Jersey counties, that a coroner was the only official who could legally arrest the sheriff in case that official needed taking into custody. As to the truth of this it is not important.

Certain it is that Billy Teller had never before found himself in such demand and prominence. He was to act in the capacity of judge, though the verdict in the case, providing one could be returned, would be given by the jury he might impanel.

There was a large throng in attendance at the town hall when the inquest began. Reporters had been sent out by metropolitan papers, for Horace Carwell was a well known figure in the sporting and the financial world, and the mere fact that there was a suspicion that his death was not from natural causes was enough to make it a good story.

Billy Teller was, frankly, unacquainted with the method of procedure, and he confessed as much to the prosecutor, an astute lawyer. As the latter would have the conducting of the case for the state in case it came to a trial in the upper courts, Mr. Stryker saw to it that legal forms were followed in the selection of a jury and the swearing in of the members of the panel. Then began the taking of testimony.

The doctors told of the finding of evidences of poison in Mr. Carwell's body. Its nature was as yet undetermined, for it was not of the common type.

This much Dr. Lambert stated calmly, and without attempting to go into technical details. Not so Dr. Baird. He spoke learnedly of Reinsch's test for arsenic, of Bloxam's method, of the distillation process. He juggled with words, and finally, when pinned down by a direct but homely question from Billy Teller, admitted that he did not know what had killed Mr. Carwell.

Testimony to the same effect was given by several chemists who had analyzed the stomach and viscera of the dead man. There was a sediment of poison present, they admitted, and sufficient had been extracted in a free state to end the lives of several guinea pigs on which it had been tested. But as to the exact nature of the poison they could not yet say. More time for analysis was needed.

It was certain that Mr. Carwell had come to his death by an active agent in the nature of some substance, as yet unknown, which he either swallowed purposely, by accident, or because some one gave it to him either knowingly or unknowingly. This was a sufficiently broad hypothesis on which to base almost anything, thought Colonel Ashley, as he sat and listened in the corner of the improvised courtroom.

There was a stir of excitement and anticipation when Viola was called, but beyond testifying that her father was in his usual health when he went with her to the golf game, she could throw no light on the puzzle, nor could the dead man's sister or any of the servants.

"Call Jean Forette," said the prosecutor, and the chauffeur, a decidedly nervous man on whom the excitement of testifying plainly told, came to the stand.

He made a poor showing, and there were several whispers that ran around the courtroom, but poor Jean's rather distressing manner was improved when Mr. Stryker took him in hand to question him. The prosecutor, observing that the man was more frightened than anything else, soon put him at his ease, and then the witness told a clear and connected story. He admitted frankly that because he had not the faculty, or, perhaps, the desire to drive the big, new car, he and his late employer were to part company at the end of the month. That was no secret, and there were no hard feelings on either side. It was in the course of business, and natural.

Yes, he had driven Mr. Carwell and his daughter to the links that day in the big red, white and blue machine. Mr. Carwell had been in his usual jolly spirits, and had greeted several acquaintances on the road. Had they stopped at any place? Oh, yes. The golfer was thirsty, and halted at a roadhouse for a pint of champagne--his favorite wine. Jean had alighted from the car to get it for him, and Viola, recalled to the stand, testified that she had seen her father drink some of the bubbling liquor. It was obvious why she had not spoken of it before, and that point was not pressed. It was known she did not share her father's love for sports and high living.

A little delay was caused while the innkeeper was sent for, but pending his arrival some other unimportant witnesses were called, among them Major Wardell, who was Mr. Carwell's rival in the golf game.

Had he heard his friend speak of feeling ill? No, not until a moment before the final stroke was made. Then Mr. Carwell had said he felt "queer," and had acted as though dizzy. The major, who was himself quite a convivial spirit, attributed it to some highballs he and his friend had had in the clubhouse just prior to the game.

Mr. Carwell had drunk nothing during his round of golf, and had associated during the progress of the game with no one except the players who were with him from the start to the finish. He was not seen to have taken any tablets or powders that might have contained poison, and a thorough search of his person and clothing after his death had revealed nothing.

At this point the innkeeper appeared. He testified to having served Mr. Carwell's chauffeur with a pint of champagne which Jean Forette was seen to carry directly from the cafe to the waiting automobile. The champagne was from a bottle newly opened, and the innkeeper himself had selected a clean glass and carefully washed it before pouring in the wine. He knew Mr. Carwell was fastidious about such matters, as he had often spent many hours in the roadhouse.

"LeGrand Blossom!"

Now something might come out. It was known that Blossom was Mr. Carwell's chief clerk, and more than one person knew of the impending partnership, for Mr. Carwell was rather talkative at times.

"Mr. Blossom," asked the prosecutor, after some preliminary questions, "it has been intimated--not here but outside--that the financial affairs of Mr. Carwell were not in such good shape as might be wished. Do you know anything about this?"

"I do, sir.

"Tell what you know."

"I know he was hard pushed for money, and had to get loans from the bank and otherwise."

"Was that unusual?"

"Yes, it was. Before he bought the big car and the yacht he carried a good balance. But I told him--"

"Never mind what you told him or he told you. That is not admissible under the circumstances. Just tell what you know."

"Well, then I know that Mr. Carwell's affairs were in bad shape, and that he was trying to raise some ready cash."

"How do you know this?"

"Because he asked me to put a large sum into his business and become a member of the firm."

"He asked you to invest money and become a partner?"

"Yes."

"Well, that is not unusual, is it? Many a business man might do the same if he wanted to branch out, mightn't he?"

"Yes. But before this Mr. Carwell had offered to take me into partnership without any advance of money on my part. Then he suddenly said he needed a large sum. He knew I had inherited eleven thousand dollars and had, moreover, made from investments."

"And did you agree to it?"

"I said I'd think it over. I was to give him my answer the day he died."

"Did you?"

"No."

"What would have been your answer?"

"It would have been 'no.' I didn't think I wanted to tie up with a man who was on the verge of ruin; and if you ask me I'll say I think he committed suicide because he was on the verge of financial ruin and couldn't face the music, and--"

"That will do!" came sternly from the prosecutor. "We didn't ask your opinion as to the suicide theory, and, what is more, we don't want it. I ask, your honor," and he turned to Billy Teller, who was secretly delighted at being thus addressed, "that the last remark of the witness be stricken from the record."

"Rub it out," ordered the coroner, looking over at the stenographer; and the latter, with a smile, ran his pen through the curious hooks and curves that represented the "opinion" of LeGrand Blossom.

He was allowed to leave the stand, and Harry Bartlett was called next. He nodded and smiled at Viola as he walked forward through the crowd, and Captain Poland, who was sitting in front, waved his hand to his rival. For the young men were friends, even if both were in love with Viola Carwell.

"Mr Bartlett," began the prosecutor, after some unimportant preliminary questions, "I have been informed that you had a conversation with Mr. Carwell shortly before his death. Is that true?"

"Yes, we had a talk."

Viola started at hearing this--started so visibly that several about her noticed it, and even Colonel Ashley turned his head.

"What was the nature of the talk?" asked Mr. Stryker.

"That I can not tell," said Bartlett firmly. "But it had nothing to do with the matter in hand."

There was a rustle of expectancy on hearing this, and the prosecutor quickly asked:

"What do you mean by 'the matter in hand'?"

"Well, his death."

"Naturally you didn't talk about his death, for it hadn't taken place," said Mr. Stryker. "Nor could it have been foreseen, I imagine. But what did you talk about?"

"I decline to answer."

There was a gasp that swept over the courtroom, and Billy Teller banged the gavel as he had seen real judges do.

"You decline to answer," repeated the prosecutor. "Is it on the ground that it might incriminate you?"

"No."

"Then I must insist on an answer. However, I will not do so now, but at the proper time. I will now ask you one other question, and I think you will answer that. Did you resume friendly relations with Mr. Carwell after your quarrel with him that day?" and Mr. Stryker fairly hurled the question at Harry Bartlett.

If this was a trap it was a most skillfully set one. For there must be an answer, and either no or yes would involve explanations.

"Answer me!" exclaimed the prosecutor. "Did you make up after the quarrel?"

There was a tense silence as Bartlett, whose face showed pale under his tan, said:

"I did not."

"Then you admit that you had a quarrel with Mr. Carwell?"

"Yes, but--"

Just at this moment Viola Carwell fainted in the arms of her aunt, the resultant commotion being such that an adjournment was taken while she was carried to an anteroom, where Dr. Lambert attended her.

"We will resume where we left off," said the prosecutor, when Bartlett again took the stand, and it might have been noticed that during the temporary recess one of the regular court constables from the county building at Loch Harbor remained close at his side. "Will you now state the nature of your quarrel with Mr. Carwell?" asked Mr. Stryker.

"I do not feel that I can."

"Very well," was the calm rejoinder. "Then, your honor," and again Billy Teller seemed to swell with importance at the title, "I ask that this witness be held without bail to await a further session of this court, and I ask for an adjournment to summon other witnesses."

"Granted," replied Teller, who had been coached what to answer.

"Held!" exclaimed Bartlett, as he rose to his feet in indignation. "You are going to hold me! On what grounds?"

"On suspicion," answered the prosecutor.

"Suspicion of what?"

"Of knowing something concerning the death of Mr. Carwell."

An exclamation broke from the crowd, and Bartlett reeled slightly. He was quickly approached by the same constable who had remained at his side during the recess, and a moment later Coroner Billy Teller adjourned court.

CHAPTER IX. 58 C. H.--I6I*

There was considerable excitement when it became known to the crowd, as it speedily did, that Harry Bartlett, almost universally accepted as the fiance of Viola Carwell, had been held as having vital knowledge of her father's death. Indeed there were not a few wild rumors which insisted that he had been held on a charge of murder.

"Oh, I can't believe it! I can't believe it!" exclaimed Viola, when they told her. "It can't be possible that they can hold him on such a charge. It's unfair!"

"Perhaps," gently admitted Dr. Lambert. "The law is not always fair; but it seeks to know the truth."

Viola and her aunt were again in the room where Viola had been revived from her indisposition caused by the shock of Bartlett's testimony. Colonel Ashley, who, truth to tell, had been expecting some such summons, went with Dr. Lambert.

"Oh, isn't it terrible, Colonel?" began Viola. "Have they a right to--to lock him up on this charge?"

"It isn't exactly a charge, Viola, my dear, and they have, I am sorry to say, a right to lock him up. But it will not be in a cell."

"Not in a--a cell?"

"No, as a witness, merely, he has a right to better quarters; and I understand that he will be given them on the order of the prosecutor."

"He'll be in jail, though, won't he?"

"Yes; but in very decent quarters. The witness rooms are not at all like cells, though they have barred windows."

"But why can't he get out on bail?" asked Viola, rather petulantly. "I'm sure the charge, absurd as it is, is not such as would make them keep him locked up without being allowed to get bail. I thought only murder cases were not bailable."

"That is usually the case," said Colonel Ashley. "But if this is not a suicide case it is a murder case, and though Harry is not accused of murder, in law the distinction is so fine that the prosecutor, doubtless, feels justified in refusing bail."

"But we could give it--I could--I have money!" cried Viola. "Aunt Mary has money, too. You'd go his bail, wouldn't you?" and the girl appealed to her father's sister.

"Well, Viola, I--of course I'd do anything for you in the world. You know that, dearie. But if the law feels that Harry must be locked up I wouldn't like to interfere."

"Oh, Aunt Mary!"

"Besides, he says he did quarrel with your father," went on Miss Carwell. "And he won't say what it was about. I don't want to talk about any one, Vi, but it does look suspicious for Mr. Bartlett."

"Oh, Aunt Mary! Oh, I'll never forgive you for that!" and poor Viola broke into tears.

They left the courtroom and returned to The Haven. Harry Bartlett sent a hastily written note to Viola, asking her to suspend judgment and trust in him, and then he was taken to the county jail by the sheriff--being assured that he would be treated with every consideration and lodged in one of the witness rooms.

"Isn't there some process by which we could free him?" asked Viola. "Seems to me I've heard of some process--a habeas corpus writ, or something like that."

"Often persons, who can not be gotten out of the custody of the law in any other way, may be temporarily freed by habeas corpus proceedings," said Colonel Ashley. "In brief that means an order from the court, calling on the sheriff, or whoever has the custody of a prisoner, to produce his body in court. Of course a live body is understood in such cases.

"But such an expedient is only temporary. Its use is resorted to in order to bring out certain testimony that might be the means of freeing the accused. In this case, if Harry persisted in his refusal not to tell about the quarrel, the judge would have no other course open but to return him to jail. So I can't see that a habeas corpus would be of any service."

"In that case, no," sighed Viola. "But, oh, Colonel Ashley, I am sure something can be done. You must solve this mystery!"

"I am going to try, my dear Viola. I'll try both for your sake and that of the memory of your father. I loved him very much."

The day passed, and night settled down on the house of death. Throughout Lakeside and Loch Harbor, as well as the neighboring seaside places, talk of the death of Mr. Carwell under suspicious circumstances multiplied with the evening editions of many newspapers.

Colonel Ashley in his pleasant room at The Haven--more pleasant it would have been except for the dark chamber with its silent occupant--was putting his fishing rod together. There came a knock on the door, and Shag entered.

"Oh!" he exclaimed at the sight of the familiar equipment. "Is we--is yo' done on dish yeah case, Colonel?"

"No, Shag. I haven't even begun yet."

"But--"

"Yes, I know. I've just heard that there's pretty good fishing at one end of the golf course that's so intimately mixed up in this mystery, and I don't see why I shouldn't keep my hand in. Come here, you black rascal, and see if you can make this joint fit any better. Seems to me the ferrule is loose."

"Yes, sah, Colonel, I'll 'tend to it immejite. I--er I done brung in--you ain't no 'jections to lookin' at papers now, has you?" he asked hesitatingly. For when he went fishing the mere sight of a newspaper sometimes set Shag's master wild.

"No," was the answer. "In fact I was going to send you out for the latest editions, Shag."

"I'se done got 'em," was the chuckling answer, and Shag pulled out from under his coat a bundle of papers that he had been hiding until he saw that it was safe to display them.

And while Shag was occupied with the rod, the colonel read the papers, which contained little he did not already know.

The next day he went fishing.

It was on his return from a successful day of sport, which was added to by some quiet and intensive thinking, that Viola spoke to him in the library. The colonel laid aside a paper he had been reading, and looked up.

In lieu of other news one of the reporters had written an interview with Dr. Baird, in which that physician discoursed learnedly on various poisons and the tests for them, such as might be made to determine what caused the death of Mr. Car-well. The young doctor went very much into details, even so far as giving the various chemical symbols of poison, dwelling long on arsenious acid, whose symbol, he told the reporter, was As_2O_5, while if one desired to test the organs for traces of strychnine, it would be necessary to use "sodium and potassium hydroxide, ammonia and alkaline carbonate, to precipitate the free base strychnine from aqueous solutions of its salts as a white, crystalline solid," while this imposing formula was given:

$$C_{21}H_{22} + NaOH \quad C_{21}H_{22} + H_2O + NaNO_3.$$

And so on for a column and a half.

"Oh, Colonel! Have you found out anything yet?" the girl besought.

"Nothing of importance, I am sorry to say."

"But you are working on it?"

"Oh, yes. Have you anything to tell me?"

"No; except that I am perfectly miserable. It is all so terrible. And we can't even put poor father's body in the grave, where he might rest."

"No, the coroner is waiting for permission from the prosecutor. It seems they are trying to find some one who knows about the quarrel between Harry and your father."

"I don't believe there was a quarrel--at least not a serious one. Harry isn't that kind. I'm sure he is not guilty. Harry Bartlett had nothing to do with his death. If my father was not a suicide--"

"But if he was not a suicide, for the sake of justice and to prove Harry Bartlett innocent, we must find out who did kill your father," said the colonel.

"You don't believe Harry did it, do you?" Viola asked appealingly.

Colonel Ashley did not answer for a moment. Then he said slowly:

"My dear Viola, if some one were ill of a desperate disease, in which the crisis had not yet been passed, you would not expect a physician to say for certainty that such a person was to recover, would you?"

"No."

"Well, I am in much the same predicament. I am a sort of physician in this mystery case. It has only begun. The crisis is still far off, and nothing can be said with certainty. I prefer not to express an opinion."

"I'm not afraid!" cried Viola. "I know Harry Bartlett is not guilty!"

"If he is not--who then?" asked the colonel.

"Oh, I don't know! I don't know what to think! I suspect--No, I mustn't say that--Oh, I'm almost distracted!" And, with sobs shaking her frame, Viola Carwell rushed from the room.

Colonel Ashley looked after her for a moment, as though half of a mind to follow, and then, slowly shaking his head, he again picked up the paper he had been reading, delving through a maze of technical poisoning detection formulae, from Vortmann's nitroprusside test to a consideration of the best method of estimating the toxicity of chemical compounds by blood hemolysis. The reporter and young Dr. Baird certainly left little to the imagination.

Colonel Ashley read until rather late that evening, and his reading was not altogether from Izaak Walton's "Compleat Angler." He delved into several books, and again read, very carefully, the article on the effects of various poisons as it appeared in the paper he had been glancing over when Viola talked with him.

As the colonel was getting ready to retire a servant brought him a note. It was damp, as though it had been splashed with water, and when the detective had read it and had noted Viola's signature, he knew that her tears had blurred the writing.

"Please excuse my impulsiveness," she penned. "I am distracted. I know Harry is not guilty. Please do something!"

"I am trying to," mused the colonel as he got into bed, and turned his thoughts to a passage he had read in Walton just before switching off his light. It was an old rhyme, the source of which was not given, but which seemed wonderfully comforting under the circumstances. It was a bit of advice given by our friend Izaak, and as part of what a good fisherman should provide specified:

"My rod and my line, my float and my lead,   My hook and my plummet, my whetstone and knife.   My basket, my baits, both living and dead,   My net and my meat (for that is the chief):   Then I must have thread, and hairs green and small,   With mine angling purse--and so you have all."

"And," reflected Colonel Ashley, as he dozed off, "I guess I'll need all that and more to solve this mystery."

The detective was up betimes the next morning, as he would have said had he been discoursing in the talk of Mr. Walton, and on going to the window to fill his lungs with fresh air, he saw a letter slipped under his door.

"From Viola, I imagine," he mused, as he picked it up. "Unless it's from Shag, telling me the fish are biting unusually well. I hope they're not, for I must do considerable to-day, and I don't want to be tempted to stray to the fields.

"It isn't from Shag, though. He never could muster as neat a pen as this. Nor yet is it from Viola. Printed, too! The old device to prevent detection of the handwriting. Well, mysterious missive, what have you to say this fine morning?"

He opened the envelope carefully, preserving it and not tearing the address, which, as he had said, was printed, not written. It bore his name, and nothing else.

Within the envelope was a small piece of paper on which was printed this:

"Ask Miss Viola what this means. 58 C. H.--161*."

Colonel Ashley read the message through three times without saying a word. Then he held the paper and envelope up to the light to see if they bore a water mark. Neither did, and the paper was of a cheap, common variety which might be come upon in almost any stationery store. The colonel read the message again, looked at the back and front of the envelope, and then, placing both in his pocket, went down to breakfast, the bell for which he heard just as he finished his simple breathing exercises.

The morning papers were at his place, which was the only one at the table. Either Viola and her aunt had already breakfasted, or would do so later. The colonel ate and read.

There was not much new in the papers. Harry Bartlett was still held as a witness, and the prosecutor's detectives were still working on the case. As yet no one had connected Colonel Ashley officially with the matter. The reporters seemed to have missed noting that a celebrated--not to say successful--detective was the guest of Viola Carwell. It was an hour after the morning meal, and the colonel was in the library, rather idly glancing over the titles of the books, which included a goodly number on yachting and golfing, when Viola entered.

"Oh, I didn't know you were here!" she exclaimed, drawing back.

"Oh, come in! Come in!" invited the colonel. "I am just going out. I was wondering if there happened to be a book on chemistry here--or one on poisons."

"Poisons!" exclaimed the girl, half drawing back.

"Yes. I have one, but I left it in New York. If there happened to be one--Or perhaps you can tell me. Did you ever study chemistry?"

"As a girl in school, yes. But I'm afraid I've forgotten all I ever knew."

"My case, too," said the colonel with a laugh. "Then there isn't a book giving the different symbols of chemicals?"

"Not that I know of," Viola answered. "Still I might help you out if it wasn't too complicated. I remember that water is H two O and that sulphuric acid is H two S O four. But that's about all."

"Would you know what fifty-eight C H one sixty-one, with a period after the C, a dash after the H and a star after the last number was?" the colonel asked casually.

Viola shook her head.

"I'm afraid I wouldn't," she answered. "That is too complicated for me. Isn't it a shame we learn so much that we forget?'

"Still it may have its uses," said the colonel. "I'll have to get a book on chemistry, I think."

He turned to go out.

"Have you learned anything more?" Viola asked timidly.

"Nothing to speak about," was the answer.

"Oh, I wish you would find out something--and soon," she murmured. "This suspense is terrible!" and she shuddered as the detective went out.

It was late that afternoon when Colonel Ashley, having seen Miss Mary Carwell and Viola walking at the far end of the garden, went softly up the stairs to the room of the girl who had summoned him to The Haven. With a skill of which he was master he looked quickly but carefully through Viola's desk, which was littered with many letters and telegrams of condolence that had been answered.

Colonel Ashley worked quickly and silently, and he was about to give up, a look of disappointment on his face, when he found a slip of paper in one of the pigeon holes. And the slip bore this, written in pencil:

58 C. H.--I6I*

CHAPTER X. A WATER HAZARD

I sn't there some place where you can take her for a few days--some relative's where she can rest and forget, as much as possible, the scenes here?"

"Yes, there is," replied Miss Mary Carwell to Colonel Ashley's question. "I'll go with her myself to Pentonville. I have a cousin there, and it's the quietest place I know of, outside of Philadelphia," and she smiled faintly at the detective.

"Good!" he announced. "Then get her away from here. It will do you both good."

"But what about the case--solving the mystery? Won't you want either Viola or me here to help you?"

"I shall do very well by myself for a few days. Indeed I shall need the help of both of you, but you will be all the better fitted to render it when you return. So take her away--go yourself, and try to forget as much of your grief as possible."

"And you will stay--"

"I'll stay here, yes. Shag and I will manage very nicely, thank you. I'm glad you have colored help. I can always get along with that kind. I've been used to them since a boy in the South."

And so Viola and Miss Carwell went away.

It was after the sufficiently imposingly somber funeral of Horace Carwell, for since the adjourned inquest--adjourned at the request of the prosecutor--it was not considered necessary to keep the poor, maimed body out of its last resting place any longer. It had been sufficiently viewed and examined. In fact, parts of it were still in the hands of the chemists.

"And now, Shag, that we're left to ourselves--" said Colonel Ashley, when Viola and Miss Carwell had departed the day following the funeral, "now that we are by ourselves--"

"I reckon as how you'll fix up as to who it were whut done killed de gen'man, an' hab him 'rested, won't yo', Colonel, sah?" asked Shag, with the kindly concern and freedom of an old and loved servant.

"Indeed I'll do nothing of the sort!" exclaimed Colonel Ashley. "I'm going fishing, Shag, and I'll be obliged to you if you'll lay out my Kennebec rod and the sixteen line. I think there are some fighting fish in that little river that runs along at the end of the golf course. Get everything ready and then let me know," and the colonel, smoking his after-breakfast cigar, sat on the shady porch of The Haven and read:

"O, Sir, doubt not that angling is an art: is it not an art to deceive a trout with an artificial fly? a trout! that is more sharp-sighted than any hawk you have named, and more watchful and timorous than your high-mettled merlin is bold; and yet I doubt not to catch a brace or two to-morrow for a friend's breakfast."

"Um," mused the colonel. "Too bad it isn't the trout season. That passage from Walton just naturally makes me hungry for the speckled beauties. But I can wait. Meanwhile we'll see what else the stream holds. Shag, are you coming?"

"Yes, sah! Comm' right d'rectly, sah! Yes, sah, Colonel!" and Shag shuffled along the porch with the fishing tackle.

And so Colonel Ashley sat and fished, and as he fished he thought, for the sport was not so good that it took up his whole attention. In fact he was rather glad that the fish were not rising well, for he had entered into this golf course mystery with a zest he seldom brought to any case, and he was anxious to get to the bottom.

"I didn't want to get into that diamond cross affair, but I was dragged in by the heels," he mused. "And now, just because some years ago Horace Carwell did me a favor and enabled me to make money in the copper market, I am trying to find out who killed him, or if, in a fit of despondency, he killed himself."

"And yet, if it was despondency, he disguised it marvelously well. And if it was an accident it was a most skillful and fateful one. How he could swallow poison and not know it is beyond me. And now to consider who might have given it to him, arguing that it was not an accident."

The colonel had walked up and down the stream at the turn of the Maraposa golf course, Shag following at a discreet distance, and, after trying out several places had settled down under a shady tree at an eddy where the waters, after rushing down the bed of the small river, met with an obstruction and turned upon themselves. Here they had worn out a place under an overhanging bank, making a deep pool where, if ever, fish might he expected to lurk.

And there the colonel threw in his bait and waited.

"And now, that I am waiting," he mused, "let me consider, as my friend Walton would, matters in their sequence. Horace Carwell is dead. Let us argue that some one gave him the poison. Who was it?"

And then, like some file index, the colonel began to pass over in his mind the various persons who had come under his observation, as possible perpetrators of the crime.

"Let us begin with one the law already suspects," mused the fisherman. "Not that that is any criterion, but that it disposes of him in a certain order--disposes of him or--involves him more deeply," and the colonel looked to where a ground spider had woven a web in which a small but helpless grass hopper was then struggling.

"Could Harry Bartlett have given the poison?" the colonel asked himself. And the answer, naturally, was that such could have been the case.

Then came the question: "Why?"

"Had he an object? What was the quarrel about, concerning which he refuses to speak? Why is Viola so sure Harry could not have done it? I think I can see a reason for the last. She loves him as much as he does her. That's natural. She's a sweet girl!"

And, being unable to decide definitely as to the status of Harry Bartlett, Colonel Ashley mentally passed that card in his file and took up another, bearing the name Captain Gerry Poland.

"Could he have had an object in getting Horace Carxvell out of the way?" mused the detective. "At first thought I'd say he could not, and, just because I would say so, I must keep him on my list. He also is in love with Viola,--just as much as Bartlett is. I shall list Captain Poland as a remote possibility. I can't afford to eliminate him altogether, as it may develop that Mr. Carwell objected to his paying his attentions to Viola. Well, we shall see."

The next mental index card bore the name Jean Forette; and concerning him Colonel Ashley had secured some information the day before. He had got, by adroit questioning, a certain knowledge of the French chauffeur, and this was now spread out on the card that, in fancy, Colonel Ashley could see in his filing cabinet.

"Forette? Oh, yes, I know him," the mechanician of the best garage in Lakeside had told the detective. "He's a good driver, and knows more about an ignition system than I ever shall. He's a shark at it. But he's a queer Dick."

"How do you mean?"

"Well, sometimes he's a regular devil at driving. Once he had a big Rilat car in here for repairs. He had to tell me what was wrong with it, as I couldn't dope it out. Then when we got it running for him, he took it out for a trial run on the road. Drive! Say, it's a wonder I have any hair on my head!"

"Did he go fast?"

"Fast? Say, a racing man had nothing on that Forette. And yet the next day, when he came to take the car away, after we'd charged the storage battery, he drove like a snail. One of my men went with him a little way, to see that everything was all right, for Mr. Carwell is very particular--I mean he was--and Forette didn't let her out for a cent My man was disappointed, for he's a fast devil, too, and he asked the Frenchman why he didn't kick her along."

"What did the chauffeur say?"

"Well, it wasn't so much what he said as how he acted. He was as nervous as a cat. Kept looking behind to see that no other machine was coming, and when he passed anything on the road he almost went in the ditch himself to make sure there was room enough to pass."

"Seemed afraid, did he?"

"That's it. And considering how bold he was the day I was out with him, I put it down that he must have had a few drinks when he took me for a-- Well, I never saw him, but how else can you account for it? Drink will make a man drive like old Nick, and get away with it, too, sometimes, though the stuff'll get 'em sooner or later. But that's how I sized it up."

"He might have taken something other than drink."

"What do you mean?"

"Dope!"

"Oh, yes, I s'pose so, and him bein' French might account for it. Anyhow he was like two different men. That one day he was as bold as brass, and I guess he'd have driven one of them there airships if any one had dared him to. Then, the next day he was like a chap trying for his license with the motor inspector lookin' on. I can't account for it. That Jean Forette sure is a card!"

"Then he really seemed afraid to speed the Dilat car?"

"That's it. And he spoke of Mr. Carwell going to get a more powerful French machine. He said then he'd never driven it to the limit, and didn't want to handle it at all. And he spoke the truth, for I heard that he and the old man didn't get along at all with that red, white and blue devil Mr. Carwell imported."

"So they say. Forette was to leave at the end of the month. Well, I'm much obliged to you. A friend of mine was going to engage him, but if he has such a reputation--not reliable, you know, I guess I'll look farther. Much obliged," and the colonel, who, it is needless to say, had not revealed his true character to the garage owner, turned aside.

"Oh, I wouldn't want what I said to keep Forette out of a place!" protested the man quickly. "If I'd thought that--"

"You needn't worry. You haven't done him any harm. He's out of a place anyhow, since Mr. Carwell died, and I'll treat what you told me in strict confidence."

"I wish you would. You know we have to be careful."

"I understand."

And this information passed again in review before the mind of the fisherman as he took Jean Forette's card from the pack.

"I wonder if he can be a dope fiend?" mused the colonel. "It's worth looking up, at any rate. He'd be a bad kind to drive a car. I'm glad he isn't in my employ, and I'm better pleased that he won't take Viola out. This dope--bad stuff, whether it's morphine, cocaine, or something else. We'll just keep this card up in front where we can get at it easily."

The next mental card had on it the name of LeGrand Blossom.

"Curious chap, him," mused the detective. "He's very fond of the sound of his own voice, particularly where he can get an audience, as he had at the inquest. Well, I don't know anything about you, Mr. Blossom, neither for nor against you, but I'll keep your card within reach, also. Can't neglect any possibilities in cases like this. And now for some others."

There were many cards in the colonel's index, and he ran rapidly over them as he waited for a bite. They bore the names of many members of the golf and yacht-ing clubs of which Mr. Carwell had been a member. There were also the names of the household servants, and the dead man's nearest relatives, including his sister and Viola. But the colonel did not linger long over any of these memoranda. The card of Viola Carwell, however, had mentally penciled on it the somewhat mystic symbol 58 C. H.--i6i* and this the colonel looked at from every angle.

"I really must get a book on chemistry," he mused. "I may need it to find out what kind of dope Forette uses--if he takes any."

And thus the colonel sat in the shade, beside the quiet stream, the little green book by his side. But he did not open it now, and though his gaze was on his line, where it cut the water in a little swirl, he did not seem to see it.

"Shag!" suddenly exclaimed the colonel, breaking a stillness that was little short of idyllic.

"Yes, sah, Colonel! Yes, sah!" and the colored man awoke with a skill perfected by long practice under similar circumstances.

"Shag, the fishing here is miserable!"

"Yes, sah, Colonel. Shall we-all move?"

"Might as well. I haven't had a nibble, and from the looks of everything--even the evidence of Mr. Walton himself--it ought to have been a most choice location. However, there will be other days, and--"

The colonel's voice was cut short by a shrill call from his delicate reel, and a moment later he had leaped to his feet and cried:

"Shag, I'm a most monumental liar!"

"Yes, sah, Colonel. Dat's whut yo' suah is!"

"I've got the biggest bite I ever had! Get that landing net and see if you can forget that you're a cross between a snail and a mud turtle!" cried the colonel excit-edly.

"Yes, sah!"

Shag moved on nimble feet, and presently stood down on the shore, near the edge of the stream, while the colonel, on the bank above the eddy, played the fish that had taken his bait and sought to depart with it to some watery fastness to de-vour it at his leisure. But the hook and tackle held him.

Up and down in the pool rushed the fish, and the colonel's rod bent to the strain, but it did not break. It had been tested in other piscatorial battles and was tried and true.

The battle progressed, not so unequal as it might seem, considering the frail means used to ensnare the big fish. And the prize was gradually being brought within reach of the landing net.

"Get ready now, Shag!" ordered the colonel.

"Yes, sah, I'se all ready!"

There was a final rush and swirl in the water. Shag leaned over, his eyes shining in delight, for the fish was an extraordinarily large one. He was about to scoop it up in the net, to take the strain off the rod which was curved like a bow, when there came a streak of something white sailing through the air. It fell with a splash into the water so close to the fish that it must have bruised its scaly side, and then, in some manner, the denizen of the stream, either in a desperate flurry, or because the blow of the white object broke its hold on the hook, was free, and with a dart scurried back into the element that was life itself.

For a moment there was portentous silence on the part of Colonel Ashley. He gazed at his dangling line and at the straightened pole. Then he solemnly said:

"Shag!"

"Yes, sah, Colonel!"

"What happened?"

"By golly, Colonel! dat's whut I'd laik t' know. Must hab been a shootin' star, or suffin laik dat! I never done see--"

At that moment a drawling voice from somewhere back of the fringe of trees and bushes broke in with:

"I fancy I made that water hazard all right, though it was a close call. Which reminds me of the perhaps interesting fact that forty-five and sixty-four hundredths cylindrical feet of water will weigh twenty-two hundred and forty pounds, figuring one cubic foot of salt water at sixty-four and three-tenths pounds, if you get my meaning!" and there was a genial laugh.

"Well, I don't get it, and I don't care to," was the rejoinder. "But I'm ready to bet you a cold bottle that you've gone into instead of over that water hazard."

"Done! Come on, we'll take a look!"

CHAPTER XI. POISONOUS PLANTS

Colonel Ashley still stood, holding his now useless rod and line, gazing first at that, then at Shag and, anon, at the little swirl of the waters, marking where the big fish had disappeared from view.

"Shag!" exclaimed the colonel in an ominously, quiet voice.

"Yes, sah!"

"Do you know what that was?"

"No, sab, Colonel, I don't."

"Well, that was a spirit manifestation of Izaak Walton. It was jealous of my success and took that revenge. It was the spirit of the old fisherman himself."

"Good land ob massy!" gasped Shag. "Does yo'--does yo' mean a--ghost?"

"You might call it that, Shag. Yes, a ghost."

The colored man looked frightened for a moment, and then a broad grin spread over his face.

"Well, sah, Colonel," he began, deferentially, "maybe yo' kin call it dat, but hit looks t' me mo' laik one ob dem li'l white balls de gen'mens an' ladies done knock aroun' wif iron-headed clubs. Dat's whut it looks laik t' me, sah, Colonel," and Shag picked up a golf ball from the water, where it floated.

"By Jove!" exclaimed the fisherman. "If it was that--"

His indignant protest was interrupted by the appearance, breaking through the underbrush on the edge of the stream, of two men, each one carrying a bag of golf clubs.

"Did you--" began one, and then, as he caught sight of Shag holding up in his black fingers the white ball, there was added:

"I see you did! Thank you. You were right, Tom. I did go into the water. I sliced worse than I thought."

Then the two men seemed, for the first time, to have caught sight of Colonel Ashley. They noticed his attitude, the dangling line and his disappointed look.

"I beg pardon," said the one who had already spoken, "but did we interfere with your fishing?"

"Did you interfere with it?" stormed the colonel. "You just naturally knocked it all to the devil, sir! That's what you did!" And then, as he saw a curious look on the faces of the two men, he added:

"I beg your pardon. I shouldn't have said that. I'm an interloper, I realize--a trespasser. It's my own fault for fishing so near the golf course. But I--"

"Excuse me," broke in the other man. "But you are Colonel Ashley, aren't you?"

"I am."

"My name is Sharwell--Tom Sharwell, and this is Bruce Garrigan. I thought I had seen you at the club. Pray excuse our interruption of your sport. We had no idea any one was fishing here."

"It's entirely my fault," declared the colonel, as he removed his cap and bowed, a courtesy the two golfers, after a moment of hesitation, returned. "I was taking chances when I threw in here."

"And did we scare the fish?" asked Garrigan. "I suppose so. Never was much of a fisherman myself. All I know about them is seventeen million, four hundred and eighty-eight thousand nine hundred and twenty one boxes of sardines were imported into the United States last year. I read it in the paper so it must be true. I know I ate the one box."

"Be quiet, Bruce," said Sharwell in a low voice, but the colonel smiled. There was no affront to his dignity, as the golfer had feared.

"I had on a most beautiful catch," said the colonel, "and then what I thought, at first, was the embodied spirit of Izaak Walton suddenly came zipping into the water just as Shag was about to land the beauty, and knocked it off the hook. Since then I have been informed by my servant that it was no spirit, but a golf ball."

"It was mine," confessed Garrigan. "I'm all kinds of sorry about it. Never had the least notion any one was here. Never saw any one fish here before; did we, Tom?""Well, I thought there were fish here, and events proved I was right," said the colonel. "I hope the water isn't posted?" he inquired anxiously, for he was a stickler for the rights of others.

"Oh, no, nothing like that!" Garrigan hastened to add. "You're welcome to fish here as long and as often as you like. Only, as this water hazard is often played from the fifth hole, it would be advisable to post a sign just outside the trees, or station your man there to give notice."

"I'll do it after this," said the colonel, as he reeled in.

"You're not going to quit just because I was so unfortunate as to spoil your first catch, are you?" asked Garrigan.

"I think I'd better," the colonel said. "I don't believe I could land anything after what happened. The fish must have thought it was a thunderbolt, from the way that ball landed."

"I did drive rather hard," admitted Garrigan. "But we can cut this out of our game, take a stroke apiece and go on with the play. That is, I'm willing. I don't feel very keen for the game to-day. How about you, Tom?"

"I'm ready to quit, and I think the least we can do, considering that we have spoiled Colonel Ashley's day, is to ask him if he won't share with us the bottle I won from you on the water hazard."

"Done!" exclaimed Garrigan. "There were eleven million, four hundred and ten thousand six hundred and six dollars' worth of soya beans imported into the United States in 1917," he added, "which, of course, has nothing to do with the number of cold bottles of champagne the steward, at the nineteenth hole, has on the ice for us. So I suggest that we adjourn and--"

"I will, on one condition," said Sharwell.

"What is it?" asked his companion.

"That you kindly refrain from telling us how many spools of thread were sent to the cannibals of the Friendly Islands for the fiscal year ending June 30, 1884."

"Done!" cried Garrigan with a laugh. "I'll never hint of it. Colonel, will you accept our hospitality? I believe you are already put up at the club?"

"Yes, Miss Carwell was kind enough to secure a visitor's card for me."

"Then let's forget our sorrows; drown them in the bubbling glasses with hollow stems!" cried Garrigan, gayly.

"Here, Shag," called the colonel, as he gave his rod to his colored servant. "I don't know when I'll be back."

"Well said!" exclaimed Sharwell.

Then they adjourned to the nineteenth hole.

If it is always good weather when good fellows get together, it was certainly a most delightful day as the colonel and his two hosts sat on the shady veranda of the Maraposa Golf Club. They talked of many things, and, naturally, the conversation veered around to the death of Mr. Carwell. Out of respect to his memory, an important match had been called off on the day of his funeral. But now those last rites were over, the clubhouse was the same gay place it had been. Though more than one veteran member sat in silent reverie over his cigar as he recalled the friend who never again would tee a ball with him.

"It certainly is queer why Harry Bartlett doesn't come out and say what it was that he and Mr. Carwell had words about," commented Sharwell. "There he stays, in that rotten jail. Bah! I can smell it yet, for I called to see if I could do anything. And yet he won't talk."

"It is queer," said Garrigan. "If he'd only let his friends speak for him it could be cleared. We all know what the quarrel was about."

"What?" asked the colonel. He had his own theory, but he wanted to see how it jibed with another's.

"It's an old story," went on Bruce Garrigan. "It goes back to the time, about three years ago, when the fair Viola and Harry began to be talked about as more than ordinary friends. Just about then Mr. Carwell lost a large sum of money in a stock deal, or a bond issue, or something--I've forgotten what--and he always said that Harry and his clique engineered the plan by which he was mulcted."

"And did Mr. Bartlett have anything to do with it?" asked the colonel.

"Well, some say he did, and some say he didn't. Harry himself denied all knowledge of it. Anyhow the colonel lost a stiffish sum, and some of Harry's people took in a goodly pile. Naturally there was a bit of coldness between the families, and I did hear Harry was told his presence around Viola wasn't desired."

"If he was so warned he didn't heed it, for they went out together as much as ever, though I can't say he called at the house very often."

"And you think it was about this he and Mr. Carwell quarreled just before Mr. Carwell was stricken?" asked the colonel.

"I think so, yes," answered Garrigan. "And I think Harry refuses to admit it, from a notion that it would be dragging in a lady's name. But it wouldn't be airing anything that isn't already pretty well known. Mr. Carwell has a violent temper--or he had one--and Harry isn't exactly an angel when he's roused, though I'll say say for him that I have rarely seen him angry. And there you are. Boy, another bottle, and have it colder than the last."

"Yes," mused the colonel, "there you are--or aren't, according to your view-point."

And so the day grew more sunshiny and mellow, and Colonel Ashley did not regret the fish that the golf ball cheated him of, for he added several new cards to his index file and jotted down, mentally, new facts on some already in it.

"Will return to-morrow. Viola too restless here."

That was the telegram Colonel Ashley received the day following his acquaintance at the nineteenth hole with Bruce Garrigan and Tom Sharwell.

"She stayed away longer than I thought she would," mused the detective, "Yes, sah!"

"See if that French chauffeur, Forette, can drive me into town."

"Yes, sah, Colonel."

A little later Jean brought the roadster to the front of the house and waited for Colonel Ashley. The latter came forth holding a slip of paper in his hand, and, to the chauffeur, he said:

"Do you know where Dr. Baird lives?"

"Oh, yes, sir."

"Take me there, please. He was one of the physicians called in when Mr. Carwell was poisoned, was he not?"

"Yes," and the chauffeur nodded and smiled. "You are not ill, I hope, monsieur. If you are, there is a physician nearer--"

"Oh, no. I'm all right. I just want to have a talk with the doctor. Did you ever consult him?"

"Me? Oh, no, monsieur, I have no need of a doctor. I am never sick. I feel most excellent!" and certainly he looked it. There was a sparkle in his eyes--perhaps too brilliant a sparkle, but he did not look like a "dope fiend."

"If you are in a hurry," went on the chauffeur, "I can--"

"No, no hurry," responded the colonel. "Why, do you feel like driving fast?"

"Very fast, monsieur. I always like to drive fast, only there is seldom call for it. Mr. Carwell, he at times would like speed, and again he was like the tortoise. But as for me--poof! What would you?" and he shrugged his shoulders and reverted to his own tongue.

"Hum," mused the colonel. "Rather a different story from the garage man's. However, we shall see."

Dr. Baird was in. In fact, being a very young doctor indeed, he was rather more in than out--too much in to suit his own inclination and pocketbook, for, as yet, the number of his patients was small.

"I did not come to see you for myself, professionally," said Colonel Ashley, as he took a seat in the office, and introduced himself. "I am trying to establish, for the satisfaction of Miss Carwell, that her father was not a suicide, and--"

"What else could it be?" asked Dr. Baird.

"I do not know. But I read with great interest the interview, you gave the Globe on the effects and detection of various poisons."

"Yes?" and young Dr. Baird rubbed his hands in delight, and stroked his still younger moustache.

"Yes. And I called to ask what poison or chemical symbol that might be."

The colonel extended a paper on which was inscribed: 58 C. H.--I6I*

"That! Hum, why that is not a chemical symbol at all!" promptly declared Dr. Baird.

"Are you sure?"

"Positive."

"Could it be some formula for poison?"

"It could not. Of course that is not to say it could not be some person's private memorandum for some combination of elements. C might stand for carbon and H for hydrogen. But that would not make a poison in the ordinary accepted meaning of the term. I am sure you are mistaken if you think that is a chemical symbol."

"I am sure, also," said the detective with a smile. "I just wanted your opinion, that is all. Then those letters and figures would mean nothing to you?"

"Nothing at all. Wait though--"

Young Dr. Percy Baird looked at the slip again. "No, it would mean nothing to me," he said finally.

"Thank you," said the colonel.

He came out of the physician's office to find Jean Forette calmly reading in his side of the car. The paper was put away at once, and with a whirr from the self-starter the motor throbbed.

"It there a free public library in town, Jean?" asked the detective.

"Yes, monsieur."

"Take me there."

The library was one built partly with the money donated by a celebrated millionaire, and contained a fair variety of books. To the main desk, behind which sat a pretty girl, marched Colonel Ashley.

"Have you any books on poisons?" he asked.

"Poisons?" She looked up at him, startled, a flush mantling her fair cheeks.

"Yes. Any works on poisons--a chemistry would do."

"Oh, yes, we have books on poisons. I'll jot down the numbers for you. We have not many, I'm afraid. It is--it isn't a pleasant subject."

"No, I imagine not."

She busied herself with the card index, and came back to him in a moment with a slip of paper.

"I'm sorry," said the pretty girl, "but we seem to have only one book on poisons, and I'm afraid that isn't what you want. It is entitled 'Poisonous Plants of New Jersey,' and is one of the bulletins of the New Jersey Agricultural Experiment Station at New Brunswick. But it is out at present. Here is the number of it, and if it comes in--"

"I should be glad to see it," interrupted the colonel pleasantly.

"Here is the number," and the pretty girl extended to him a slip which read: 58 C. H--i6i*

"What is the star for?" asked the colonel.

"It indicates that the book was donated by the state and was not purchased with the endowment appropriation," she informed him.

"And it is out now. I wonder if you could tell me who has it?"

"Why, yes, sir. Just a moment."

She looked at some more cards, and came back to him. She looked a bit disturbed.

"The book, 'Poisonous Plants of New Jersey' was taken out by Miss Viola Carwell," said the girl.

CHAPTER XII. BLOSSOM'S SUSPICIONS

Characteristic as it was of Colonel Ashley not to show surprise, he could hardly restrain an indication of it when he reached The Haven, and found Miss Mary Carwell and Viola there. They were not expected until the next day, but while her niece was temporarily absent Miss Carwell explained the matter.

"She couldn't stand it another minute. She insisted that I should pack and come with her. Something seemed to drive her home."

"I hope," said the Colonel gently, "that she didn't imagine that I wasn't doing all possible, under the circumstances."

"Oh, no, it wasn't anything like that. She just wanted to be at home. And I think, too," and Miss Carwell lowered her voice, after a glance at the door, "that she wanted to see him."

"You mean--?"

"Mr. Bartlett! There's no use disguising the fact that his family and ours aren't on friendly terms. I think he did a grave injustice to my brother in a business way, and I'll never forgive him for it. I don't want to see Viola marry him--that is I didn't. I hardly believe, now, after he has been arrested, that she will. But there is no doubt she cares for him, and would do anything to prove that this charge was groundless."

"Well, yes, I suppose that's natural," assented the detective. "I'd be glad, myself, to believe that Harry Bartlett had nothing to do with the death of Mr. Carwell."

"But you believe he did have, don't you?"

"I haven't yet made up my mind," was the cautious answer. "The golf course mystery, I don't mind admitting, is one of the most puzzling I've ever run across. It won't do to make up one's mind at once."

"But my brother either committed suicide, or else he was deliberately poisoned!" insisted Miss Carwell. "And those of us who knew him feel sure he would never take his own life. He must have been killed, and if Harry Bartlett didn't do it who did?"

"I don't know," frankly replied the colonel. "That's what I'm going to try to find out. So Miss Viola feels much sympathy for him, does she?"

"Yes. And she wants to go to see him at the jail. Of course I know they don't exactly call it a jail, but that's what I call it!"

Miss Carwell was nothing if not determined in her language.

"Would you let her go if you were I--go to see him?" she asked.

"I don't see how you are going to prevent it," replied the colonel. "Miss Viola is of legal age, and she seems to have a will of her own. But I hardly believe that she will see Mr. Bartlett."

"Oh, but she said she was going to. That's one reason she made me come home ahead of time, I believe. She says she's going to see him, and what she says she'll do she generally does."

"However I don't believe she'll see him," went on the detective. "The prosecutor has given orders since yesterday that no one except Mr. Bartlett's legal adviser must communicate with him; so I don't believe Miss Viola will be admitted."

This proved to be correct. Viola was very insistent, but to no avail. The warden at the jail would not admit her to the witness rooms, where Harry Bartlett paced up and down, wondering, wondering, and wondering. And much of his wonder had to do with the girl who tried so hard to see him.

She had sent word by his lawyer that she believed in his innocence and that she would do all she could for him, but he wanted more than that. He wanted to see her--to feast his hungry eyes on her--to hold her hand, to--Oh, well, what was the use? he wearily asked himself. Would the horrible tangle ever be straightened out? He shook his head and resumed his pacing of the rooms--for there were two at his disposal. He was weary to death of the dismal view to be had through the barred windows.

"Did you see him?" asked her aunt, when Viola, much dispirited, returned home.

"No, and I suppose you're glad of it!"

"I am. There's no use saying I'm not."

"Aunt Mary, I think it's perfectly horrid of you to think, even for a moment, that Harry had anything to do with this terrible thing. He'd never dream of it, not if he had quarreled with my father a dozen times. And I don't see what they quarreled about, either. I'm sure I was with Harry a good deal of the time before the game, and I didn't hear him and my father have any words."

"Perhaps, as it was about you, they took care you shouldn't hear."

"Who says it was about me?"

"Can't you easily guess that it was, and that's why Harry doesn't want to tell?" asked Miss Mary.

"I don't believe anything of the sort!" declared Viola.

"Well," sighed Miss Carwell, "I don't know what to believe. If your poor, dear father wasn't a suicide, some one must have killed him, and it may well have been--"

"Don't dare say it was Harry!" cried Viola excitedly. "Oh, this is terrible! I'm going to see Colonel Ashley and ask him if he can't end this horrible suspense."

"I wish that as eagerly as you do," said Miss Mary. "You'll find the colonel in the library. He's poring over some papers, and Shag, that funny colored man, is getting some fish lines ready; so it's easy enough to guess where the colonel is going. If you want to speak to him you'd better hurry. But there's another matter I want to call to your attention. What about our business affairs? Have we money enough to go on living here and keeping up our big winter house? We must think of that, Viola."

"Yes, we must think of that," agreed the girl. "That's one of the reasons why I wanted to come back. Father's affairs must be gone into carefully. He left no will, and the lawyer says it will take quite a while to find out just how things stand. If only Harry were here to help. He's such a good business man."

"There are others," sniffed Miss Mary. "Why don't you ask the colonel--or Captain Poland?"

"Captain Poland!" exclaimed Viola, startled. "Yes. He helped us out in the matter of the bank when more collateral was asked for, and he'll be glad to go over the affairs with us, I'm sure."

"I don't want him to!" snapped Viola. "Mr. Blossom is the proper one to do that. He is the chief clerk, and since he was going to form a partnership with father he will, most likely, know all the details. We'll have him up here and ask him how matters stand."

"Perhaps that will be wise," agreed Miss Carwell. "But I can't forget how careless LeGrand Blossom was in the matter of the loan your father had from the bank. If he's that careless, his word won't be worth much, I'm afraid."

"Oh, any one is likely to make a mistake," said Viola. "I'll telephone to Mr. Blossom and ask him to come here and have a talk with us. It will give me something to think about. Besides--"

She did not finish, but went to the instrument and was soon talking to the chief clerk in the office Mr. Carwell maintained while at his summer home.

"He'll be up within an hour," Viola reported. "Now I'm going to have a talk with the colonel," and she hastened to the library.

The old detective was smoking a cigar, which he hastened to lay aside when Viola made her entrance, but she raised a restraining hand.

"Smoke as much as you like," she said. "I am used to it."

"Thank you," and he pulled forward a chair for her.

"Oh, haven't you found out anything yet?" she burst out. "Can't you say anything definite?"

Colonel Ashley shook his head in negation.

"I'm sorry," he said softly. "I'm just as sorry about it as you are. But I have seldom had a case in which there were so many clews that lead into blind allies. I was just trying to arrange a plan of procedure that I thought might lead to something."

"Can you?" she asked eagerly.

"I haven't finished yet. What I need most is a book on poisons-a comprehensive chemistry would do, but I haven't been able to find one around here," and he glanced at the books lining the library walls. "Your father didn't go in for that sort of thing."

"No. But can't you send to New York for one?"

"I suppose I could--yes. I wonder if they might have one in the local library?"

"I'm sure I don't know," and Viola leaned over to pick a thread from the carpet. "I don't draw books from there. When it was first opened I took out a card, but when I saw how unclean some of the volumes were I never afterward patronized the place."

"Then you wouldn't know whether they had a book on poisons, or poison plants or not?"

"I wouldn't in the least," she answered, as she arose. "As I said, I don't believe I have been in the place more than twice, and that was two years ago."

"Then I'll have to inquire myself," said the colonel, and he remained standing while Viola left the room. And for some little time he stood looking at the door as it closed after her. And on Colonel Ashley's face there was a peculiar look.

LeGrand Blossom came to The Haven bearing a bundle of books and papers, and with rather a wry face--for he had no heart for business of this nature. Miss Mary Carwell sat down at the table with him and Viola.

"We want to know just where we stand financially," said Viola. "What is the condition of my father's affairs, Mr. Blossom?"

The confidential clerk hesitated a moment before answering. Then he said slowly:

"Well, the affairs are anything but good. There is a great deal of money gone, and some of the securities left are pledged for loans."

"You mean my father spent a lot of money just before he died?" asked Viola.

"He either spent it or--Well, yes, he must have spent it, for it is gone. The car cost ten thousand, and he spent as much, if not more, on the yacht."

"But they can be sold. I don't want either of them. I'm afraid in the big car," said Viola, "and the yacht isn't seaworthy, I've heard. I wouldn't take a trip in her."

"I don't know anything about that," said LeGrand Blossom. "But even if the car and yacht were sold at a forced sale they would not bring anything like what they cost. I have gone carefully over your father's affairs, as you requested me, and I tell you frankly they are in bad shape."

"What can be done?" asked Miss Carwell.

"I don't know," LeGrand Blossom frankly admitted. "You may call in an expert, if you like, to go over the books; but I don't believe he would come to any other conclusion than I have. As a matter of fact, I bad a somewhat selfish motive in look-ing into your father's affairs of late. You know I was thinking of going into partner-ship with him, and--and--" He did not finish.

Viola nodded.

"Perhaps I might say that he was good enough to offer me the chance," the young man went on. "And, as I was to invest what was, to me, a large sum, I wanted to see how matters were. So I examined the books carefully, as your father pressed me to do. At that time his affairs were in good shape. But of late he had lost a lot of money."

"Will it make any difference to us?" and Viola included her aunt in her gesture.

"Well, you, Miss Carwell," and Blossom nodded to the older lady, "have your own money in trust funds. Mr. Carwell could not touch them. But he did use part of the fortune left you by your mother," he added to Viola.

"I don't mind that," was her steady answer. "If my father needed my money he was welcome to it. That is past and gone. What now remains to me?"

"Very little," answered LeGrand Blossom. "I may be able to pull the business through and save something, but there is a lot of money lost--spent or gone somewhere. I haven't yet found out. Your father speculated too much, and unwisely. I told him, but he would pay no heed to me."

"Do you think he knew, before his death, that his affairs were in such bad shape?" asked the dead man's sister.

"He must have, for I saw him going over the books several times."

"Do you think this knowledge impelled him toto end his life?" faltered Viola.

LeGrand Blossom considered a moment before answering. Then he slowly said:

"It was either that, or--or, well, some one killed him. There are no two ways about it."

"I believe some one killed him!" burst out Viola. "But I think the authorities have made a horrible mistake in detaining Mr. Bartlett," she added. "Don't you, Mr. Blossom?"

"I--er--I don't know what to think. Your father had some enemies, it is true. Every business man has. And a person with a temper easily aroused, such as--"

LeGrand Blossom stopped suddenly.

"You were about to name some one?" asked Viola.

"Well, I was about to give, merely as an instance, Jean Forette the chauffeur. Not that I think the Frenchman had a thing to do with the matter. But he has a violent temper at times, and again he is as meek as any one I ever knew. But say a person did give way to violent passion, such as I have seen him do at times when something went wrong with the big, new car, might not such a person, for a fancied wrong, take means of ending the life of a person who had angered him?"

"I never liked Jean Forette," put in Miss Carwell, "and I was glad when I heard Horace was to let him go."

"Do you think--do you believe he had anything to do with my father's death?" asked Viola quickly.

"Not the least in the world," answered the head clerk hastily. "I just used him as an illustration."

"But he quarreled with my father," the girl went on. "They had words, I know."

"Yes, they did, and I heard some of them," admitted LeGrand Blossom. "But that passed over, and they were friendly enough the day of the golf game. So there could not have been murder in the heart of that Frenchman. No, I don't mean even to hint at him: hut I believe some one, angry at, and with a grudge against, your father, ended his life."

"I believe that, too!" declared Viola firmly. "And while I feel, as you do, about Jean, still it is a clew that must not be overlooked. I'll tell Colonel Ashley."

"I fancy he knows it already," said LeGrand Blossom. "There isn't much that escapes that fisherman."

CHAPTER XIII. CAPTAIN POLAND CONFESSES

When LeGrand Blossom had taken his departure, carrying with him the books and papers, he left behind two very disconsolate persons.

"It's terrible!" exclaimed Mr. Carwell's sister. "To think that poor Horace could be so careless! I knew his sporting life would bring trouble, but I never dreamed of this."

"We must face it, terrible as it is," said Viola. "Nothing would matter if he--if he were only left to us. I'm sure he never meant to spend so much money. It was just because--he didn't think."

"That always was a fault of his," sighed Miss Mary, "even when a boy. It's terrible!"

"It's terrible to have him gone and to think of the terrible way he was taken," sighed Viola. "But any one is likely to lose money."

She no more approved of many of her late father's sporting proclivities than did her aunt, and there were many rather startling stories and rumors that came to Viola as mere whispers to which she turned a deaf ear. Since her mother's death her father had, it was common knowledge, associated with a fast set, and he had been seen in company with persons of both sexes who were rather notorious for their excesses.

"Well, Mr. Blossom will do the best he can, I suppose," said Miss Carwell, with rather an intimation that the head clerk's best would be very bad indeed.

"I'm sure he will," assented Viola. "He knows all the details of poor father's affairs, and he alone can straighten them out. Oh, if we had only known of this before, we might have stopped it."

"But your father was always very close about his matters," said his sister. "He resented even your mother knowing how much money he made, and how. I think she felt that, too, for she liked to have a share in all he did. He was kindness itself to her, but she wanted more than that. She wanted to have a part in his success, and he kept her out--or she felt that he did. Well, I'm sure I hope all mistakes are straightened out in Heaven. It's certain they aren't here."

Viola pondered rather long and deeply on what LeGrand Blossom had told her. She made it a point to go for a drive the next afternoon with Jean Forette in the small car, taking a maid with her on a pretense of doing some shopping. And Viola closely observed the conduct of the chauffeur.

On her return, the girl could not help admitting that the Frenchman was all a careful car driver should be. He had shown skill and foresight in guiding the car through the summer-crowded traffic of Lakeside, and had been cheerful and polite.

"I am sorry you are going to leave us, Jean," she said, when he had brought her back to The Haven.

"I, too, am regretful," he said in his careful English. "But your father had other ideas, and I--I am really afraid of that big new car. It is not a machine, mademoiselle, it is--pardon--it is a devil! It will be the death of some one yet. I could never drive it."

"But if we sold that car, Jean, as we are going to do--"

"I could not stay, Miss Viola. I have a new place, and to that I go in two weeks. I am sorry, for I liked it here, though--Oh, well, of what use?" and he shrugged his shoulders.

"Was there something you did not like? Did my father not treat you well?" asked Viola quickly.

"Oh, as to that, mademoiselle, I should not speak. I liked your father. We, at times, did have difference; as who has not? But he was a friend to me. What would you have? I am sorry!" And he touched his hat and drove around to the garage.

As Viola was about to enter the house she chanced to look down the street and saw Minnie Webb approaching. She looked so thoroughly downcast that Viola was surprised.

"Hello, Minnie!" she exclaimed pleasantly. "Anything new or startling?"

"Nothing," was the somewhat listless reply. "Is there anything new here?" and

Minnie Webb's face showed a momentary interest.

"I can't say that there is," returned Viola. She paused for a moment. "Won't you come in?"

"I don't think so-not to-day," stammered the other girl. And then as she looked at Viola her face began to flush. "I--I don't feel very well. I have a terrible headache. I think I'll go home and lie down," and she hurried on without another word.

"There is certainly something wrong with Minnie," speculated Viola, as she looked after her friend. "I wonder if it is on account of LeGrand Blossom."

She did not know how much Minnie Webb was in love with the man who had been her father's confidential clerk and who was now in charge of Mr. Carwell's business affairs, and, not knowing this, she could, of course, not realize under what a strain Minnie was now living with so many suspicions against Blossom.

Divesting herself of her street dress for a more simple gown, Viola inquired of the maid whether Colonel Ashley was in the house. When informed that he had gone fishing with Shag, the girl, with a little gesture of impatience, took her seat near a window to look over some mail that had come during her absence.

As she glanced up after reading a belated letter of sympathy she saw, alighting from his car which had stopped in front of The Haven, Captain Gerry Poland. He caught sight of her, and waved his hand.

"Oh, dear!" exclaimed Viola. "If he hadn't seen me I could have said I was not at home, but now--"

She heard his ring at the door and resigned herself to meeting him, but if the captain had not been so much in love with Viola Carwell he could not have helped noticing her rather cold greeting.

"I called," he said, "to see if there was anything more I could do for you or for your aunt. I saw Blossom, and he says he is working over the books. I've had a good deal of experience in helping settle up estates that were involved. I mean--" he added hastily--"where no will was left, and, my dear Viola, if I could be of any assistance--"

"Thank you," broke in Viola rather coldly, "I don't know that there is anything you can do. It is very kind of you, but Mr. Blossom has charge and--"

"Oh, of course I realize that," went on Captain Poland quickly. "But I thought there might be something."

"There is nothing," and now the yachtsman could not help noticing the cold- ness in Viola's voice. He seemed to nerve himself for an effort as he said:

"Viola"--he paused a moment before adding--"why can't we be friends? You were decent enough to me some days ago, and now--Have I done anything--said anything? I want to be friends with you. I want to be--"

He took a step nearer her, but she drew back.

"Please don't think, Captain Poland, that I am not appreciative of what you have done for me," the girl said quickly. "But--Oh, I really don't know what to think. It has all been so terrible."

"Indeed it has," said the captain, in a low voice. "But I would like to help."

"Then perhaps you can!" suddenly exclaimed Viola, and there was a new note in her voice. "Have you been to see Harry Bartlett in--in jail?" and she faltered over that word.

"No, I have not," said the captain, and there was a sharp tone in his answer. "I understood no one was allowed to see him."

"That is true enough," agreed Viola. "They wouldn't let me see him, and I wanted to--so much. I presume you know how he comes to be in prison."

"It isn't exactly a prison."

"To him it is-and to me," she said. "But you know how he comes to be there?"

"Yes. I was present at the inquest. By the way, they are to resume it this week, I heard. The chemists have finished their analyses and are ready to testify."

"Oh, I didn't know that."

"Yes. But, speaking of Harry--poor chap--it's terrible, of course, but he may be able to clear himself."

"Clear himself, Captain Poland? What do you mean?" and indignant Viola faced her caller.

"Oh, well, I mean--" He seemed in some confusion.

"I want to know something," went on Viola. "Did you bring it to the attention of the coroner or the prosecutor that Harry Bartlett saw my father just before- before his death, and quarreled with him? Did you tell that, Captain Poland?"

Viola Carwell was like a stem accuser now.

"Did you?" she demanded again.

"I did," answered Captain Poland, not, however, without an effort. "I felt that it was my duty to do so. I merely offered it as a suggestion, however, to one of the prosecutor's detectives. I didn't think it would lead to anything. I happened to hear your father and Harry having some words-about what I couldn't catch-and I thought it no more than right that all the facts should be brought out in court. I made no secret about it. I did not send word anonymously to the coroner, as I might have done. He knew the source of the information, and he could have called me to the stand had he so desired."

"Would you have told the same story on the stand?"

"I would. It was the truth."

"Even if it sent him--sent Harry to jail?"

"I would--yes. I felt it was my duty, and--"

"Oh-duty!"

Viola made a gesture of impatience.

"So-you-you told, Captain Poland! That is enough! Please don't try to see me again."

"Viola!" he pleaded. "Please listen--"

"I mean it!" she said, sternly. "Go! I never want to see you again! Oh, to do such a thing!"

The captain, nonplussed for a moment, lingered, as though to appeal from the decision. Then, without a word, he turned sharply on his heel and left the room.

Viola sank on a sofa, and gave way to her emotion.

"It can't be true! It can't!" she sobbed. "I won't believe it. It must not be true! Oh, how can I prove otherwise? But I will! I must! Harry never did that horrible thing, and I will prove it!

"Why should Captain Poland try to throw suspicion on him? It isn't right. He had no need to tell the detective that! I must see Colonel Ashley at once and tell him what I think. Oh, Captain Poland, if I--"

Viola twisted in her slender hands a sofa cushion, and then threw it violently from her.

"I'll see Colonel Ashley at once!" she decided.

Inquiry of a maid disclosed the fact that the colonel was still fishing, and from Patrick, the gardener, she learned that he had gone to try his luck at a spot in the river at the end of the golf course where Patrick himself had hooked more than one fish.

"I'll follow him there," said Viola. "I suppose he won't want to be interrupted while he's fishing, but I can't help it! I must talk to some one--tell somebody what I think."

She donned a walking skirt and stout shoes, for the way to the river was rough, and set out. On the way she thought of many things, and chiefly of the man pacing his lonely walk back and forth behind windows that had steel bars on them.

Viola became aware of some one walking toward her as she neared the bend of the river whither Patrick had directed her, and a second glance told her it was the faithful Shag.

He bowed with a funny little jerk and took off his cap.

"Is the colonel there?" and she indicated what seemed to be an ideal fishing place among the willows.

"He was, Miss Viola, but he done gone now."

"Gone? Where? Do you mean back to the house?"

"No'm. He done gone t' N'York."

"New York?"

"Yes'm. On de afternoon train. He say he may be back t'night, an' mebby not 'twell mornin'."

"But New York-and so suddenly! Why did he go, Shag?"

"I don't know all de 'ticklers, Miss Viola, but I heah him say he got t' git a book on poisons."

"A book on poisons?" and Viola started.

"Yes'm. He done want one fo' de case he's wukin' on, an' he can't git none at de library, so he go to N'York after one. I'se bringin' back his tackle. De fish didn't bite nohow, so he went away, de colonel did."

"Oh!"

Viola stood irresolute a moment, and then turned back toward the house, Shag walking beside her.

CHAPTER XIV. THE PRIVATE SAFE

Divided as she was among several opinions, torn by doubts and sufferings from grief, Viola Carwell found distinct relief in a message that awaited her on her return to the house after her failure to find Colonel Ashley. The message, given her by a maid, was to the effect:

"The safe man has come."

"The who?" asked Viola, not at first understanding.

"The safe man. He said you sent for him to open a safe and--"

"Oh, yes, I understand, Jane. Where is he?"

"In the library, Miss Viola."

Viola hastened to the room where so many fateful talks had taken place of late, and found there a quiet man, beside whose chair was a limp valise that rattled with a metallic jingle as his foot brushed against it when he arose on her entrance.

"Have you come from the safe company?" she asked.

"Yes. I understood that there was one of our safes which could not be opened, and they sent me. Here is the order," and he held out the paper.

He spoke with quiet dignity, omitting the "ma'am," from his salutation. And Viola was glad of this. He was a relief from the usual plumber or carpenter, who seemed to lack initiative.

"It is my father's private safe that we wish opened," she said. "He alone had the combination to it, and he--he is dead," she added softly.

"So I understood," he responded with appreciation of what her grief must be. "Well, I think I shall be able to open the safe without damaging it. That was what you wanted, was it not?"

"Yes. Father never let any one but himself open the safe when he was alive. I don't believe my mother or I saw it open more than ten times, and then by accident.

In it he kept his private papers. But, now that he is--is gone, there is need to see how his affairs stand. The lawyer tells me I had better open the safe.

"When we found that none of us knew the combination, and when it was not found written down anywhere among father's other papers, and when his clerk, Mr. Blossom, did not have it, we sent to the company."

"I understand," said the safe expert. "If you will show me--"

Viola touched a button on the wall, a button so cleverly concealed that the ordinary observer would never have noticed it, and a panel slid back, revealing the door of the safe.

"It was one of father's ideas that his strong box was better hidden this way," said Viola, with a little wan smile. "Is there room enough for you to work? The safe is built into the wall."

"Oh, there is plenty of room, thank you. I can very easily get at it. It isn't the first safe I've had to work on this way. Many families have safes hidden like this. It's a good idea."

He looked at the safe, noted the manufacturer's number, and consulted a little book he carried with him. Then he began to turn the knob gently, listening the while, with acute and trained ears, to the noise the tumblers made as they clicked their way, unseen, amid the mazes of the combination.

"Will it be difficult, do you think?" asked Viola. "Will it take you long?"

"That is hard to say."

"Do you mind if I watch you?" she asked eagerly. She wanted something to take her mind off the many things that were tearing at it as the not far distant sea tore at the shore which stood as a barrier in its way.

"Not at all," answered the expert. Then he went on with his work.

In a way it was as delicate an operation as that which sometimes confronts a physician who is in doubt as to what ails his patient. There was a twisting and a turning of the knob, a listening with an ear to the heavy steel door, as a doctor listens to the breathing of a pneumonia victim. Then with his little finger held against the numbered dial, the expert again twirled the nickel knob, seeking to tell, by the vibration, when the little catches fell into the slots provided for them.

It was rather a lengthy operation, and he tried several of the more common and usual combinations without result. As he straightened up to rest Viola asked:

"Do you think you can manage it? Can you open it?"

"Oh, yes. It will take a little time, but I can do it. Your father evidently used a more complicated combination than is usually set on these safes. But I shall find it."

Viola's determination to open the safe had been arrived at soon after the funeral, when it was found that, as far as could be ascertained, her father had left no will. A stickler for system, in its many branches and ramifications, and insisting for minute detail on the part of his subordinates, Horace Carwell did what many a better and worse man has done--put off the making of his will. And that made it necessary for the surrogate to appoint an administrator, who, in this case, Viola renouncing her natural rights, was Miss Mary Carwell.

"I'd rather you acted than I," Viola had said, though she, being of age and the direct heir, could well and legally have served.

Miss Carwell had agreed to act. Then it became necessary to find out certain facts, and when they were not disclosed by a perusal of the papers of the dead man found in his office and in the safe deposit box at the bank, recourse was had to the private safe. LeGrand Blossom knew nothing of what was in the strong box--not even being entrusted with the combination.

"There! It's open!" announced the expert at length, and he turned the handle and swung back the door.

"Thank you," said Viola. Then, as she looked within the safe, she exclaimed:

"Oh, there is an inner compartment, and that's locked, too!"

"Only with a key. That will give no trouble at all," said the man. He proved it by opening it with the third key he tried from a bunch of many he took from his valise.

That was all there was for him to do, save to set the combination with a simpler system, which he did, giving Viola the numbers.

"Was it as easy as you thought?" she asked, when the expert was about to leave.

"Not quite--no. The combination was a double one. That is, in two parts. First the one had to be disposed of, and then the other worked."

"Why was that?"

"Well, it is on the same principle as the safe deposit boxes in a bank. The depositor has one key, and the bank the other. The box cannot be opened by either party alone. Both keys must be used. That insures that no one person alone can get into the box. It was the same way with this safe. The combination was in two parts."

"And did my father set it that way?"

"He must have done so, or had some one arrange the combination for him."

"Then he--he must have shared the combination with some one else!" There was fright in Viola's eyes, and a catch in her voice.

"Yes," assented the expert. "Either that or he set it that way merely for what we might call a 'bluff,' to throw any casual intruder off the track. Your father might have possessed both combinations himself."

"And yet he might have shared them with--with another person?"

"Yes."

"And the other--the other person"--Viola hesitated noticeably over the word--"would have to be present when the safe was opened?" She did not say "he" or "she."

"Well, not necessarily," answered the expert. "He might have had the combination in two parts, and used both of them himself. It is often done. Though, of course, he could, at any time, have shared the secret of the safe with some one else."

"That would only be in the event of there being something in it that both he and some other person would want to take out at the same time; something that one could not get at without the knowledge of the other; would it not?"

"Naturally, yes. But, as I say, it might be the other way--that the double combination was used merely as an additional precaution."

"Thank you," said Viola.

She sat for several minutes in front of the opened safe after the expert had gone, and did not offer to take out any of the papers that were now exposed to view. There was a strange look on her face.

"Two persons!" she murmured. "Two persons! Did he share the secrets of this safe with some one--some one else?"

Viola reached forth her hand and took hold of a bundle of papers tied with a red band-tape it was, of the kind used in lawyers' offices. The bundle appeared to contain letters--old letters, and the handwriting was that of a woman.

"I wonder if I had better get Aunt Mary?" mused the girl. "She is the administrator, and she will have to know. But there are some things I might keep from her--if I had to."

She looked more closely at the letters, and when she saw that they were in the well-remembered hand of her mother she breathed more easily.

"If he kept--these--it must be--all right!" she faltered to herself. "I will call Aunt Mary."

The two women, seeing dimly through their tears at times, went over the contents of the private safe. There were letters that told of the past--of the happy days of love and courtship, and of the early married life. Viola put them sacredly aside, and delved more deeply into the strong box.

"It was like Horace to keep something away from every one else," said his sister. "He did love a secret. But we don't seem to be getting at anything, Viola, that will tell us where there is any more money, and that's what we need now, more than anything else. At least you do, if LeGrand Blossom is right, and you intend to keep on living in the style you're used to."

"I don't have to do that, Aunt Mary. Being poor would not frighten me."

"I didn't think it would. Fortunately I have enough for both of us, though I won't spend anything on a big yacht nor a car that looks like a Fourth of July procession, however much I love the Star Spangled Banner.

"Oh, no, we mustn't dream of keeping the big car nor the yacht," said Viola. "They are to be sold as soon as possible. I only hope they will bring a good price. But here are more papers, Aunt Mary. We must see what they are. Poor father had so many business interests. It's going to be a dreadful matter to straighten them all out."

"Well, LeGrand Blossom and Captain Poland will help us."

"Captain Poland?" questioned Viola.

"Yes. Why not? He is a fine business man, and he has large interests of his own. Have you any objection?"

"Oh, I don't know. Of course not!" she added quickly, as she caught sight of a rather odd look on her aunt's face. "If we have to--I mean if you find it necessary, you can ask his advice, I suppose."

"Wouldn't you?"

"Why, yes, I believe I would--just as a matter of business."

Viola's voice was calm and cool, but it might have been because her attention was focused on a bundle of papers she was taking from the safe. And a casual perusal of these showed that they had a bearing on subjects that might explain certain things.

"Look, Aunt Mary!" the girl exclaimed. "Father seems to have kept a diary. It tells--it tells about that trouble he had with Harry--Rather, it wasn't with Harry at all. It was Harry's uncle. It's that same old trouble father so often referred to. He always declared he was cheated in a certain business deal, but I always imagined it was because he didn't make as much money as he thought he ought to. Father was like that. But see-this puts a different face on it."

Together they looked over the papers, and among them-among the memoranda, copies of contracts and other documents--was a diary, or perhaps it might be called a business man's journal. Both Viola and her aunt were familiar enough with business to understand the import of what they read.

It was to the effect that Mr. Amos Bartlett, Harry's paternal uncle, had been associated with Mr. Carwell in several transactions involving some big business deals. Mr. Bartlett had been smart enough, by forming a directorate within a directorate and by means of a dummy company, to get a large sum to his credit, while Mr. Carwell was left to face a large deficit.

"And Harry Bartlett acted as agent for his uncle in the transactions!" exclaimed Miss Carwell as she looked over the papers.

"But I don't believe he knew anything wrong was being done!" declared Viola. "I'm positive he didn't. Harry isn't that kind of a man."

"These papers don't say so."

"Naturally you wouldn't expect father to say a good word for one he considered his business rival, not to say enemy. I don't believe Harry had anything more to do with it than he had with--with poor father's death."

Miss Carwell said nothing. She was busy looking over some other papers which the opening of the private safe had revealed. And then, while her aunt was engaged with these, Viola found a little bundle that had on it her name.

For a moment she debated with herself whether or not to open it. The handwriting was that of her father, and it seemed as though something stayed her. But she broke the string at last and there tumbled into her lap some photographs of herself, taken at different ages, a number of them--in fact, most of them--amateur attempts, some snapped by her mother and some by her father, as Viola knew from seeing them. She recalled some very well--especially one taken on the back of a little Shetland pony. On the reverse of this picture Mr. Carwell had written: "My dear little girl!"

Viola burst into tears, and her aunt, seeing the cause, felt the strings of her heart being tugged.

"Well, one thing seems to be proved," said the older woman, when they were again going over the papers, sorting out some to be shown to the lawyer who was advising them on the conduct of the estate, "and that is that your father didn't think very much of Harry Bartlett."

"That was his fault--I mean father's," retorted Viola. "He had no reason for it, even with what this paper says. I don't believe Harry would do such a thing."

"Do you suppose the quarrel could have been about this?" and Miss Carwell held out the journal.

"I don't know what to think," said Viola. "But here is another memorandum. We must see what this is."

Together they bent over the remaining documents the safe had given up--secrets of the dead.

As they read a strange look came over Viola's face.

Miss Carwell, perusing a document, recited:

"Memo. of certain matters between Captain Poland and myself. And while I think of it let me state that but for his timely and generous financial aid I would have been ruined by that scoundrel Bartlett. Captain Poland saved me. And should the stock of the concern ever be on a paying basis I intend to repay him not only all he advanced me but any profit I may secure shall be divided with him in gratitude. That there will be a profit I very much doubt, though this does not lessen my gratitude to Captain Poland for his aid."

There was a little gasp from Viola as she heard this.

"Captain Poland saved father from possible ruin," she murmured, "and I--I treated him so! Oh! oh!"

CHAPTER XV. POOR FISHING

Have a drink, Colonel?"

"Eh?"

"I said--Here, boy! A Scotch high and a mint julep."

Colonel Ashley, roused from his reverie as he sat in his club, gazing out on the busy, fashionable, hurrying, jostling, worried, happy, sad, and otherwise throngs that swept past the big Fifth avenue windows, shifted himself in the comfortable leather chair, and looked at his cigar. It had gone out, and he decided that it was not worth relighting.

"Cigars, too!" ordered Bruce Garrigan.

"Oh, were you speaking to me?" and the colonel seemed wholly awake now.

"Not only to you, but in your interests," went on Garrigan, with a smile. "Hope I didn't disturb your nap, but--"

"Oh, no," the colonel hastened to assure his companion with his usual affability. "I had finished sleeping."

"So I inferred. Do you know how many hours, minutes and seconds the average human being has passed in sleep when he reaches the age of forty-five years?" and Garrigan smiled quizzically.

"No, sir," answered Colonel Ashley, "I do not."

"Neither do I," confessed Mr. Garrigan as he sank down in a chair beside the colonel and accepted the glass from a tray which the much-buttoned club attendant held out to him. "I don't know, and I don't much care."

Then, when cigars were glowing and the smoke arose in graceful clouds, an aroma as of incense shrouding the two as they gazed out on the afternoon throngs, Garrigan remarked:

"I didn't know you were here. In fact, I didn't know you were a member of this club."

"You wouldn't know it if my attendance here were needed to prove it," said the colonel with a smile. "I don't get here very often, but I had to run up on some business, and I found this the most convenient stopping place."

"Are you going back to Lakeside?"

"Oh, yes!" There was prompt decision in the answer.

"Then you haven't finished that unfortunate affair? You haven't found out what caused the death of Mr. Carwell?"

"Oh, yes, I know what killed him."

"But not who?"

"Not yet."

"Do you hold to the suicide theory?"

"I don't hold to anything, my dear Mr. Garrigan," answered the colonel, who was in a sufficiently mellow mood to be amused by the rather vapid talk of his host--for such he had constituted himself on the ordering of the drinks and cigars. "That is I haven't such a hold on any theory that I can't let go and take a new one if occasion warrants it."

"I see. And so you came up to get away from the rather gruesome atmosphere down there?"

"Not exactly. I came up on business--I have a business in New York you know, in spite of the fact that I am here," and the colonel smiled as he looked about the room where were gathered men of wealth and leisure, who did not seem to have a care or worry in the world.

"Oh, yes, I know that," agreed Garrigan. "Well, has your trip been satisfactory?"

"I can't say that it has. In fact it's pretty poor fishing around here, and I'm thinking of going back. I want to hear the click of the reel and the music of the brook. I wasn't cut out for a city man, and the longer I stay here the worse I hate the place, even if I do have a business here."

"Then you don't care for--this," and Garrigan waved his hand at the congestion of automobiles and stages which had come to a halt opposite the big windows of the exclusive and fashionable club.

It was four in the afternoon, just when traffic both of automobiles and pedestrians is at its height on the avenue. Of horse-drawn equipages they were so few as to be a novelty.

"I care so little for it that I am going back to-night," the detective responded.

"Then you have found what you came looking for?"

"I told you the fishing was very poor," said the colonel with a smile. "My friend Mr. Walton, were he alive now, would never forgive me for deserting the place I left to come here. When did you come up?"

"Last night. They insisted I had to put in an appearance at the office merely to take away the salary that's been accumulating for me--said it cluttered up the place. So I obliged. Do you know how many automobiles pass this window every twenty-four hours?" Garrigan asked suddenly.

"I do not."

"Neither do I. It would be interesting to know, however. I think I shall count them, when I have nothing else to do. I understand there is a checking or tabulating machine made for such purposes. But perhaps I am keeping you from--"

"You are merely keeping me from ordering another portion of liquid refreshment," interrupted the colonel with a smile. "Boy!"

And once again there was diffused the aroma of mint and the more pronounced odor of the Scotch.

"Yes, it's pretty poor fishing," mused the colonel, when Garrigan had gone off to engage in a game of billiards with some insistent friends, whose advent the detective was thankful for, as he wanted to be alone. He was gregarious by nature, but there were times when he had to be alone, and it was because of this trait in his nature that he had taken up with the rod and reel, becoming a disciple of Izaak Walton.

Until dusk began to fall, changing the character of the throngs on the avenue, the colonel lingered in his easy chair before the broad, plate windows. And then, as the electric lights began to sparkle, as had the diamonds on some of the over-dressed women in the afternoon, he arose and started out.

"Will you be dining here, sir?" asked one of the stewards.

"Mr. Garrigan asked me to inquire, sir, and, if you were, to say that he would appreciate it if you would be his guest."

"Thank him for me, and tell him I can't stay." And the colonel, tossing aside the cigar which had gone out and been frequently relighted, soon found himself making a part of the avenue's night throng.

It was a warm summer evening-altogether too warm to be in New York when one had the inclination and means to be elsewhere, but the colonel, in spite of the fact that he had been in a hurry to leave the club, seemed to find no occasion for haste now.

He sauntered along, seemingly without an object, though the rather frequent consultations he made of his watch appeared to indicate otherwise. Finally, he seemed either to have come to a sudden decision or to have noted the demise of the time he was trying to kill, for with a last quick glance at his timepiece he put it back into his pocket, and, turning a corner where there was a taxicab stand, he entered one of the vehicles and gave an order to the chauffeur.

"Columbia College-yes, sir!" and the driver looked rather oddly at the figure of the colonel.

"Wonder what he teaches, and what he's going up there this time of night for?" was the mental comment of the chauffeur. "Maybe they have evening classes, but this guy looks as though he could give em a post-graduate course in poker."

Colonel Ashley sat back in the corner of the cab, glad of the rather long ride before him. He scarcely moved, save when the sway or jolt of the vehicle tossed him about, and he sat with an unlighted cigar between his teeth.

"Yes," he murmured once, "pretty poor fishing. I might better have stayed where I was. Well, I'll go back to-morrow."

Leaving the taxicab, the colonel made his way along the raised plaza on which some of the college buildings front, and turned into the faculty club, where he stayed for some time. When he came out, having told his man to wait, he bore under his arm a package which, even to the casual observer, contained books.

"Pennsylvania station," was the order he gave, and again he sat back in the corner of the cab, scarcely glancing out of the window to note the busy scenes all about him.

It was not until he had purchased his ticket and was about to board the last Jersey Shore train, to take him back to the 'scene of the death of Horace Carwell, that Colonel Ashley, as he caught sight of a figure in the crowd ahead of him, seemed galvanized into new life.

For a moment he gazed at a certain man, taking care to keep some women with large hats between the object of his attention and himself. And then, as he made sure of the identity, the colonel murmured:

"Poor fishing did I say? Well, it seems to me it's getting better."

He looked at his watch, made a rapid calculation that showed him he had about five minutes before the train's departure, and then he hurried off to his right and down the stairs that led to the lavatories.

It was Colonel Robert Lee Ashley, as Bruce Garrigan had seen him at the Fifth Avenue club, who entered one of the pay compartments where so many in-coming and out-going travelers may, for the modest sum of ten cents, enjoy in the railroad station a freshening up by means of soap, towels and plenty of hot water.

But it was a typical Southern politician, with slouch hat, long frock coat, a moustache and goatee, who emerged from the same private wash-room a little later, carrying a small, black valise.

"I don't like to do this," said Colonel Ashley, making sure the spirit gum had set, so his moustache and goatee would not come off prematurely, "but I have to. This fishing is getting better, and I don't want any of the fish to see me."

Then he went down the steps to the train that soon would be whirling him under the Hudson river, along the Jersey meadows, and down to the cool shore. He passed through the string of coaches until he came to one where he found a seat behind a certain man. Into this vantage point the colonel, looking more the part than ever, slumped himself and opened his paper.

"Yes, the fishing is getting better--decidedly better," he mused. "I shouldn't wonder but what I got a bite soon."

CHAPTER XVI. SOME LETTERS

When Jean Forette, whose month was not quite up and who had not yet completed arrangements for his new position, alighted from the Shore Express at Lakeside and made his way-afoot and not in a machine--to the Three Pines, the picturesque figure of the Southern gentleman followed.

"I wonder," mused Colonel Ashley, "whether he takes Scotch Highballs or absinthe, and what dope he mixes with it? Absinthe is rather hard to get out here, I should imagine, but they might have a green brand of whiskey they'd sell for it. But that Frenchman ought to know the genuine stuff. However, we'll see."

Carrying his limp, leather bag, which had served him in such good stead when he entered the lavatory, the colonel slouched silently along the road. It was close to midnight, and there would be no other trains to the shore that day.

The lights of the Three Pines glowed in pleasant and inviting fashion across the sandy highway. Out in front stood several cars, for the tavern was one much patronized by summer visitors, and was a haven of refuge, a "life-saving station," as it had been dubbed by those who fancied they were much in need of alcoholic refreshment.

Jean Forette entered, and Colonel Ashley, waiting a little and making sure that the "tap room," as it was ostentatiously called, was sufficiently filled to enable him to mingle with the patrons without attracting undue notice, followed.

He looked about for a sight of the chauffeur, and saw him leaning up against the bar, sipping a glass of beer, and, between imbibitions, talking earnestly to the white-aproned bartender.

"I'd like to hear what they're saying," mused the colonel. "I wonder if I can get a bit nearer."

He ordered some rye, and, having disposed of it, took out a cigar, and began searching in his pockets as though for a match.

"Here you are!" observed a bartender, as he held out a lighted taper.

The colonel had anticipated this, and quickly moved down the mahogany rail toward the end where Jean Forette was standing. At that end was a little gas jet kept burning as a convenience to smokers.

"I'll use that," said the colonel. "I don't like the flavor of burnt wood in my smoke."

"Fussy old duck," murmured the barkeeper as he let the flame he had ignited die out, flicking the blackened end to the floor.

And, being careful to keep his face as much as possible in the shadow of his big, slouch hat, Colonel Ashley lighted his cigar at the gas flame.

And, somehow or other, that cigar required a long and most careful lighting. The smoker got the tip glowing, and then inspected it critically. It was not to his satisfaction, as he drew a few puffs on it, and again he applied the end to the flame.

He sent forth a perfect cloud of smoke this time, and it seemed to veil him as the fog, blowing in from the sea, veils the tumbling billows. Once more there was a look at the end, but the "fussy old duck" was not satisfied, and, again had recourse to the flame.

All this while Colonel Ashley was straining his ears to catch what Jean Forette was saying to the attendant who had drawn the frothing glass of beer for him.

But the men talked in too low a tone, or the colonel had been a bit too late, for all he heard was a murmur of automobile talk. Jean seemed to be telling something about a particularly fast car he had formerly driven.

"The fishing isn't as good as I hoped," mused the colonel.

Then, as he turned to go out, he heard distinctly:

"Sure I remember you paying for the drink. I can prove that if you want me to. Are they tryin' to double-cross you?"

"Something like that, yes."

"Well, you leave it to me, see? I'll square you all right."

"Thanks," murmured Jean, and then he, too, turned aside.

"There may be something in it after all," was the colonel's thought, and then he, too, hurried from the Three Pines, passing beneath the big trees, with their sighing branches, which gave the name to the inn.

On toward The Haven, through the silence and darkness of the night, went the detective. And at a particularly dark and lonely place he stopped. The pungent, clean smell of grain alcohol filled the air, and a little later a man, devoid of goatee and moustache, passing out into the starlight, while a black, slouch hat went into the bag, and a Panama, so flexible that it had not suffered from having been thrust rather ruthlessly into the valise, came out.

"I don't like that sort of detective work," mused the colonel, "but it has its uses."

Viola Carwell, alone in her room, sat with a bundle of letters on a table before her. They were letters she had found in a small drawer of the private safe--a drawer she had, at first, thought contained nothing. The discovery of the letters had been made in a peculiar manner.

Viola and Miss Carwell, going over the documents, had sorted them into two piles--one to be submitted to the lawyer, the other being made up of obviously personal matters that could have no interest for any but members of the family.

Then Miss Carwell had been called away to attend to some household matters, and Viola had started to return to the safe such of the papers as were not to go to the lawyer.

She opened a small drawer, to slip back into it a bundle of letters her mother had written to Mr. Carwell years before. Then Viola became aware of something else in the drawer. It was something that caught on the end of her finger nail, and she was stung by a little prick-like that of a pin.

"A sliver--under my nail!" exclaimed Viola. "The bottom of the wooden drawer must be loose."

It was loose, as she discovered as soon as she looked in the compartment. But it was a looseness that meant nothing else than that the drawer had a false bottom.

It was not such a false bottom as would have been made use of in the moving pictures. That is to say it was very poorly made, and an almost casual glance would have revealed it. All that had been done was to take a piece of wood the exact size and shape of the bottom of the drawer, and fit it in. This extra piece of wood covered anything that might be put in the drawer under it, and then, on top of the false bottom other things might be placed so that when they were taken out, and the person doing it saw bare wood, the conclusion would naturally follow that all the contents of the drawer had been removed.

But such was not the case. Beneath the smooth-fitting piece of wood, which had sprung loose and been the means of driving a splinter under Viola's nail, thus apprising her of the fact that there was something in the drawer she had not seen, had been found some letters. And Viola had not told her aunt about them.

"I want to see what they are myself, first," the girl decided.

Now they were spread out on her dressing table in front of her. She sat with her glorious blue-black hair unbound, and falling over her shoulders, which gleamed pink through the filmy thinness of her robe.

"I wonder if I shall be shocked when I read them?" she mused.

That was what Viola had been living in continual fear of since her father's death--that some disclosure would shock her--that she might come upon some phase of his past life which would not bear the full light of day. For Horace Carwell had not stinted himself of the pleasures of life as he saw them. He had eaten and drunk and he had made merry. And he was a gregarious man--one who did not like to take his pleasures alone.

And so Viola was afraid.

The letters were held together with an elastic band, and this gave some hope.

"If they were from a woman, he wouldn't have used a rubber band on them," reasoned Viola. "He was too sentimental for that. They can't be mother's letters--they were in another compartment. I wonder--"

Viola had done much wondering since her mother's death, and considerable of it had been due to the life her father led. That he would marry again she doubted, but he was fond of the society of the men, and particularly the women of their own set, and some sets with which Viola preferred to have nothing to do.

And if Mr. Carwell had no intentions of marrying again, then his interest in women--

But here Viola ceased wondering.

With a more resolute air she reached forth hand to the bundle of letters and took one out. There was distinct relief in her manner as she quickly turned to the signature and read: "Gerry Poland."

And then, quickly, she ascertained that all the letters comprised correspondence between her father and the yacht club captain.

"But why did he hide these letters away?" mused Viola. "They seem to be about business, as the others were--the others showing that Captain Poland perhaps saved my father from financial ruin. Why should they be under the false bottom of the drawer?"

She could not answer that question.

"I must read them all," she murmured, and she went through the entire correspondence. There were several letters, sharp in tone, from both men, and the subject was as Greek to Viola. But there was one note from the captain to her father that brought a more vivid color to her dark cheeks, for Captain Poland had written:

"You care little for what I have done for you, otherwise you would not so oppose my attentions to your daughter. They are most honorable, as you well know, yet you are strangely against me. I can not understand it."

"Oh!" murmured Viola. "It is as if I were being bargained for! How I hate him!"

Almost blinded by her tears she read another letter. It was another appeal to her father to use his influence in assisting the captain's suit.

But this letter--or at least that portion of it relating to Viola--had been torn, and all that remained was:

"As members of the same lo--"

"What can that have meant?" she mused. "Is it the word 'lodge'?"

She read on, where the letter was whole again:

"I must ask you to reconsider your actions. Let me hear from you by the twenty-third or--"

Again was that mystifying and tantalizing tear. Viola hastily searched among the other letters, hoping the missing pieces might be found.

"I simply must see what it meant," she said. "I wonder if they can be in another part of the safe? I'm going to look!"

She started for her bath robe, and, at that moment, with a suddenness that unnerved her, there came a knock on her door.

CHAPTER XVII. OVER THE TELEPHONE

Viola's first movement was of concealment--to toss over the scattered letters on her desk a lace shawl she had been wearing earlier in the evening. Then satisfied that should the unknown knocker prove to be some one whom she might admit--her Aunt Mary or one of the maids--satisfied that no one would, at first glance, see the letters which might mean nothing or much, Viola asked in a voice that slightly trembled:

"Who is it?"

"I did not mean to disturb you," came the answer, and with a sense of relief Viola recognized the voice of Colonel Ashley. "But I have jus returned from New York, and, seeing a light under your door, I thought I would-report, as it were."

"Oh, thank you-thank you!" the girl exclaimed, relief evident in her voice.

"Is there anything I can do for you?" the colonel went on, as he stood outside the closed door. "Has anything happened since I went away?"

"No--no," said Viola, rather hesitatingly. "There is nothing new to tell you. I was sitting up--reading."

Her glance went to the desk where the letters were scattered.

"Oh," answered the colonel. "Well, don't sit up too late. It is getting on toward morning."

"Have you anything to tell me, Colonel Ashley?" asked Viola. "Did you discover anything?"

There was silence on the other side of the door for a moment, and then came the answer, given slowly:

"No, nothing to report. I will have a talk with you in the morning."

And then the footsteps of the detective were heard, lessening in their sound, as he made his way to his room.

Viola, perplexed, puzzled, and bewildered, went back to her desk. She took up the letters again. The torn one with its strange reference: "As members of the same--"

What could it be? Was it some secret society to which her father and Gerry Poland belonged, the violation of the secrets of which carried a death penalty?

No, it could not be anything as sensational as that. Clearly the captain was in love with her--he had frankly confessed as much, and Viola knew it anyhow. She was not at all sure whether he loved her for her position or because she was good to look upon and desirable in every way.

As for her own heart, she was sure of that. In spite of the fact that she had tried to pique him that fatal day, merely to "stir him up," as she phrased it, Viola was deeply and earnestly in love with Harry Bartlett, and she was sure enough of his feeling toward her to find in it a glow of delight.

Then there was in the letter the hint of a threat. "Let me hear from you by the twenty-third, or--"

"Oh, what does it mean? What does it mean?" and Viola bent her weary head down on the letters and her tears stained them. Puzzled as she was over the contents of the letters--torn and otherwise--which she had found hidden in the drawer of the private safe, Viola Carwell was not yet ready to share her secret with her Aunt Mary or Colonel Ashley. These two were her nearest and most natural confidants under the circumstances.

"I would like to tell Harry, but I can't," she reasoned, when she had awakened after a night of not very refreshing slumber. "Of course Captain Poland could explain--if he would. But I'll keep this a secret a little longer. But, oh! I wonder what it means?"

And so, when she greeted Colonel Ashley at the breakfast table she smiled and tried to appear her usual self.

"I did not hear you come in," said Miss Carwell, as she poured the coffee.

"No, I did not want to disturb any one," answered the colonel. "I saw a light under Miss Viola's door, and reported myself to her," he went on. "But I don't imagine you slept much more than I did, for your eyes are not as bright as usual," and he smiled at the girl.

"Aren't they?" countered Viola. "Well, I did read later than I should. But tell me, Colonel Ashley, are you making any progress at all?"

He did not answer for a moment. He seemed very much occupied in buttering a piece of roll--trying to get the little dab of yellow in the exact center of the white portion. Then, when it was arranged to his satisfaction, he said:

"I am making progress, that is all I can say now."

"And does that progress carry with it any hope that Harry Bartlett will be proved innocent?" asked Viola eagerly.

"That I can not say--now. I hope it will, though."

"Thank you for that!" exclaimed Viola earnestly.

Miss Carwell said nothing. She had her own opinion, and was going to hold to it, detectives or no detectives.

"Will you send Shag to me?" the colonel requested a maid, as he arose from the table. "Tell him we are going fishing."

"Isn't there anything you can do--I mean toward--toward the--case?" faltered Viola. "Not that I mean--of course I don't want to seem--"

"I understand, my dear," said the colonel gently. "And I am not going fishing merely to shirk a responsibility. But I have to think some of these puzzles out quietly, and fishing is the quietest pastime I know."

"Oh, yes, I know," Viola hastened to add. "I shouldn't have said anything. I wish I could get quiet myself. I'm almost tempted to take your recipe."

"Why don't you?" urged the colonel. "Come along with me. I can soon teach you the rudiments, though to become a finished angler, so that you would be not ashamed to meet Mr. Walton, takes years. But I think it would rest you to come. Shall I tell Shag to fit you out with one of my rods?"

Viola hesitated a moment. This might give her an opportunity for talking with the colonel in secret and confidence. But she put it aside.

"No, thank you," she answered. "I'll go another time. I must stop at the office and leave some bills that have come here to the house. Mr. Blossom attends to the payment."

"Let me leave them for you," offered the colonel. "I have to go into town for some bait, and I can easily stop at the office for you."

"If you will be so good," returned Viola, and she got the bundle of bills--some relating to Mr. Carwell's funeral and others that had been mailed to the house instead of to the office.

The colonel might have sent Shag to purchase the shedder crabs he was going to use for bait that day in fishing in the inlet, and the colored servant might have left the bills. But the colonel was particular about his bait, and would let none select it but himself. Consequently he had Jean Forette drive him in, telling Shag to meet him at a certain dock where they would drop down the inlet and try for "snappers," young bluefish, elusive, gamy and delicious eating.

"You have not yet found a place?" asked the colonel of the chauffeur, as they rolled along.

"No, monsieur--none to my satisfaction, though I have been offered many. One I could have I refused yesterday."

"You liked it with Mr. Carwell, then?"

"Truly the situation was in itself delightful. But I could not manage the big car as he liked, and we had to part. There was no other way."

The detective narrowly observed the driver beside whom he sat. Jean did not look well. He had much of the appearance of the "morning after the night before," and his hand was not very steady as he shifted the gear lever.

"How much longer have you to stay here, Jean?"

"About two weeks. My month will be up then."

"And then you go--"

"I do not know, monsieur. Probably to New York. That is a great headquarters."

"So I believe."

"If monsieur should hear of a family that--"

"Yes, I'll bear you in mind, Jean. You are steady and reliable, I presume?" and the colonel smiled.

"I have most excellent letters!" he boasted, and for the moment he seemed to rouse himself from the sluggishness that marked him that morning.

"I'll bear it in mind," said the colonel again.

But as they drove on, and Colonel Ashley noted with what exaggerated care Jean Forette passed other cars--giving them such a wide berth that often his own machine was almost in the ditch--the impression grew on the detective that the Frenchman was not as skillful as he would have it believed.

"He drives Like an amateur, or a woman out alone in her machine for the first time," mused the colonel. "He'd never do for a smart car. Wonder what ails him. He wasn't drunk last night by any means, and yet--"

They reached the town, and paused at the only place where there was any congestion of traffic--where two main seashore highways crossed in the center of Lakeside. Jean held the runabout there so long, waiting for other traffic to pass, that the officer who was on duty called:

"What's the matter--going to sleep there?"

Then Jean, with a start, threw in the clutch and shot ahead.

"That's queer," mused the colonel. "He seems afraid."

The purchase of the shedder crabs was gone into care fully, and having questioned the bait-seller as to the best location in the inlet, the detective again got into the machine and was driven to the office of the late Horace Carwell. It was a branch of the New York office, and thither, every summer, came LeGrand Blossom and a corps of clerks to manage affairs for their employer.

Colonel Ashley, who by this time was known to the office boy at the outer gate, was admitted at once.

"Mr. Blossom is at the telephone," said the lad, "but you can go right in and wait for him."

This the colonel did, having left Jean outside in the car.

The telephone in LeGrand Blossom's private office was in a booth, put there to get it away from the noise of traffic in the street outside. And, as the boy had said, Blossom was in this booth as Colonel Ashley entered.

It so happened that the chief clerk was standing in the booth with his back turned to the main door, and did not see the colonel enter. And the latter, coming in with easy steps, as he always went everywhere, heard a snatch of the talk over the telephone that made him wonder.

Though the little booth was meant to keep sounds from entering, as well as coming out, the door was not tightly closed and as LeGrand Blossom spoke rather loudly Colonel Ashley heard distinctly.

"Yes," said the head clerk over the wire, "I'll pay the money tonight sure. Yes, positive." There was a period of waiting, while he listened, and then he went on: "Yes, on the Allawanda. I'll be there. Yes, sure! Now don't bother me any more."

Colonel Ashley, through the glass door of the telephone booth, saw LeGrand Blossom make a move as though to hang up the receiver. And then the detective turned suddenly, and swung back, as though he had entered the room at the moment Blossom had emerged from the booth.

"Oh!" exclaimed the head clerk, and, for a second, he seemed nonplused. But Colonel Ashley took up the talk instantly.

"I will keep you but a minute," he said. "Miss Viola asked me to leave these bills for you. I came in to town to buy some bait. There they are. I'm going fishing," and before LeGrand Blossom could answer the colonel was saying good-bye and making his way out.

"I wonder," mused the colonel, as he started for the car where Jean awaited him, "what or who or where the Allawanda is? I must find out."

He found further cause for wonder as he started off in the car with the French chauffeur for the boat dock, at the conduct of Jean himself.

For the man appeared to be a wholly different person. His face was all smiles, and there was a jaunty air about him as though he had received good news. His management of the car, too, left nothing to be desired. He started off swiftly, but with a smoothness that told of perfect mastery of the clutch and gears. He took chances, too, as he dashed through town, cutting corners, darting before this car, back of the other until, used as the colonel was to taxicabs in New York, he held his breath more than once.

"What's the matter--in a hurry?" he asked Jean, as they narrowly escaped a collision.

"Oh, no, monsieur, but this is the way I like to drive. It is much more--what you call pep!"

"Yes," mused the colonel to himself, "it's pep all right. But I wonder what put the pep into you? You didn't have it when we started out. Some French dope you take, I'll wager. Well, it may put pep into you now, but it'll take the starch out of you later on."

Jean left the colonel at the dock, whither Shag had already made his way, coming in a more prosaic trolley car from The Haven, and soon they were ready to row down the inlet in a boat.

"Shall I call for you?" asked Jean, as he prepared to drive back.

"No," answered the colonel, "I can't tell what luck I'll have. We'll come home when it suits us."

"Very good, monsieur."

And so the colonel went fishing, and his thoughts were rather more on the telephone talk he had overheard than on his rod and line.

Contrary to the poor luck that had held all week, so the dockman said, the colonel's good luck was exceptional. Shag had a goodly string of snappers of large size to carry back with him.

"How'd you do it?" asked the boatman, as he made fast the skiff.

"Oh, they just bit and I hauled 'em in," said he colonel. "By the way," he went on, "is there a place around here called Allawanda?"

"Yes, there's a little village named that, about ten miles back in the country," said the boatman.

"Nothing there, though, but a few houses and one store."

"Oh, I thought it might be quite a place."

"No, and nobody'd know it was there if there wasn't a boat around here named after it."

"Is there a boat called that?" asked the colonel, and he tried to keep the eagerness out of his voice.

"Yes. The ferryboat that runs from Lakeside to Loch Elarbor is named that. Seems that one of the men in the company that owns it used to live at Allawanda when he was a boy, and he called the boat that. It's an old tub of a ferry, though, about like the town itself, I guess. Well, you sure did have good luck!"

"Yes, indeed," agreed the colonel, and his luck was better than the boatman guessed, and of a different kind.

It was in pursuance of this same luck that caused the colonel, later that day, when the shadows of evening were falling, to take his limp satchel and slip out of the house. He went afoot to the ferry dock, and when the Allawanda floundered in like a porpoise he went on board. It was his first visit to this part of the inlet that separated Lakeside from Loch Harbor, and this means of getting to the yachting center was seldom used by any guests of The Haven. They went around by the highway in automobiles.

"Well," mused the colonel, as he went to the men's cabin with his limp valise,

"I hope Mr. Blossom keeps his promise and comes here to-night. I shall be interested in noting to whom he pays the money."

Then, seeing that the little cabin of the ramshackle boat was deserted at that hour, the colonel went to a dark corner, and from it emerged, a little later, with a beard on that would have done credit to the most orthodox inhabitant of New York's Ghetto.

Still the colonel did not look like a Jew, and he was not going to attempt that character. He made his way to the stern of the craft, where he could watch all who came aboard, and finding a deck hand who was sweeping, said:

"I'm not feeling very well. Thought maybe a ride back and forth across the inlet would do me good if I stayed out in the air. So if you see me here don't think I'm trying to beat my fare. Here's a dollar, you may keep the change."

"Thanks--ride all you like," said the man. At five cents a trip, with the boat stopping at midnight, there would still be a good tip in it for him. The colonel ensconced himself in a dark corner and waited.

The first two trips over and back were fruitless as far as his object was concerned. But just as the Allawanda was about to pull out for her third voyage across the inlet, there came on board a woman, with a shawl so closely wrapped about her that her features were completely hidden. There were only a few oil lamps on the old-fashioned craft, and the illumination was poor.

The colonel thought there was something vaguely familiar about the figure, but he was not certain. He tried to get near enough to her, in a casual walk up and down the deck, to view her countenance, but, either by accident or design, she turned away and looked over the rail. He was close enough, however, to note that the shawl was of fine texture and of a peculiar pattern.

Retiring again to his corner in the stern of the boat, and noting that the woman kept her place there, Colonel Ashley waited in patience. And he had his reward.

The Allawanrda was whistling to tell the deck hands to cast off the mooring ropes, when LeGrand Blossom came running down the inclined gangway and got on board. He seemed in a hurry and excited, and, apparently unaware of the presence of the detective in the dark corner, he went directly to the woman in the shawl. The boat began to move from her slip.

"Did you think I was never coming?" asked LeGrand Blossom.

"No, I was detained," the woman answered, and at the sound of her voice Colonel Ashley started and uttered a smothered exclamation. "I but just arrived," the woman went on. "Did you bring it?"

"Hush! Yes. Not so loud. Some one may hear you."

"There is no one here. One man, with a heavy beard, passed by me as I came on board. At first I thought it was you, disguised, but when I saw it was not I kept to myself. There is no one here."

"I hope not," murmured LeGrand Blossom, as he looked cautiously around. The after deck was but dimly lighted.

For a time the woman and man talked in tones so low that the detective could hear nothing, and he dared not leave his hidden corner to come closer.

But, just as the Allawanda was nearing her slip on the other side, the man spoke in louder tones. "And so we come to the end!" he said.

"No, please don't say that!" begged the woman.

"I must," Blossom answered. "We can't go on this way any longer. Here is what I promised you. It is all I can raise, and I had a hard time doing that. Every one is suspicious, and that detective is all eyes and ears. It is the best I can do. You must not bother me any more."

The lights from a passing boat fell on the couple as they stood close to the rail, and, from his vantage point in the darkness, the colonel saw LeGrand Blossom hand the woman in the shawl a package. She took it eagerly, and thrust it into her bosom. Then, turning to the man, she said reproachfully:

"You say this is the end. Then you don't love me any more?"

LeGrand Blossom did not answer for a moment.

"You don't--do you?" the woman insisted.

"No," was the slow reply. "I might as well be brutally frank about it, and say I don't. And you don't care either."

"Oh, I do! I do!" she eagerly protested.

"No, you only think you do. It is better for both of us to have it end this way. But let us make sure that it is an end. There must be no more of it. I have given you all I can. You must go away as you promised."

"Yes, I suppose I must," and her voice was broken. "Oh, I wish I had never met you!"

"Perhaps it would have been better that way," was Blossom's cold response. "However, it's too late for that now. Good-bye," he added, as the boat was grating her way along the Loch Harbor slip. "I'm not going to get off. Don't telephone me again. This is all I can ever give you."

"Oh, yes, I suppose, now you've finished, you can get rid of me. Well, let it be so," she said bitterly. And then, as the boat bumped to a landing she cried: "If I could only find--"

But the rattle of the chains and the clatter of the wheels on the ferry bridge drowned her voice. She rushed away from LeGrand Blossoms's side and, clutching her shawl close around her as if to make sure of the package the man had given her, she disappeared into the interior of the ferryboat.

Colonel Ashley started to follow, but as LeGrand Blossom remained on board he decided to watch him instead of the woman, though he was vaguely disquieted trying to remember where he had heard her voice before.

CHAPTER XVIII. A LARGE BLONDE LADY

Reaching The Haven, Colonel Ashley, who had trailed LeGrand Blossom to the latter's boarding place without anything having developed, was met by Shag, who was up later than usual, for it was now close to midnight.

"What now, Shag!" exclaimed the colonel. "Don't tell me there are any more detective cases for me to work on. I simply won't listen. I wish I hadn't to this one. It's getting more and more tangled every minute, and the fish are biting well. Hang it all, Shag, why did you let me take up this golf course mystery?"

"I didn't do it, Colonel, no, sah!"

"What's the use of talking that way, Shag! You know you did!"

"Yes, sah, Colonel. Dat's whut I did!" confessed Shag with a grin. When the colonel was in this mood there was nothing for it but to agree with him.

"And it's the worst tangle you ever got me into!" went on Shag's master. "There's no head or tail to it."

"Den it ain't laik a fish; am it?" asked Shag, with the freedom of long years of faithful service.

"No, it isn't--worse luck!" stormed the colonel. "I never saw such a case. The diamond cross mystery was nothing like it."

"But I thought, Colonel, sah, dat de mo' of a puzzle it were, de bettah yo' laiked it!" ventured Shag.

Colonel Ashley tried to repress a smile.

"Get to bed, you black rascal!" he said with an affectionate pat on Shag's back. "Get to bed! What are you staying up so late for, anyhow?"

"To gib yo' a message, Colonel, sah," answered Shag. "Miss Viola done say I was t' wait up, an', when yo' come in, t' tell yo' dat she wants t' see you."

"Oh, all right. Where is she?"

"In de liberry, Colonel, sah!"

The detective made his way through the dimly-lighted hall, and, on tapping at the library door, was bidden by Viola to enter.

"Still up?" he asked. "It was time for you to be asleep long ago if you want your eyes to keep as bright as they always are."

"They don't feel very bright," she answered, with a little laugh. "They seem to be full of sticks. But I wanted to ask you something--to consult with you--and I didn't want to go to sleep without doing it. I want you to read these," and she spread out before him the letters she had found hidden in the drawer of the safe.

Colonel Ashley, in silence, looked over one document after another, including the torn ones. When he had finished he looked across the table at Viola.

"What do you make of it?" she asked. "I don't know," he frankly confessed. "But we must find out if your father owed the captain anything--for money advanced in an emergency, or for anything else. Who would know about the money affairs?"

"Mr. Blossom. He has full charge of the office now, and access to all the books. Aunt Mary and I have to trust to him for everything. It is all we can do."

"Yes, I suppose so," agreed the detective. And he did not speak of the scene of which he had recently been a witness.

"Then if you will come with me, we will go the first thing in the morning to father's office and see LeGrand Blossom," decided Viola. "We will ask Mr. Blossom if he knows anything about the debt between my father and Captain Poland."

"It would be wise, I think."

And as the colonel retired that night he said, musingly:

"Another angle, and another tangle. I must read a little Izaak Walton to compose my mind."

So he opened the little green book and read this observation from the Venator:

"And as for the dogs that we use, who can commend their excellency to that height which they deserve? How perfect is the hound at smelling, who never leaves or forsakes his first scent, but follows it through so many changes and varieties of other scents, even over and in the water, and into the earth."

"Ah," mused the colonel, "I think I must cling to my first scent, and follow it through or over the water or into the earth."

Then, laying aside the little green book, with its atmosphere of calm delight, he picked up a little thin volume, which bore on its title page "The Poisonous Plants of New Jersey."

And in that he read:

> "The water hemlock (Cicuta maculata L.) is the most poisonous plant in the flora of the United States, and has probably destroyed more human lives than all our other toxic plants combined. As a member of the parsley family (Umbellifera) it resembles in general appearance the carrot and parsnip of the same group of plants. It grows in swampy land. The poisoning of the human is chiefly with the fleshy roots.

> "The active principle of this cicuta is the volatile alkaloid canine, common also to the poison hemlock (Conium macula turn L.) The symptoms of the poisoning are many, including violent contraction of the muscles, dilated pupils and epilepsy... No antidote for canine poisoning is known... The active canine... was the poison employed by the Greeks in putting prisoners to death, Socrates being one of its illustrious victims."

And having read that much, Colonel Ashley looked at a little slip in the book. It bore the penciled memorandum "58 C. H.--~I6I*."

"I wonder--I wonder," mused the colonel, and so wondering, and with fitful dreams attending his slumbers, he passed the night.

Jean Forette drove the colonel and Viola to the office. They arrived rather early. In fact LeGrand Blossom was not yet in, and when he did enter, a few minutes later, he was plainly surprised to see them.

"Is anything the matter?" asked the confidential clerk, as he quickly opened his desk. "I am sorry I was late this morning. But I had some matters to look after--"

"No apology necessary," said Colonel Ashley, quickly. "We have not been waiting long. We have discovered something."

If his life had depended on it LeGrand Blossom could not, at that moment, have concealed a start of surprise.

"You mean you have found out who killed Mr. Carwell?" he asked, and his tongue went quickly around his dry lips.

"Not that," the colonel answered. "But we have found some letters that seem to need explaining. Here they are."

Then when Viola had told how she discovered them, she asked:

"Did my father ever owe Captain Poland any money?"

"Yes," answered LeGrand Blossom, frankly, "he did."

"How much?"

"Fifteen thousand dollars."

"Was it ever paid back?" asked Colonel Ashley.

"That I cannot say," replied the head clerk. "The papers in that particular transaction are missing. I looked for them the other day, but failed to find them. I was intending to ask you, Miss Carwell, if you knew anything about them. Now, it seems you do not. The fact remains that your father was at one time indebted to the captain for fifteen thousand dollars. Whether it was repaid I can not say."

"Who would know?" asked Colonel Ashley.

"Why, Captain Poland, of course," answered Mr. Blossom. "One would think that it would be paid by check, but in that case the canceled one would come back from the bank, which it has not. It is possible that Mr. Carwell had an account in some other bank, or he may have paid the captain in cash. In either case a receipt would be given, I should say. Captain Poland is the only one who now would know."

"Then we had better see him," suggested Colonel Ashley. "Shall we call on him, Viola?"

She hesitated a moment before answering, and then replied in a low voice:

"I think it would be better. We must end this mystery!"

They left LeGrand Blossom and again entered the car. Jean Forette was driving, and the detective again noticed the strange and sudden change in his manner. Whereas he had been morose and sullen the first part of the trip, timid and watchful of every crossing and turning, now he put on full speed and drove with the confidence of an expert.

"He must have had another shot of dope," mused the colonel. "I'll have to keep an eye on you, my Frenchie, else you may be ramming a stone wall when you're feeling pretty well elated."

They were half way to the home of Captain Poland when Viola suddenly changed her mind.

"I--I don't believe I care to go to see him," she said. "Can't you go without me, Colonel Ashley? You can find out better than I can. I--I really don't feel equal to it."

"Of course, I can," was the ready answer. "Drive Miss Carwell home, Jean, and then I'll go on to see Captain Poland myself."

The car was swung around, and was soon in front of The Haven. The colonel, with his usual gallantry, walked with Viola to the steps. As the maid opened the door she said to her mistress:

"There is a lady to see you."

"A lady to see me?" exclaimed Viola, in some surprise.

"Yes. She is in the library, waiting. I said I did not know how long you would be away, but she said she was a friend of the family and would wait."

"Who is she?" asked Viola.

"I don't know. But she is a large, blonde lady."

"I can't imagine," murmured Viola. "Won't you come in, Colonel Ashley? It may be some one I would want you to see, also."

As Viola, followed at a little distance by the colonel, entered the library, a large, blonde woman arose to meet her.

"I am so glad to see you, my dear Miss Carwell," began the woman, and then Colonel Ashley had one of his questions answered. The voice was the same as that of the shawled woman LeGrand Blossom had met on the ferryboat the night before, and it was the voice of Annie Tighe, alias Maude Warren, alias Morocco Kate, one of the cleverest of New York's de luxe crooks.

"So you have a hand in the game, have you, my dear?" mused the colonel, as he caught the now well-remembered tones. "Well, I guess you don't want to see me right away, and I don't want you to."

He had kept behind Viola during the walk down the hall, and the large blonde had not noticed him, he hoped. He whispered to Viola, who stood just at the entrance to the room:

"Learn all you can from her. I'll be back pretty soon--as soon as she has gone. Find out where she's stopping. Don't mention me."

The hall was dimly lighted, and he had a chance to say this to Viola without getting into full view of the caller, and without her overhearing. Then, turning quickly, Colonel Ashley hurried out of the house.

"Morocco Kate," he mused as he got into the car again, and told Jean to drive to Captain Poland's. "Morocco Kate! I wonder if she is just beginning her game, or if this is merely a phase of it, started before Mr. Carwell's death? Another link added to the puzzle."

He was still pondering over this when he reached the captain's home. It was a rather elaborate summer "cottage," with magnificent grounds, and the captain's mother kept house for him. But there was a curious deserted air about the place as Jean drove up the gravel road. A man was engaged in putting up boards at the windows.

"Is the captain here?" asked the colonel.

"The place is being closed for the season, sir," answered the man, evidently a caretaker.

"Closed? So early?" exclaimed the colonel, in surprise.

"The captain has gone away," the man went on. "I got orders yesterday to close the place for the season. Captain Poland will not be back."

"Oh!" softly exclaimed the colonel. And then to himself he added: "He won't be back! Well, perhaps I shall have to bring him back. Another link! There may be three people in this instead of two!"

CHAPTER XIX. "UNKNOWN"

So sweet of you to see me, Miss Carwell, in all your grief, and I must apologize for troubling you."

Miss Tighe, alias Morocco Kate, fairly gushed out the words as she extended a hand to Viola in the library. The first glance at the "large blonde," as the maid had described her, shocked the girl. She could hardly repress a shudder of disgust as she looked at the bleached hair. But, nerving herself for the effort, Viola let her hand rest limply for a moment in the warm moist grip of Miss Tighe.

"Won't you sit down?" asked Viola.

"Thank you. I won't detain you long. I called merely on business, though I suppose you think I'm not a very business-like looking person. But I am strictly business, all the way through," and she tittered. "I find it pays better to really dress the part," she added.

"I was so sorry to hear about your dear father's death. I knew him--quite well I may say--he was very good to me."

"Yes," murmured Viola, and somehow her heart was beating strangely. What did it all mean? Who was this--this impossible person who claimed business relations, yes, even friendliness, with the late Mr. Carwell?

"And now to tell you what I came for," went on Miss Tighe. "Your dear father--and in his death I feel that I have lost a very dear friend and adviser--your dear father purchased many valuable books of me. I sell only the rarest and most expensive bindings, chiefly full morocco. Your father was very fond of books, wasn't he?"

Viola could not help admitting it, as far as purchasing expensive, if unread, editions was concerned. The library shelves testified to this.

"Yes, indeed, he just loved them, and he was always glad when I brought his attention to a new set, my dear Miss Carwell. Well, that is what I came about now.

Just before his terrible death--it was terrible, wasn't it? Oh, I feel so sorry for you," and she dabbed a much-perfumed handkerchief to her eyes. "Just before his lamented death he bought a lovely white morocco set of the Arabian Nights from me. Forty volumes, unexpurgated, my dear. Mind you that--unexpurgated!" and Morocco Kate seemed to dwell on this with relish. "As I say, he bought a lovely set from me. It was the most expensive set I ever sold--forty-five hundred dollars."

"Forty-five hundred dollars for a set of books!" exclaimed Viola, in unaffected wonder.

"Oh, my dear, that is nothing. These were some books," and she winked understandingly.

"It isn't everybody who could get them! The edition was limited. But I happened on a set and I knew your father wanted them, so I got them for him. He made the first payment, and then he died--I read it in the papers. Naturally I didn't want to bother you while the terrible affair was so fresh, so I waited. And now I'm here!"

She seemed to be--very much so, as she settled herself back in the big leather chair, and made sure that her hair was properly fluffed around her much-powdered face.

"You are here to--" faltered Viola. "To get the balance for the books--that's it, dear Miss Carwell. Naturally I'm not in for my health, and of course I don't publish books myself. I'm only a poor business woman, and I work on commission. The firm likes have all contracts cleaned up, but in this case they didn't press matters, knowing Mr. Carwell was all right; or, if he wasn't, his estate was. I've sold him many a choice and rare book--books you don't see in every library, my dear. Of course there were--ahem--some you wouldn't care to read, and I can't say I care much about 'em myself. A good French novel is all right, I say, but some of 'em well, you know!" and she winked boldly, and dabbed her face with the handkerchief which was quickly filling the room with an overpowering odor.

"You mean my father owes you money?" faltered Viola.

"Well, not me, exactly--the firm. But I don't mind telling you I get my rake-off. I have to so I can live. The balance is only three thousand dollars, and if you could give me a check--"

"Excuse me," interrupted Viola, "but I have nothing to do with the business end of my father's affairs."

"You're his daughter, aren't you?"

"Yes."

"And you'll get all his property?" Morocco Kate was getting vindictive now.

"I cannot discuss that with you," said Viola, simply. "All matters of business are attended to at the office. You will have to see Mr. Blossom."

"Huh! LeGrand Blossom! No use seeing him. I've tried. But I'll try again, and say you sent me." The voice was back to its original dulcet tones now. "That's what I'll do, my dear Miss Carwell. I'll tell LeGrand Blossom you sent me. He needn't think he can play fast and loose with me as he has. If he doesn't want to pay this bill, contracted by your father in the regular way--and I must say he was very nice to me--well, there are other ways of collecting. I haven't told all I know."

"What do you mean?" demanded Viola hotly. "Oh, there's time enough to tell later," was the answer. "I haven't been in the rare edition business for nothing, nor just for my health. But wait until I see LeGrand Blossom. Then I may call on you again!" And with this rather veiled threat Morocco Kate took her leave.

"What horrible person was that?" asked Miss Mary Carwell, who met Viola in the hail after her visitor's departure. "She was positively vulgar, I should say, though I didn't see her."

"Oh, she was just a book agent. I sent her to Mr. Blossom."

"To Mr. Blossom, my dear! I didn't know he was literary."

"Neither was this person, Aunt Mary. I think I shall go and lie down. I have a headache."

And as she locked herself in her room shed bitter tears on her pillow. Who was this person who seemed to know Mr. Carwell so well, who boasted of how "good" he was to her? Why did Colonel Ashley want to gain all the information he could about her?

"Oh, what does it all mean?" asked Viola in shrinking terror. "Is there to be some terrible--some horrible scandal?"

She put the question to Colonel Ashley a little later.

"Who is this woman?"

The colonel considered a moment before replying. Then, with a shrewd look at Viola, he replied:

"Well, my dear, she isn't your kind, of course, but I've known her, and known of her, for several years. She, and those she associates with, work the de luxe game."

"The de luxe game? What is it?"

"In brief, it's a blackmailing scheme. A woman of the type of Miss Tighe, to give her one of her names, associates herself with some men. They arrange to have a set of some books--usually well known enough and of a certain value--bound in expensive leather--full morocco--hand tooled and all that. They call on rich men and women, and induce them to buy the expensive and rare set, of which they say there is only one or two on the market.

"Sometimes the sales are straight enough--particularly where women are the buyers--but the books, even if delivered, are not worth anything like the price paid.

"But, in the case of wealthy men the game is different."

"Different?"

"Yes, particularly where a woman like Morocco Kate is the agent. They are not satisfied with the enormous profit made on selling a common edition of books, falsely dressed in a garish binding, but they endeavor to compromise the man in some business or social way, and then threaten to expose him unless he pays a large sum,--ostensibly, of course, for the books.

"Morocco Kate, who called on you, has more than one killing to her credit in this game, and she has managed to keep out of jail because her victims were afraid of the publicity of prosecuting. And it was so foolish of them for, in most cases, it was just mere foolishness on their part, and nothing criminally, or even morally, wrong, though they may have been indiscreet."

"And you think my father--"

"I don't know anything about it, Viola, my dear!" was the prompt answer. "Your father may have dealt in a legitimate way with this woman, buying books from her because she cajoled him into it, though he could have done much better with any reputable house. As I say, he may have simply bought some books from her, and not have made the final payments on account of his death. Whether the contract he entered into is binding or not I can't say until I have seen it."

"But I found nothing about books among his papers!"

"No? Then perhaps it was a verbal contract. Or he may have been--" The colonel stopped. Viola guessed what he intended to say.

"Do you think he was--Do you think this woman may make trouble?" she asked bravely.

"I don't know. We must find out more about her. If she comes again, hold her and send for me. I didn't want her to see me to-day to know that I was on this case. But I don't mind now."

"Oh, suppose there should be some--some disgrace?"

"Don't worry about that, Viola. But now, I have some rather startling news for you."

"Oh, more--"

"Not exactly trouble. But Captain Poland has gone away--his place is closed."

"The captain gone away!" faltered the girl.

"Yes. I wondered if you knew he was going. Did he intimate to you anything of the kind?"

The colonel watched Viola narrowly as he asked this question.

"No, I never knew he contemplated ending the season here so early," Viola said. "Usually he is the last to go, staying until late in October. Is there anything--"

"That is all I know--he is gone," said the detective. "I wanted to ask him about that fifteen-thousand-dollar matter, but I shall have to write, I suppose. And the sooner I get the letter off the better."

"Please write it here," suggested Viola, indicating the table where pens, ink and stationery were always kept. "I am going to look again among the papers of the private safe to see if there was anything about books--the Arabian Nights, she said it was."

"Yes, that's her favorite set. But don't worry, my dear. Everything will come out all right."

And as Viola left him alone in the library, the detective added to himself:

"I wonder if it will?"

Colonel Ashley wrote a brief, business-like letter to Captain Poland, addressing it to his summer home at Lakeside, arguing that the yachtsman would have left some forwarding address.

Then, lighting a cigar, the colonel sat back in a deep, leather chair--the same one Morocco Kate had sat in and perfumed--and mused.

"There are getting to be too many angles to this," he reflected. "I need a little help. Guess I'll send for Jack Young. He'll be just the chap to look after Jean and follow that French dope artist to his new place, provided he leaves here suddenly. Yes, I need Jack."

And having telephoned a telegram, summoning from New York one of his most trusted lieutenants, Colonel Ashley refreshed himself by reading a little in the "Compleat Angler."

Jack Young appeared at Lakeside the next day, well dressed, good looking, a typical summer man of pleasing address.

"Another diamond cross mystery?" he asked the colonel.

"How is your golf?" was the unexpected answer.

"Oh, I guess I can manage to drive without topping," was the ready answer. "Have I got to play?"

"It might be well. I'll get you a visitor's card at the Maraposa Club here, and you can hang around the links and see what you can pick up besides stray balls. Now I'll tell you the history of the case up to the present."

And Jack Young, having heard, and having consumed as many cigarettes as he considered the subject warranted, remarked:

"All right. Get me a bag of clubs, and I'll see what I can do. So you want me to pay particular attention to this dope fiend?"

"Yes, if he proves to be one, and I think he will. I'll have my hands full with Blossom, Morocco Kate and some others."

"What about Poland and Bartlett?"

"Well, Harry is still held, but I imagine he'll be released soon, Jack."

"Nothing on him?"

"I wouldn't go so far as to say that. You know my rule. Believe no one innocent until proved not guilty. I can keep my eye on him. Besides, he's pretty well anchored."

"You mean by Miss Viola?"

"Yes."

"How about the captain?"

"He's a puzzle, at present. But I wish you'd find out if that chauffeur has a girl. That's the best way to do, or undo, a man that I know of. Find out if he has a girl.

That'll be your trick."

"All right--that and golf. I'm ready."

And Jack Young worked to such good advantage that three days later he had a pretty complete report ready for his chief.

"Jean Forette has a girl," said Jack; "and she's a little beauty, too. Mazi Rochette is her name. She's a maid in one of the swell families here, and she's dead gone on our friend Jean. I managed to get a talk with her, and she thinks he's going to marry her as soon as he gets another place. A better place than with the Carwells, she says he must have. This place was pretty much on the blink, she confided to me."

"Or words to that effect," laughed the colonel.

"Exactly. I'm not much on the French, you know. Still I got along pretty well with her. She took a notion to me."

"I thought you might be able to get something in that direction," said the colonel with a smile. "Did you learn where Jean was just prior to the golf game which was the last Mr. Carwell played?"

"Yes, he was with her, the girl says, and she didn't know why I was asking, either, I flatter myself. I led around to it in a neat way. He was with her until just before he drove Mr. Carwell to the links. In fact, Jean had the girl out for a spin in the new car, she says. She's afraid of it, though. Revolutionary devil, she calls it."

"Hum! If Jean was with her just before he picked up Carwell to go to the game--well, the thing is turning out a bit different from what I expected. Jack, we still have plenty of work before us. Did I tell you Morocco Kate was mixed up in this?"

"No! Is she?"

"Seems to be."

"Good night, nurse! Whew! If he fell for her--"

"I don't believe he did, Jack. My old friend was a sport, but not that kind. He was clean, all through."

"Glad to hear you say so, Colonel. Well, what next?"

They sat talking until far into the night.

There was rather a sensation in Lakeside two days later when it became known that the coroner's jury was to be called together again, to consider more evidence in the Carwell case.

"What does it mean?" Viola asked Colonel Ashley. "Does it mean that Harry will be--"

"Now don't distress yourself, my dear," returned the detective, soothingly. "I have been nosing around some, and I happen to know that the prosecutor and coroner haven't a bit more evidence than they had at first when they held Mr. Bartlett."

"Does that mean Harry will be released?"

"I think so."

"Does it mean he will be proved innocent?"

"That I can't say. I hardly think the verdict will be conclusive in any case. But they haven't any more evidence than at first--that he had a quarrel with your father just before the fatal end. As to the nature of the quarrel, Harry is silent--obstinately silent even to his own counsel; and in this I can not uphold him. However, that is his affair."

"But I'm sure, Colonel, that he had nothing to do with my father's death; aren't you?"

"If I said I was sure, my dear, and afterward, through force of evidence and circumstance, were forced to change my opinion, you would not thank me for now saying what you want me to say," was the reply. "It is better for me to say that I do not know. I trust for the best. I hope, for your sake and his, that he had nothing to do with the terrible crime. I want to see the guilty person discovered and punished, and to that end I am working night and day. And if I find out who it is, I will disclose him--or her--no matter what anguish it costs me personally--no matter what anguish it may bring to others. I would not be doing my full duty otherwise."

"No, I realize that, Colonel. Oh, it is hard--so hard! If we only knew!"

"We may know," said the colonel gently.

"Soon?" she asked hopefully.

"Sooner than you expect," he answered with a smile. "Now I must attend the jury session."

It was brief, and not at all sensational, much to the regret of the reporters for the New York papers who flocked to the quiet and fashionable seaside resort. The upshot of the matter was that the chemists for the state reported that Mr. Carwell had met his death from the effects of some violent poison, the nature of which resembled several kinds, but which did not analyze as being any particular one with which they were, at present, familiar.

There were traces of both arsenic and strychnine, but mingled with them was some narcotic of strange composition, which was deadly in its effect, as had been proved on guinea pigs, some of the residue from the stomach and viscera of the dead man having been injected into the hapless animals.

Harry Bartlett was not called to the stand, but, pale from his confinement, sat an interested and vital spectator of the proceedings.

The prosecutor announced that the efforts of his detectives had resulted in nothing more. There was not sufficient evidence to warrant accusing any one else, and that against Harry Bartlett was of so slender and circumstantial a character that it could not be held to have any real value before the grand jury nor in a trial court.

"What is your motion, then?" asked the coroner.

"Well, I don't know that I have any motion to make," said Mr. Stryker. "If this were before a county judge, and the prisoner's counsel demanded it, I should have to agree to a nolle pros. As it is I simply say I have no other evidence to offer at this time."

"Then the jury may consider that already before it?" asked Billy Teller.

"Yes."

"You have heard what the prosecutor said, gentlemen," went on the coroner. "You may retire and consider your verdict."

This they did, for fifteen minutes--fifteen nerve-racking minutes for more than one in the improvised courtroom. Then the twelve men filed back, and in answer to the usual questions the foreman announced:

"We find that Horace Carwell came to his death through poison administered by a person, or persons, unknown."

There was silence for a moment, and then, as Bartlett started from his seat, a flush mantling his pale face, Viola, with a murmured "Thank God!" fainted.

CHAPTER XX. A MEETING

Harry Bartlett walked from the court a free man, physically, but not mentally. He felt, and others did also, that there was a stain on him--something unexplained, and which he would not, or could not, clear up--the quarrel with Mr. Carwell just before the latter's death. And even to Viola, when, in the seclusion of her home, she asked Harry about it after the trial, or rather, the verdict, he replied:

"I can not tell. It was nothing that concerns you or me or this case. I will never tell."

And Colonel Ashley, hearing this, pondered over it more and more.

The little green book was all but forgotten during these days, and as for the rods, lines, and reels, Shag arranged them, polished them and laid them out, in hourly expectation of being called on for them, but the call did not come. The colonel was after bigger fish than dwelt in the sea or the rivers that ran into the sea.

It was a week after the rather unsatisfactory verdict of the coroner's jury that Bartlett, out in his "Spanish Omelet," came most unexpectedly on Captain Gerry Poland, some fifty miles from Lakeside. The captain was in his big machine, and he seemed surprised on meeting Bartlett.

"Oh!" he exclaimed. "Then you are--"

"Out, at any rate," was the somewhat bitter reply. "Where have you been, Gerry?"

"Away. I couldn't stand it around there."

"I suppose you know they have been looking for you?"

"Looking for me? Oh, you mean Colonel Ashley wanted some information about certain business matters. Well, I didn't see that I owed him any explanation about private matters between Mr. Carwell and myself, so I didn't answer.

"You know what the imputation is, Gerry?" questioned Bartlett, as each man sat in his car, near a lonely stretch of woods.

"I don't know that I do," was the calm reply.

"Well, Viola has told me of the finding of the papers in her father's private safe. I told her I would see you, if I could, and get an explanation. I did not think I would find you so soon."

"I didn't know you were looking, Harry, or I would have come to you. What do you mean about papers in a private safe?"

"I mean those which indicate that Mr. Carwell owed you fifteen thousand dollars."

"Well, he did owe me that," said the captain calmly.

"He did?" and Harry Bartlett accented the last word.

"Yes, but it was paid. He did not owe me a dollar at the time of his death."

"That is astonishing news! There is no record of the money having been paid!"

"Nevertheless the debt is canceled," insisted the captain. "I sent the receipt and the canceled note to LeGrand Blossom."

"It's false!" cried Bartlett. "He hasn't any such documents!"

For a moment Captain Poland seemed about to leap from his car and attack the man who had given him the lie direct. Then, by an effort, he composed himself, and quietly answered:

"I can prove every word I say, and I will take immediate steps to do so. Mr. Carwell paid me the fifteen thousand dollars on the twenty-third, and I--"

"He paid you the money on the twenty-third? the very day he died?" cried Harry.

"Yes."

"Then--Why, good heavens, man! Don't you see what this means? It means you were with him just before his death, the same as I was. We're both in the same boat as far as that goes!"

"Yes, I admit that I was with him, and that he paid me the fifteen thousand dollars shortly before his unfortunate end," returned Captain Poland. "But our meeting was a most peaceful one, even friendly, and--"

"You mean that I--Oh, I see!" and Bartlett's voice was full of meaning. "So that's what you are driving at. Well, two can play at that game. I've learned something, anyhow!"

There was a grinding of gears, and the "Spanish Omelet" shot away. Captain Poland watched it for a moment, and then, with a shrug of his shoulders, threw in the clutch and speeded down the road in the opposite direction.

Harry Bartlett lost no time in acquainting Colonel Ashley with the admission made by Captain Poland.

"So the wind is veering," the detective murmured. "I shall watch him. I wondered why he didn't answer my letters. Now we must see LeGrand Blossom."

"I'll come with you," offered Bartlett. "I want to see this thing through now. Shall we tell her?" and he motioned toward Viola's room.

"Not now. We'll see Blossom first."

If the head clerk was perturbed at all by the visit to the office of Colonel Ashley and Harry Bartlett, he did not disclose it. He welcomed the two visitors, and took them to his private room.

Colonel Ashley went bluntly into the business in hand.

"Have you any papers to show that Captain Poland acknowledged the receipt of the fifteen thousand dollars owed to him by Mr. Carwell?"

"I have not," was the frank answer. "I have been searching for something to prove that the debt was paid, as I knew of its contraction. It was not canceled as far as I can find."

"Yet Captain Poland says it was paid," said Bartlett, "and that he sent you the receipt."

"I never got it!" insisted LeGrand Blossom. Harry Bartlett and Colonel Ashley looked at one another, and then the detective, with an effort at cheerfulness which he did not feel, said:

"Oh, well, perhaps in the confusion the papers were mislaid. I shall ask Viola about them. Another search must be made."

And so the two went back to The Haven, not much more enlightened than when they left it.

"'What is to be done?" asked Bartlett. "Blossom says he knows nothing of it."

"Then I must know a little more about Mr. Blossom," mentally decided the colonel. "I think I shall shadow him a bit. It may prove fruitful."

And when two nights later LeGrand Blossom left his boarding place and met a veiled woman at a lonely spot on the beach, Colonel Ashley, who had been waiting as he so well knew how to do, hid himself on the sand behind some sedge grass and began to think that the game was coming his way after all.

"For a man who pretends to be open and above board, his actions are very queer," mused the detective, as he silently crawled nearer to where LeGrand Blossom and the woman stood talking in low tones on the lonely sands. "I don't see what object he could have in making away with Carwell, and yet it begins to look black for him. Maybe there is more than the fifteen thousand dollars involved. There are so many angles to the case now. I must find out who this woman is."

And when she spoke in louder tones than usual, drawing from LeGrand Blossom an impatient "Hush!" the colonel had his answer.

"Morocco Kate again! What's her part now?"

The detective was near enough now to hear some of the talk.

"Did you bring it?" asked the woman eagerly.

"Hush! can't you?" snapped LeGrand Blossom.

"Pooh! What's the harm? There's no one in this lonely place! It gives me the creeps. Li'l ole Broadway for mine!"

"You never know who's anywhere these days!" muttered LeGrand. "That infernal detective seems to be all over. He looks at me--oh, he looks at me, and I don't like it."

Morocco Kate laughed.

"Shut up!" ordered the head clerk. "Do you think this is funny?"

"It used to be," was the answer. "It used to be funny, when you thought you were in love with me. Oh, it was delicious!"

"I was a bigger fool than I ever thought I'd be!" growled LeGrand Blossom.

"You aren't the only one," was the consoling answer. "But what I'm interested in now, is--did you bring the mazumma--the cush--the dope?"

"All I could get," was the answer. "I'm in a devil of a mess, and the estate hasn't been settled yet. I may get some more out of it then, but you'll have to quit bleeding me. I'm through with you, I tell you!"

"But I'm not with you," was the sharp rejoinder. "I'll take this now, but I'll need more. The game isn't going as it used to. Mind, I'll need more, and soon."

"You won't get it!"

"Oh, won't I? Well, there are others that'll pay well for what I'm able to tell, I guess. I rather think you'll see me again, Lee. So-long now, but I'll see you again!"

She moved off in the darkness, laughing mirthlessly, and with muttered imprecations LeGrand Blossom turned in the opposite direction, passing within a few feet of the hidden detective. "Blackmail, or is it a division of the spoils?" mused Colonel Ashley. "I've got to find out which. Mr. Blossom, I think I'll have to stick to you until you fall into the sear and yellow leaf."

The next day as Colonel Ashley sat trying to fix his attention on a passage from Walton, a messenger brought him a note. It was from a young man who, at the colonel's suggestion, had been given a clerical place in the office of the late Horace Carwell. Not even Viola knew that the young man was one of the colonel's aides.

"Blossom just sent out a note to a Miss Minnie Webb," the screed, which the colonel perused, read. "He's going to meet her in the park at Silver Lake at nine to-night. Thought I'd let you know."

"I'm glad he did," mused the detective. "I'll be there."

And he was, skillfully though not ostentatiously attired as a loitering fisherman of the native type, of which there were many in and about Lakeside.

The fisherman strolled about the little park in the center of which was a body of fresh water known as Silver Lake. It was little more than a pond, and was fed by springs and by drainage. In the park were trees and benches, and it was a favorite trysting spot.

Up and down the paths walked Colonel Ashley, his clothes odorous of fish, and he was beginning to think he might have his trouble for his pains when he saw a woman coming along hesitatingly.

It needed but a second glance to disclose to the trained eyes of the detective that it was none other than Minnie Webb, whom he had met several times at the home of Viola Carwell. Minnie advanced until she came to a certain bench, and she stopped long enough to count and make sure that it was the third from one end of a row, and the seventh from the other end.

"The appointed place," mused the colonel as he sauntered past. And then, making a detour, he came up in the rear and hid in the bushes back of the bench, where he could hear without being observed--in fact the bench was in such shadow that even the casual passerby in front could not after darkness had fallen tell who occupied it.

Minnie Webb sat in silence, but by the way she fidgeted about the colonel, hearing the shuffling of her feet on the gravel walk, knew she was nervous and impatient.

Then quick footsteps were heard coming along through the little park. They increased in sound, and came to a stop in front of the bench on which sat the shrouded and dark figure of the girl.

"Minnie?"

"LeGrand! Oh, I'm so glad you came! What is it? Why did you send me a note to meet you in this lonely place? I'm so afraid!"

"Afraid? Lonely? Why, it's early evening, and this is a public park," the man answered in a low voice. "I wanted you to come here as it's the best place for us to talk--where we can't be overheard."

"But why are you so afraid of being overheard?"

"Oh, things are so mixed up--one can't be too careful. Minnie, we must settle our affairs."

"Settle them? You mean--?"

"I mean we can't go on this way. I must have you! I've waited long enough. You know I love you--that I've never loved any one else as I've loved you! I can't stand it any longer without you. I have asked you to marry me several times. Each time you have put it off for some reason or other. Now we must settle it. Are you going to marry me or not? No matter what your folks say about me and this Carwell affair. Do you--do you care for me?"

The answer was so low and so muffled that the colonel was glad he could not hear it.

"Confound it all!" he murmured, "that's the worst of this business! I don't mind anything but the love-making. I hate to break in on that!"

There was an eloquent silence, and then LeGrand Blossom said:

"I am very happy, Minnie."

"And so am I. Now what shall we do?"

"Get married as soon as possible, of course. I've got to wind up matters here, and as soon as I can I may take up an offer that came from Boston. It's a very good one. Would you go there with me?"

"Yes, LeGrand. I'd go anywhere with you--you know that."

"I'm glad I do, my dear. It may be necessary to go very soon, and--well, we won't stop to say good-bye, either."

"Why! what do you mean," and the hidden detective knew that the girl had drawn away from the young man.

"Oh, I mean that we won't bother about the fuss of a farewell-party. I'm not tied to the Carwell business. In fact I'd be glad to chuck it. There's nothing in it any more, since there's no chance for a partnership. We'll just go off by ourselves and be happy--won't we, Minnie?"

"I hope so, LeGrand. But must we go away? Can't you get something else here?"

"I think we must, yes."

"You haven't had trouble with--with Viola, have you?"

"No. What made you think of that?"

"Oh, it was just a notion. Well, if we have to leave we will. I shall hate to go, however. But, I'll be with you--" and again the words were smothered.

"I wonder what sort of a double-cross game he's playing," mused the colonel when the two had left the park and he, rather stiff from his position, shuffled to the lonely spot where he had before made a change of garments. Attired as his usual self, he went back to The Haven, and spent rather a restless night.

Minnie Webb was perplexed. She loved LeGrand Blossom--there was no doubt of that--but she did not see why he should have to leave the vicinity of Lakeside where she had lived so many years--at least during the summer months. All her friends and acquaintances were there.

"I wonder if Viola has given him notice to leave since she came into her father's property," mused Minnie. "I'm going to ask her. He may never get such a good place in Boston as he has here. I'll see if I can't find out why he wants to leave. It can't be just because father does not care much for him."

So she called on Viola, as she had done often of late, and found her friend sitting silent, and with unseeing eyes staring at the rows of books in the library.

"Oh, Minnie, it was so good of you to come! I'm very glad to see you. Since father went it has been very lonely. You look extremely well."

"I am well--and--happy. Oh, Viola, you're the first I have told, but--but Mr.

Blossom has--asked me to marry him, and--"

"Oh, how lovely! And you've said 'yes!' I can tell that!" and Viola smiled and kissed her friend impulsively. "Tell me all about it!"

"And so it's all settled," went on Minnie, after much talk and many questions and answers. "Only I'm sorry he's going to leave you."

"Going to leave me!" exclaimed Viola. Her voice was incredulous.

"Well, I mean going to give up the management of your business. I'm sure you'll miss him."

"I shall indeed! But I did not know Mr. Blossom was going to leave. He has said nothing to me or Aunt Mary about it. In fact, I--"

"Oh, is there something wrong?" asked Minnie quickly, struck by something in Viola's voice.

"Well, nothing wrong, as far as we know. But--"

"Oh, please tell me!" begged Minnie. "I am sure you are concealing something."

"Well, I will tell you!" said Viola at last. "I feel that I ought to, as you may hear of it publicly. It concerns fifteen thousand dollars," and she went into details about the loan, which one party said had been paid, and of which Blossom said there was no record.

"Oh!" gasped Minnie Webb. "Oh, what does it mean?" and, worried and heartsick, lest she should have made a mistake, she sat looking dumbly at Viola...

CHAPTER XXI. THE LIBRARY POSTAL

My dear, I am sorry if I have told you anything that distresses you," said Viola gently. "But I thought--"

"Oh, yes, it is best to know," was the low response. "Only--only I was so happy a little while ago, and now--"

"But perhaps it may all be explained!" interrupted Viola. "It is only some tiresome business deal, I'm sure. I never could understand them, and I don't want to. But it does seem queer that there is no record of that fifteen thousand dollars being paid back."

"What does Captain Poland say about it?"

"Oh, he told Harry, very frankly, that father paid the money, and that the receipt was sent to Mr. Blossom. But the latter says it can not be found."

"And do you suspect Mr. Blossom?" asked Minnie, and her voice held a challenge.

"Well," answered Viola slowly, "there isn't much of which to suspect him. It isn't as if Captain Poland claimed to have paid father the fifteen thousand dollars, and the money couldn't be found. It's only a receipt for money which the captain admits having gotten back that is missing. But it makes such confusion. And there are so many other things involved--"

"You mean about the poisoning?"

"Yes. Oh, I wish it were all cleared up! Don't let's talk of it. I must find out about Mr. Blossom going away. We shall have to get some one in his place. Aunt Mary will be so disturbed--"

"Don't say that I told you!" cautioned Minnie. "Perhaps I should not have mentioned it. Oh, dear, I am so miserable!" And she certainly looked it.

"And so am I!" confessed Viola. "If only Harry would tell what he is keeping back."

"You mean about that quarrel with your father?"

"Yes. And he acts so strangely of late, and looks at me in such a queer way. Oh, I'm afraid, and I don't know what I'm afraid of!"

"I'm the same way, Viola!" admitted Minnie.

"I wonder why we two should have all the trouble in the world?"

And the two were miserable together.

They were not the only ones to suffer in those days. Captain Gerry Poland could not drive Viola from his mind. To the yachtsman, she was the most beautiful woman he had ever met, and he wondered if fortune would ever make it possible for him to approach her again on the subject that lay so close to his heart.

And then there was Bartlett. It was true he walked the streets--or rather rode around them in his "Spanish Omelet"--a free man; yet the finger of suspicion was constantly pointed at him.

More than once in the town he met people who sneered openly at him, as if to say, "You are guilty, but we can't prove it." And once on the golf course he went up to three men who had formerly been quite friendly and suggested a game of golf, upon which one after another the others made trivial excuses and begged to be excused. Upon this occasion the young man had rushed away, his face scarlet, and he had only calmed down after a mad tour of many miles in his racing machine.

"It's an outrage!" he had muttered to himself. "A dastardly outrage! But what is a fellow going to do?"

Meanwhile Colonel Ashley and Jack Young were puzzling their heads over many matters connected with the golf course mystery. Jack had obeyed the colonel's instructions to the letter. He had played many rounds on the links and had gotten to a certain degree of friendship with Jean Forette. He had even formed a liking for Bruce Garrigan, who, offhand, informed him that the amount of India ink used in tattooing sailors during the past year was less by fifteen hundred ounces than the total output of radium salts for 1916, while the wheat crop of Minnesota for the same period was 66,255 bushels. All of which information, useful in a way, no doubt, was accepted by Jack with a smile. He was there to look and listen, and, well, he did it.

"But I've got to pass it up," he told Colonel Ashley. "I've stuck to that Jean chap until I guess he must think I want him for a chauffeur if ever I'm able to own a car bigger than a flivver. And aside from the fact that he does use some kind of dope, in which he isn't alone in this world, I can't get a line on him."

"No, I didn't expect you would," said Colonel Ashley, with a smile. "But are you well enough acquainted with him to have a talk with his sweetheart?"

"You mean Mazi?"

"Yes."

"Well, I s'pose I might get a talk with her. But what's the idea?"

"Nothing special, only I'd like to see if she tells you the same story she told me. Have a try at it when you get a chance."

"On the theory, I suppose, of in any trouble, look for the lady?"

"Somewhat, yes."

They were talking in The Haven, for Jack had been put up there as a guest at the request of Colonel Ashley. And when the bell rang, indicating some one at the door, they looked at one another questioningly.

Then came the postman's whistle, for Lakeside, though but a summer resort, with a population much larger in summer than in winter, boasted of mail delivery.

A maid placed the letters in their usual place on the hall table, and the colonel quickly ran through them, for he had reports sent him from his New York office from time to time.

"Here's one for you, Jack," he announced, handing his assistant a letter.

While Jack Young was reading it the colonel caught sight of a postal, with the address side down, lying among the other missives. It was a postal which bore several lines of printing, the rest being filled in by a pen, and the import of it was that a certain library book, under the number 58 C. H--16I* had been out the full time allowed under the rules, and must either be returned for renewal, or a fine of two cents a day paid, and the recipient was asked to give the matter prompt attention.

The colonel turned the card over. It was addressed to Miss Viola Carwell at The Haven.

"So the book is out on her card," murmured the detective. "I must look for her copy of 'Poison Plants of New Jersey,' and see if it is like the one I have."

"Were you speaking to me?" asked Jack, having finished his letter.

"No, but I will now. We've got to get busy on this case, and close it up. I've been too long on it now. Shag is getting impatient."

"Shag?"

"Yes, he wants me to go fishing."

"Oh, I see. Well, I'm ready. What are the orders?"

Two busy days on the part of Colonel Ashley and his assistant followed. They went on many mysterious errands and were out once all night. But where they went, what they did or who they saw they told no one.

It was early one evening that Colonel Ashley waited for his assistant in the library of The Haven. Jack had gone out to send a message and was to return soon. And as the colonel waited in the dim light of one electric bulb, much shaded, he saw a figure come stealing to the portieres that separated the library from the hall. Cautiously the figure advanced and looked into the room. A glance seemed to indicate that no one was there, for the colonel was hidden in the depths of a big chair, "slumping," which was his favorite mode of relaxing.

"I wonder if some one is looking for me?" mused the colonel. "Well, just for fun, I'll play hide and seek. I can disclose myself later." And so he remained in the chair, hardly breathing the silent figure parted the heavy curtains, within, dropped something white on the floor, and then quickly hurried away, the feet making no sound on the thick carpet of the hall.

"Now," mused the colonel to himself, "I wonder that is a note for me, or a love missive for one the maids from the butler or the gardener, who too bashful to deliver it in person. I'd better look."

Without turning on more light the colonel picked up the thing that had fluttered so silently to the floor. It was a scrap of paper, and as he held it under the dimly glowing bulb he saw, scrawled in printed letters:

"Viola Carwell has a poison book."

"As if I didn't know it!" softly exclaimed the colonel.

And then, as he resumed his comfortable, but not very dignified position, he heard some one coming boldly along the hall, and the voice of Jack asked:

"Are you in here, Colonel?"

"Yes, come in. Did you get a reply?"

"Surely. Your friend must have been waiting for your telegram."

"I expected he would be. Let me see it," and the detective read a brief message which said:

"Thomas much better after a long sleep."

"Ah," mused the colonel. "I'm very glad Thomas is better."

"Is Thomas, by any chance, a cat?" asked Jack, who read the telegram the colonel handed him.

"He is--just that--a cat and nothing more. And now, Jack, my friend, I think we're about ready to close in."

"Close in? Why--"

"Oh, there are a few things I haven't told you yet. Sit down and I'll just go over them. I've been on this case a little longer than you have, and I've done some elimination which you haven't had a chance to do."

"And you have eliminated all but--"

"Captain Poland and LeGrand Blossom."

At these words Jack started, and made a motion of silence. They were still in the library, but more lights had been turned on, and the place was brilliant.

"What's the matter?" asked the colonel, quickly. "I thought I heard a noise in the hall," and Jack stepped to the door and looked out. But either he did not see, or did not want to see, a shrinking figure which quickly crouched down behind a chair not far from the portal.

"Guess I was mistaken," said Jack. "Anyhow I didn't see anything." Did he forget that coming out of a light room into a dim hall was not conducive to good seeing? Jack Young ought to have remembered that.

"One of the servants, likely, passing by," suggested the colonel. "Yes, Jack, I think we must pin it down to either the captain or Blossom."

"Do you really think Blossom could have done it?"

"He could, of course. The main question is, did he have an object in getting Mr. Carwell out of the way?"

"And did he have?"

"I think he did. I've been trailing him lately, when he didn't suspect it, and I've seen him in some queer situations. I know he needed a lot of money and--well, I'm going to take him into custody as the murderer of Mr. Carwell. I want you to--"

But that was as far as the detective got, for there was a shriek in the hall--a cry of mortal anguish that could only come from a woman--and then, past the library door, rushed a figure in white.

Out and away it rushed, flinging open the front door, speeding down the steps and across the lawn.

"Quick!" cried Colonel Ashley. "Who was that?"

"I don't know!" answered Jack. "Must have been the person I thought I heard in the hall."

"We must find out who it was!" went on the detective. "You make some inquiries. I'll take after her."

"Could it have been Miss Viola?"

The question was answered almost as soon as it was asked, for, at that moment, Viola herself came down the front stairs.

"What is it?" she asked the two detectives. "Who cried out like that? Is some one hurt?"

"I don't know," answered Colonel Ashley. "Mr. Young and I were talking in the library when we heard the scream. Then a woman rushed out."

"It must have been Minnie Webb!" cried Viola. "She was here a moment ago. The maid told me she was waiting in the parlor, and I was detained upstairs. It must have been Minnie. But why did she scream so?"

Colonel Ashley did not stop to answer.

"Look after things here, Jack!" he called to his assistant. "I'm going to follow her. If ever there was a desperate woman she is."

And he sped through the darkness after the figure in white.

CHAPTER XXII. THE LARGE BLONDE AGAIN

The trail was not a difficult one to follow. The night was particularly black, with low-hanging clouds which seemed to hold a threat of rain, and the wind sighed dolefully through the scrub pines. Against this dim murkiness the figure of the woman in white stood out ghostily.

"Poor Minnie Webb!" mused Colonel Ashley, as he hurried on after her. "She must be desperate now--after what she heard. I wonder--"

He did not put his wonder into words then, but his suspicion was confirmed as he saw her head for the bridge that spanned a creek, not far from where the ferry ran over to Loch Harbor.

At certain times this creek was not deep enough to afford passage for small rowboats, but when the tide was in there was draught enough for motor launches.

"And the tide is in now," mused the colonel, as he remembered passing among the sand dunes late that afternoon, and noting the state of the sea. "Too bad, poor little woman!" he added gently, as he followed her. "Not so fast! Not so fast! There is no need of rushing to destruction. It comes soon enough without our going out to meet it. Poor girl!"

He went on through the darkness, following, following, following distracted Minnie, who, with the fateful words still ringing in her ears, hardly knew whither she hurried.

Colonel Ashley, in spite of the desperate manner in which the chase had begun, felt that he was safe from observation. He had on dark clothes, which did not contrast so strongly with the night as did the light and filmy dress of Minnie Webb. Besides, she was too distracted to notice that she was being followed.

"She is going to the bridge, and the tide is in," mused the detective. "I didn't think she had that much spunk--for it does take spunk to attempt anything like this in the dark. However, I'll try to get there as soon as she does."

The fleeing girl in white passed over an open moor, fleeced here and there with scanty bushes, which gave the detective all the cover he needed. But the girl did not look back, and the night was dark. The clouds were thicker too, and the very air seemed so full of rain that an incautious movement would bring it spattering about one's head, as a shake of a tree, after a shower, precipitates the drops.

And then there suddenly loomed, like grotesque shadows on the night, two other figures at the very end of the bridge that Minnie Webb sought to cross. They seemed to bar her way, and yet they were as much startled as she, for they drew back on her approach.

And Colonel Ashley, stealing his way up unseen, heard from Minnie Webb the startled ejaculation:

"LeGrand! You here? And who--who is this?"

Then, as if in defiance, or perhaps to see who the challenger was, the figure standing beside that of LeGrand Blossom flashed a little pocket electric torch. And by the gleam of it Colonel Ashley saw the large blonde woman again.

"Morocco Kate!" he murmured. "So she is mixed up in it after all! I think I begin to see daylight in spite of the darkness. Morocco Kate!"

Then, crouching down behind some bushes, he waited and listened and thought swiftly.

"Speak to me!" implored Minnie of the young man. "What does it mean, LeGrand? Why are you here with--with--"

"He knows my name well enough, if he wants to tell it," broke in the other. "I'm not ashamed of it, either. But who are you, I'd like to know? I never saw you before!" and the blonde woman flashed her light full on Minnie's white face.

And as the girl shrank back, Morocco Kate, so called, sneered:

"Some one else he's got on a string, I suppose! Ho! It's a merry life you lead, LeGrand Blossom!"

"Stop!" the young man exclaimed. "I can't let you go on this way. Minnie, please leave us for a moment. I'll come to you as soon as I can."

"Oh, yes! Of course!" sneered the other. "She's younger and prettier than I-- quite a flapper. I was that way--once. And I suppose you said the same thing to some one else you wanted to get rid of before you took me on. Oh, to the devil with the men, anyhow!"

Minnie gasped.

"Shocked you, did I, kid? Well, you'll hear worse than that, believe me. If I was to tell--"

"Stop!" and LeGrand Blossom snapped out the words in such a manner that the desperate woman did stop.

"Minnie, go away," he pleaded, more gently. "I'll come to you as soon as I can, and explain everything. Please believe in me!"

"I--I don't believe I can--again, LeGrand," faltered Minnie. "I--I heard what you said to her just now--that you couldn't do anything more for her. Oh, what have you been doing for her? Who is she? Tell me! Oh, I must hear it, though I dread it!"

"Yes, you shall hear it!" cried LeGrand Blossom, and there was desperation in his voice. "I was going to tell you, anyhow, before I married you--"

"Oh, you're really going to marry her, are you?" sneered the blonde. "Really? How interesting!"

"Will you be quiet?" said LeGrand, and there was that in his voice which seemed to cow the blonde woman.

"Minnie," went on LeGrand Blossom, "its a hard thing for a man to talk about a woman, but sometimes it has to be done. And it's doubly hard when it's about a woman a man once cared for. But I'm going to take my medicine, and she's got to take hers."

"I'm no quitter! I'm a sport, I am!" was the defiant remark. "So was Mr. Carwell--Old Carwell we used to call him. But he had more pep than some of you younger chaps.

"Leave his name out of this!" growled LeGrand, like some dog trying to keep his temper against the attacks of a cur.

"This woman--I needn't tell you her name now, for she has several," he went on to Minnie. "This woman and I were once engaged to be married. She was younger then--and--different. But she began drinking and--well, she became impossible. Believe me," he said, turning to the figure beside him, "I don't want to tell this, but I've got to square myself."

"Yes," and the other's voice was broken. "I may as well give up now as later.

If anything can be saved out of the wreck--my wreck--go to it! Shoot, kid! Tell the worst! I'll stand the gaff!"

"Well, that makes it easier," resumed Blossom. "We were going to be married, but she got in with a fast crowd, and I couldn't stand the pace. I admit, I wasn't sport enough."

"I'm glad you weren't," murmured Minnie, her breast heaving.

"The result was," went on Blossom, "that she and I separated. It was as much her wish as mine--toward the end. And she married a Frenchman with whom she seemed to be fascinated."

"Yes, he sure had me hypnotized," agreed the blonde woman. "It was more my fault than yours, Lee. Perhaps if you'd taken a whip to me, and made me behave-- Some of us women need a beating now and then. But it's too late now." Of a sudden she seemed strangely subdued.

LeGrand Blossom went on with the sordid tale.

"Well, the marriage didn't turn out happily. It was--"

"It was hell! I'm not afraid to use the word!" interrupted the blonde. "It was just plain, unadulterated hell! And I went into it with my eyes open. That's what it was--hell! I've had such a lot here on earth that maybe they'll give me a discount when I get--well, when I get where I'm going!" and she laughed, but there was no mirth in it.

Minnie shuddered, and drew nearer to LeGrand. And it did not seem to be because of the chill night wind, either.

"It was the same old story," went on the clerk. "No need of going over that, Minnie. It doesn't concern the question now. In the end the Frenchman cast her off, and she had to live, somehow. She came to me, and I, for the sake of old times, agreed to help her. I didn't think I was doing anything wrong; but it seems I was. I thought the rare and expensive book publishing business she said she was in was legitimate. Instead it was--"

"Yes, it was a blackmailing scheme!" interrupted Morocco Kate, not without some curious and perverted sense of pride. "I admit that. I got you in wrong, LeGrand, but it wasn't because I hated you, for I didn't. I really loved you, and I was a fool to take up with Jean. But that's past and gone. Only I didn't really mean to make trouble for you. I thought you might be able to wiggle out, knowing business men as you did."

"Instead," said the clerk, "I only became the more involved. It began to look as though I was a partner in the infernal schemes, and she and those she worked with held the threat over my head to extort money from me."

"Believe me, LeGrand, I didn't do that willingly," interrupted Morocco Kate. "The others had a hold over me, and they forced me to use you as their tool. They bled me, as I, in turn, bled you. Oh, it was all a rotten game, and I'm glad the end's at hand. I suppose it's all up now?" she asked Blossom.

"The end is, as far as it concerns you and me," he said. "I'm going to confess, and take my medicine. Minnie, I've lied to give this woman money to prevent her exposing me. Now I'm through. I've told my last lie, and given my last dollar. Thank God--who has been better to me than I deserve--thank God! I'm still young enough to make good the money I've lost. The lies I can't undo, but I can tell the truth. I'm going to confess everything!"

"Oh, LeGrand!" cried Minnie, and she held out her hands to him. "Not--not everything!"

"Yes, the whole rotten business. That's the only way to begin over again, and begin clean. I'll come through clean!"

"Oh!" murmured Minnie. "It will be so--so hard!"

"Yes," and LeGrand gritted his teeth, "it isn't going to be easy; but it'll be a bed of roses compared to what I've been lying on the last year. This woman had such a hold on me that I couldn't clear myself before--that is, clear myself of grave charges. But now I can. This is the end. I can prove that I wasn't mixed up in the Roswell de luxe book case, and that's what she's been holding over me."

"The Roswell case!" faltered Minnie.

"Yes, you don't know about it, but I'll tell you, later. Now I'm free. This is the end. I came here to-night to tell her so. How you happened to follow me I don't know."

"I didn't follow, LeGrand. It was all an accident."

"Then it's a lucky accident, Minnie. This is the end. From now on--"

"Yes, it's the end!" bitterly cried the other woman. "It's the end of everything. Oh, if I could only make it the end for Jean Carnot, I'd be satisfied. He made me what I am--an outcast from the world. If I could find Jean Carnot--"

And then, with the suddenness of a bird wheeling in mid air, the blonde woman turned and rushed away in the darkness.

For an instant Colonel Ashley hesitated in his hiding place. And then he murmured:

"I guess you'll keep, LeGrand Blossom, and you, too, Minnie Webb. Morocco Kate needs watching. And I think, now, she'll lead me right where I've been wanting to go for a long time. The darkness is fast fading away," which was a strange thing to say, seeing that the night was blacker than ever.

Back on the desolate moor, near the bridge under which the black tide was now hurrying, murmuring and whispering to the rushes tales of the deep and distant sea, stood two figures.

"Do you believe in me, Minnie?" asked the man brokenly.

There was a pause. The murmuring of the tide grew louder, and it seemed to sing now, as it rose higher and higher.

"Do you?" he repeated, wistfully.

"Yes," was the whispered reply. "And, Lee, I'll help you to come through-- clean! I believe in you!"

And the tide washed up the shores of the creek so that, even in the darkness, the white sands seemed to gleam.

CHAPTER. XXIII. MOROCCO KATE, ALLY

Who are you? Who is trailing me? Is that you, LeGrand?"
The challenge came sharply out of the darkness, and Colonel Ashley, who had been following Morocco Kate, plodding along through the sand, stumbling over the hillocks of sedge grass, halted.

"Who's there?" was the insistent demand. "I know some one is following me. Is it you, LeGrand Blossom? Have you--have you--"

The voice died out in a choking sob. "She's gamer than I thought," mused the detective. "And, strange as it may seem, I believe she cares." Then he answered, almost as gently as to a grieving child:

"It is not LeGrand Blossom. But it is a friend of his, and I want to be a friend to you. Wait a moment."

Then, as he came close to her side and flashed on his face a gleam from an electric torch he always carried, she started back, and cried:

"Colonel Ashley! Heavens!"

"Exactly!" he chuckled. "You didn't expect to see me here, did you? Well, it's all right."

"Then you're not after me for--" She gasped and could not go on. "That last deal was straight. I'm not the one you want."

"Don't get Spotty's habit, and throw up your hands just because you see me, Kate," went on the colonel soothingly. "I'm not after you professionally this time. In fact, if things turn out the way I want, I may shut my eyes to one or two little phases of your--er--let us call it career. I may ignore one or two little things that, under other circumstances, might need explaining."

"You mean you want me for a stool pigeon?"

"Something like that, yes."

"And suppose I refuse?"

"That's up to you, Kate. I may be able to get along without you--I don't say I can, but I may. However it would mean harder work and a delay, and I don't mind, seeing it's you, saying that I'd like to get back to my fishing. So if you'll come to reason, and tell me what I want to know, it will help you and--Blossom."

"Blossom!" she gasped. "Then you know--"

"I may as well tell you that I was back there--a while ago," and the colonel nodded vaguely to the splotch of blackness from whence Morocco Kate had rushed with that despairing cry on her lips.

"I'm a friend of LeGrand Blossom's--at least, I am now since I overheard what he had to say to you and Miss Webb," went on the detective. "Now then, if you'll tell me what I want to know, I'll help him to come across--clean, and I'll help you to the extent I mentioned."

Morocco Kate seemed to be considering as she stood in the darkness. Then a long sigh came from her lips, and it was as though she had come to the end of everything.

"I'll tell," she said simply. "What do you want to know? But first, let me say I didn't no more have an idea that Sport Carwell was going to die than you have Do you believe that?" she asked fiercely.

"I believe you, Kate. Now let's get down to brass tacks. Who is Jean Carnot, and where can I find him?"

"Oh!" she murmured. "You want him?"

"Very much, I think. Don't you?"

"Yes, I do! I--I would like to tear out his eyes! I'd like to--"

"Now, Kate, be nice! No use losing your temper. That's got you into trouble more than once. Try to play the lady--you can do it when you have to. Calling names isn't going to get us anywhere. Just tell me where I can find your former husband--or the one you thought was your husband--Jean Carnot."

"You're right, Colonel Ashley, I did think him my husband," said Morocco Kate simply. "And when I found out he had tricked me by a false marriage, and wouldn't make it good--well, I just went to the devil and hell--that's all."

"I know it, Kate, and I appreciate your position. I'm not throwing any stones at you. I've seen enough of life to know that none of us can do that with impunity.

Now tell me all you can. And I'll say this--that after this is all over, if you want to try and do as Blossom is going to do--come through clean--I'll help you to the best of my ability."

"Will you, Colonel?" the big blonde woman asked eagerly.

"I will--and here's my hand on it!"

He reached out in the darkness, but there was no answering clasp. The woman seemed to shrink away. And then she said:

"I don't believe it would be of any use. I guess I'm too far down to crawl up. But I'll help you all I can."

"Don't give up, Kate!" said the detective gently. "I've seen lots worse than you--you notice I'm not mincing words--I've seen lots worse than you start over again. All I'll say is that I'll give you the chance if you want it. There's nothing in this life you're leading. You know the end and the answer as well as I do. You've seen it many a time."

"God help me--I have!" she murmured. "Well, I--I'll think about it."

"And, meanwhile, tell me about this Jean Carnot," went on the colonel. "You were married to him?"

"I thought I was."

"What sort of man was he? Come, sit down on this sand dune and tell me all about it. I think I want that man."

"No more than I do," she said fiercely. "He left me as he would an old coat he couldn't use any more! He cast me aside, trampled on me, left me like a sick dog! Oh, God--"

For a moment she could not go on. But she calmed herself and resumed. Then, by degrees, she told the whole, sordid story. It was common enough--the colonel had listened to many like it before. And when it was finished, brokenly and in tears, he put forth his hand on the shoulder of Morocco Kate and said:

"Now, Kate, let's get down to business. Are you willing to help me finish this up?"

"I'll do all I can, Colonel Ashley. But I don't see how we're going to find this devil of a Jean."

"Leave that to me. Now where can I find you when I want you--in a hurry, mind. I may want you in a great hurry. Where can I find you?"

"I'm stopping in the village. I'll arrange to be within call for the next few days. Will it take long?"

"No, not very. If I can I'll clean it all up tomorrow. Things are beginning to clear up. And now allow me the pleasure of walking back to town with you. It's getting late and beginning to rain. I have an umbrella, and you haven't."

And through the rain which began to fall, as though it might wash away some of the sordid sin that had been told of in the darkness, the strangely different couple walked through the dark night, Morocco Kate as an ally of Colonel Ashley.

The clean, fresh sun was shining in through the windows of Colonel Ashley's room at The Haven when he awakened the next morning. As he sprang up and made ready for his bath he called toward the next apartment:

"Are you up, Jack?"

"Just getting. Any rush?"

"Well, I think this may be our busy day, and again it may not. Better tumble out."

"Just as you say. How you feeling, Colonel?"

"Never better. I feel just like fishing, and you--"

"'Nough said. I'm with you."

And then, as he started toward his bath, the colonel saw a dirty slip of paper under the door of his room.

"Ha!" he ejaculated. "Another printed message. The writer is getting impatient. I think it's time to act."

And he read:

"Why does not the great detective arrest the poisoner of her father? If he will look behind the book case he will find something that will prove everything--the poison book and--something else."

The printed scrawl was signed: "Justice."

"Well, 'Justice,' I'll do as you say, for once," said the colonel softly, and there was a grim smile on his face.

And so it came about that after his bath and a breakfast Colonel Ashley, winking mysteriously to Jack Young, indicated to his helper that he was wanted in the library.

"What is it?" asked Jack, when they were alone in the room. "A new clew?"

"No, just a blind trail, but I want to clean it up. Help me move out some of the bookcases."

"Good night! Some job! Are you looking for a secret passage, or is there a body concealed here?" and Jack laughed as he took hold of some of the heavy furniture and helped the colonel move it.

Not until they had lifted out the third massive case of volumes was their search successful. There was a little thud, as though something had fallen to the floor, and, looking, the colonel said:

"I have it."

He reached in and brought out a thin volume. Its title page was inscribed "The Poisonous Plants of New Jersey."

Something was in the book--something more bulky than a mere marker; and, opening the slender volume at page 4, a spray of dried leaves and some thin, whitish roots were disclosed.

"Somebody trying to press wild flowers?" asked Jack. "Why all this trouble for that? Hum! Doesn't smell like violets," he added, as he picked up the spray of leaves and roots.

"No, it doesn't," agreed the colonel. "But if you are not a little careful in handling it you'll be a fit subject for a bunch of violets--tied with crepe."

"You mean--"

Jack was startled, and he dropped the dried leaves on the library floor.

"A specimen of the water hemlock," went on the colonel. "One of the deadliest poisons of the plant world. And as we don't want any one else to suffer the fate of Socrates, I'll put this away."

He looked at the compound leaves, the dried flowers, small, but growing in the characteristic large umbels, and at the cluster of fleshy roots, though now pressed flat, and noted the hollow stems of the plant itself. The bunch of what had been verdure once had made a greenish, yellow stain in the book, which, as the colonel noted, was from the local public library, and bore the catalogue number 58 C. H.--I6I*.

"Well, maybe you see through it, but I don't," confessed Jack. "Now, what's the next move?"

"Get these book cases back where they belong."

This was done, and then the colonel, sitting down to rest, for the labor was not slight, went on:

"You are sure that the French chauffeur has been told that The Haven is to be closed, and that he will be no longer required here, nor in the city? That he must leave at once though his month is not up?"

"Oh, yes, I heard Miss Viola tell him that herself. She told me she didn't see why you wanted that done, but as you had charge of the case the house would be closed, even if they had to open it again, for they stay here until late in the fall, you know.

"Yes, I know. Then you are sure Forette thinks they are all going away and that he will have to go, too?"

"Oh, yes, he's all packed. Been paid off, too, I believe, for he was sporting a roll of bills."

"And he is to see Mazi--when?"

"This evening."

"Very good. Now I don't want you to let him out of your sight. Stick to him like a life insurance agent on the trail of a prospect. Don't let him suspect, of course, but follow him when he goes to see the pretty little French girl to-night, and stay within call."

"Very good. Is that all?"

"For now, yes."

"What are you going to do, Colonel?"

"Me? I'm going fishing. I haven't thrown a line in over a week, and I'm afraid I'll forget how. Yes, I'm going fishing, but I'll see you some time to-night."

And a little later Shag was electrified by his master's call:

"Get things ready!"

"Good lan' ob massy, Colonel, sah! Are we suah gwine fishin'?"

"That's what we are, Shag. Lively, boy!"

"I'se runnin', sah, dat's whut I'se doin'! I'se runnin'!" And Shag's hands fairly trembled with eagerness, while the colonel, opening a little green book, read:

"Of recreation there is none
So free as fishing is alone;

All other pastimes do no less
Than mind and body both possess;
My hand alone my work can do,
So I can fish and study too!"

"Old Isaac never wrote a truer word than that!" chuckled the colonel. "And now for a little studying."

And presently he was beside a quiet stream.

Luck was with the colonel and Shag that day, for when they returned to The Haven the creel carried by the colored man squeaked at its willow corners, for it bore a goodly mess of fish.

"Oh, Colonel, I've been so anxious to see you!" exclaimed Viola, when the detective greeted her after he had directed Shag to take the fish to the kitchen.

"Sorry I delayed so long afield," he answered with a gallant bow. "But the sport was too good to leave. What is it, my dear? Has anything happened?" Her face was anxious.

"Well, not exactly happened," she answered; "but I don't know what it means. And it seems so terrible! Look. I just discovered this--or rather, it was handed to me by one of the maids a little while ago," and she held out the postal from the library, telling of the overdue book.

"Well?" asked the colonel, though he could guess what was coming.

"Why, I haven't drawn a book from the library here for a long time," went on Viola. "I did once or twice, but that was when the library was first opened, some years ago. This postal is dated a week ago, but the maid just gave it to me."

"Very likely it was mislaid."

"That's what I supposed. But I went at once to the library, and I found that the book had been taken out on my card. And, oh, Colonel Ashley, it is a book on--poisons!"

"I know it, my dear."

"You know it! And did you think--"

"Now don't get excited. Come, I'll show you the very book. It's been here for some time, and I've known all about it. In fact I have a copy of it that I got from New York. There isn't anything to be worried about."

"But a book on poisons--poisonous plants it is, as I found out at the library--and poor father was killed by some mysterious poison! Oh--"

She was rapidly verging on an attack of hysterics, and the colonel led her gently to the dining room whence, in a little while, she emerged, pale, but otherwise self-possessed.

"Then you really want Aunt Mary and me to go away?" she asked.

"Yes, for a day or so. Make it appear that the house is closed for the season. You dismissed Forette, didn't you, as I suggested?"

"Yes, and paid him in full. I never want to see him again. He's been so insolent of late--he'd hardly do a thing I asked him. And he looked at me in such a queer, leering, impudent way."

"Don't worry about that, my dear. Everything will soon be all right."

"And will--will Harry be cleared?"

The colonel did not have time to answer, for Miss Mary Carwell appeared just then, lamenting the many matters that must be attended to on the closing of the house for even a short time. The colonel left her and Viola to talk it over by themselves.

On slowly moving pinions, a lone osprey beat its way against a quartering south-east wind to the dead tree where the little birds waited impatiently in the nest, giving vent to curious, whistling sounds. Slowly the osprey flew, for it had played in great luck that day, and had swooped down on a fish that would make a meal for him and his mate and the little ones. The fish was not yet dead, but every now and then would contort its length in an effort to escape from the talons which were thrust deeper and deeper into it, making bright spots of blood on the scaly sides.

And a man, walking through the sand, looked up, and in the last rays of the setting sun saw the drops of blood on the sides of the fish.

"A good kill, old man! A good kill!" he said aloud, and as though the osprey could hear him. "A mighty good kill!"

When it was dark a procession of figures began to wend its way over the lonely moor and among the sand dunes to where a tiny cottage nestled in a lonely spot on the beach. From the cottage a cheerful light shone, and now and then a pretty girl went to the door to look out. Seeing nothing, she went back and sat beside a table, on which gleamed a lamp.

By the light of it a woman was knitting, her needles flying in and out of the wool. The girl took up some sewing, but laid it down again and again, to go to the door and peer out.

"He is not coming yet, Mazi?" asked the woman in French.

"No, mamma, but he will. He said he would. Oh, I am so happy with him! I love him so! He is all life to me!"

"May you ever feel like that!" murmured the older woman.

Soon after that, the first of the figures in the procession reached the little cottage. The girl flew to the door, crying:

"Jean! Jean! What made you so late?"

"I could not help it, sweetheart. I but waited to get the last of my wages. Now I am paid, and we shall go on our honeymoon!"

"Oh, Jean! I am so happy!"

"And I, too, Mazi!" and the man drew the girl to him, a strange light shining in his eyes.

They sat down just outside the little cottage, where the gleam from the lamp would not reflect on them too strongly, and talked of many things. Of old things that are ever new, and of new things that are destined to be old.

The second figure of the procession that seemed to make the lonely cottage on the moor a rendezvous that evening, was not far behind that of the lover. It was a figure of a man in a natty blue serge suit. A panama hat of expensive make sat jauntily on top of his head on which curled close, heavy black hair.

"I wonder if the colonel is coming?" mused Jack Young, as he stopped to let Jean Forette hurry on a little in advance. Then a backward lance told him that two other figures were joining the procession. These last two--a man and a woman--walked more slowly, and they did not talk, except now and then to pass a few words.

"Then the marriage was legal, after all?" the woman asked.

"Yes, Kate, it was," answered Colonel Ashley. "You are his lawful wife."

"And he only told me I wasn't, so as to shame me--to make me leave him, and render me desperate?"

"That, and for other reasons. But the fact remains that you are his wife."

"And this other ceremony--this other woman?"

"No legal wife at all."

"I am sorry for her."

"Yes, she is but a girl. If I had known in time I might have stopped it. But it is too late now. Is he there, Jack?" he asked, as he joined the man in the panama hat.

"Yes, sitting outside with Mazi. Going to close in?"

"Might as well. Watch him carefully. He's desperate, and--"

"I know--full of dope. Well I'm ready for him."

And so the trio--the last of the procession, if we except Fate--went closer to the cottage whence so cheerfully gleamed the light.

"Who is there? What do you want?"

It was the snarling voice of Jean Forette, late chauffeur for the Carwells, challenging.

"Who is it?" he cried.

The three figures came on.

Suddenly there was a blinding flash, and the gleam from a powerful electric torch shone in the faces of Jack Young, Morocco Kate and Colonel Ashley.

There was a gasp of surprise and terror from the man beside Mazi--the man who had thrust out the torch to see who it was advancing and closing in on him through the darkness.

"Ah!" sneered the Frenchman, recovering his self-possession. "It is my friend the officer. Ah, I am glad to see you--but just now--not!" and he seemed to spit out the words.

"Maybe not. I can't always come when I'm expected, nor where I'm wanted," said Colonel Ashley coolly. "Now, my friend--Jack!" he cried sharply.

"I've got him, Colonel," was the cool answer, and there was a cry of agony from the chauffeur as his wrist was turned, almost to the breaking point, while there dropped from his paralyzed hand a magazine pistol, thudding to the sand at his feet.

"Go on, Colonel," said Jack, who had slipped off to one side, out of the focus of the glaring light, just in time to prevent Jean Forette from using the weapon he had quickly taken from a side pocket. "Go on, close in. I've drawn his stinger."

"Messieurs, what does this mean?" demanded the girl beside Jean. "Who are you? What do you want? Ah, it is you--and you!" and she turned first to Colonel

Ashley and then to Jack Young. "You who have talked so kindly to me--who have asked me so much about--about my husband! It is you who come like thieves and assassins! Speak to them, Jean! Tell them to go!"

The Frenchman was breathing heavily, for Jack had a merciless grip on him.

"Speak to them, Jean!" implored the girl, while her mother, standing in the door with her knitting, looked wonderingly on. "Why do they come to take you like a traitor?"

"It--it's all a mistake!" panted the chauffeur.

"You've got me wrong, messieurs. I--I didn't do it. It was all an accident. He--I--Oh, my God! You!" and he started back as Morocco Kate stepped toward him, pulling from her face the veil that had covered it when the glaring light showed. Jack Young now held the electric torch.

"You!" he murmured hoarsely.

"Yes, I!" she cried. "The woman you kicked out like a sick dog! I've found you at last, and now I'll make you suffer all I did and more--you--devil!"

"Softly, Kate, softly!" murmured the colonel. But she did not heed him.

"You--you spawn of hell!" she cried. "It was you who sent me down where I am--where not a decent woman will look at me and a decent man won't speak to me. You did it--you left me to rot in my shame so you could find some one else--some one younger and prettier to fondle and kiss and--Oh, God!"

She sank in a shuddering heap on the sand at the feet of the man who had broken her body and spirit, and lay there, sobbing out her anger.

"Let her stay there a little," said the colonel softly. "She'll feel better after this outburst."

"Jean! Jean! What is it all about?" begged the girl who still maintained her place beside him. "Oh, speak to me! Tell me! Who is she?" and she pointed to the huddled figure on the sand.

"I'll tell you who she is," said Colonel Ashley. "She is the legal wife of Jean Carnot, alias Jean Forette, and--"

A scream from Mazi stopped him.

"Tell me it isn't true, Jean! Tell me it isn't true!" begged the girl.

Jean Carnot did not speak.

"He knows it is true," said the colonel. "And now, my French auto friend, I've come to take you into custody on a charge of--"

"I didn't do it! I didn't do it!" cried the man. "I swear I didn't do it. I was going to throw the glass away but he grabbed it from me, and--"

"I arrest you on a charge of bigamy," went on the calm voice of Colonel Ashley. And then, as he saw Mazi stagger as though about to fall, he added:

"All right, Jack. I'll take care of her. You put the bracelets on him. And see that they're good and tight. We don't want him slipping out and getting married again. He doesn't have much regard for bonds of any sort, matrimonial or legal."

And then he lifted poor, little Mazi up and carried her into the cottage, while Morocco Kate got slowly to her feet and sat down on the bench in the darkest shadows, sobbing.

CHAPTER XXIV. STILL WATERS

The records show that Henri Margot, alias Jean Carnot alias Jean Forette was married to Isabel Pelubit in Paris on March 17, four years ago, and that she died under suspicious circumstances three months later, leaving her husband all of a snug little fortune she possessed.

"All lies, monsieur--all lies! I do not believe anything you tell me!"

"Well, that's very foolish of you, Mazi, for you can easily prove for yourself everything I tell you, and it will be better for you, in the end, if you do believe."

"I do not. But go on with--more lies!" She shrugged her shoulders contemptuously.

Colonel Ashley leafed over a sheaf of papers he had spread out on the table in front of him. He and Mazi sat in a room in police headquarters in Lakeside. It was the day following the procession to the cottage on the moor.

"The records show," went on the detective, "that Henri Margot was arrested in Paris, charged with having poisoned his wife so that he might spend on another woman the money she possessed. But he was not convicted, chiefly because the chemists could not agree on the kind of poison that had caused death."

"All lies--I do not believe," said Mazi, stolidly.

"Um!" mused the colonel. "Well, Mazi, you're more stubborn than I thought. But it doesn't make any difference to me, you know. I'm paid for all this. Now let's see--what's next? Oh, yes. Then the records show that Henri, or Jean, whichever you choose to call him, came to this country. He fell in love with a pretty girl--she wasn't as pretty as you, Mazi, I'll say that--but he fell in love with her and married her--or pretended to. However, it was a fake ceremony, and she couldn't prove anything when he had spent all her money and tossed her aside. So there wasn't anything we could do to him that time."

"More lies," said Mazi, calmly--or at least with the appearance of calmness.

"The records show," went on the inexorable voice of Colonel Ashley, "that next Jean Carnot, as he called himself then, became infatuated with a pretty girl-- and this time I'll say she was just about as pretty as you, Mazi--and her name was Annie Tighe. She was an Irish girl, and she insisted on being married by a priest, so there wasn't any faking there. Jean was properly married at least."

"What do I care for all these lies?" sneered the girl, impatiently tapping her foot on the floor. "Why do you bore me? I am not interested! I should like to see Jean. Ha! Where have you put him?"

"You'll see him soon enough, Mazi. I've got just a few more records to show you, and then I'm done. Now we come to the time when, after he found he couldn't get out of a legal marriage, Jean put his foot in it, so to speak. He was tied right, this time, so he took refuge in a lie when he wanted to shake off the bonds of matrimony, as my friend Jack Young would say. He told his wife--and she was his wife, and is yet--he told her the ceremony was a fake, that the priest was a false one, in his pay."

"All lies! What do I care?" sneered Mazi, again shrugging her shoulders.

"Well, now let's get along. After our friend Jean found he was tired of his wife he shamed her into leaving him and she went--well, that isn't pleasant to dwell on, either. Except that he's the villain responsible for her going to the dogs. He sent her there just as he would have sent you, Mazi, except for what has happened."

"You mean he is not my husband?"

"Not in the least."

"I do not believe you. It is all lies. These women are but jealous. Proceed."

"That's about all there is to it, Mazi, except to show you the letter from your own priest, who confirms the fact that the priest who married Jean Carnot and An-nie Tighe was legally authorized to do so, both by the laws of his own church and those of New York State, where the ceremony took place. You will believe Father Capoti, won't you?" and he laid beside the girl a letter which she read eagerly.

This time she said nothing about lies, but her face turned deadly pale.

"And this is the last exhibit," went on the colonel, as he laid a photograph before Mazi. It showed a man and a girl, evidently in their wedding finery, and the face of the man was that of Jean Forette, and that of the girl was of the woman who had groveled on the sand at the feet of the chauffeur the night before,--Morocco Kate.

"Look on the back," suggested the detective, and when Mazi turned the photograph over she read:

"The happiest day of my life--Jean Carnot."

"If you happen to have any love letters from him--and I guess you have," went on the colonel, "you might compare the writing and--"

"I have no need, monsieur," was the low answer. "I--God help me.--I believe now! Oh, the liar! If I could see him now--"

"I rather thought you'd want to," murmured the colonel. "Bring him in!" he called.

The door opened, and, handcuffed to a stalwart officer, in slunk Jean of the many names.

Mazi sprang to her feet, her face livid. She would have leaped at the prisoner, but the colonel held her back. But he could not hold back the flood of voluble French that poured from her lips.

"Liar! Dog!" she hissed at him. "And so you have deceived me as you deceived others! You lied--and I thought he lied!" and she motioned to the colonel. "Oh, what a silly fool I've been! But now my eyes are open! I see! I see!"

With a quick gesture, before the colonel could stop her, she tore in half the picture that had swept away all her doubts.

"Mustn't do that!" chided the colonel, as he picked up the pieces which she was about to grind under her feet. "I'll need that at the trial."

"You--you beast!" whispered the girl, but the whisper seemed louder than a shout would have been. "You beast! No longer will I lie for you. Why you wanted me to, I do not know. Yes, I do! It was so that you might be with some one else when you should have been with me. Listen, all of you!" she cried, as she flung her arms wide. "No longer will I shield him. He told me to say that he was with me when that golf man--Monsieur Carwell died--before he died--but he was not. No more will I lie for you, Jean of the many names! You were not with me! I did not even see you that day. Bah! You were kissing some other fool maybe! Oh, my God! I--I--"

And the colonel gently laid the trembling, shrieking girl down on a bench, while the eyes of the shrinking figure of Jean the chauffeur followed every movement.

He raised his free hand, and seemed to be struggling to loosen his collar that appeared to choke him. For a moment the attention of Colonel Ashley was turned toward Mazi, who was sobbing frantically. Then, when he saw that she was becoming quieter, he turned to the prisoner.

"You heard all that went on, I know," said the detective. "That's why I put you in the next room."

"Yes, I heard," was the calm answer. "But what of it? You can prove nothing only that women are fools. I shall hire a good lawyer and--poof! What would you have--a man must live. Bigamy, it is not such a serious charge."

"Oh, no, there are worse," said the colonel calmly. "You're going to hear one presently. She told me just what I wanted to know, as I thought she would if I could get her roused up enough against you. So, you weren't riding, as you said, with her the day Mr. Carwell came to his end. I never thought you were, Jean of the many names. And now, officer, if you'll take him back and lock him up, I guess this will be about all to-day."

"But I want to get bail!" exclaimed the prisoner. "I have a right to be bailed. My lawyer says so."

"There isn't any bail in your case," said the detective.

"Pooh! Nonsense! Bigamy, it is not such a serious charge."

"Oh, didn't I tell you? I meant to," said the colonel gently. "You're under another accusation now. Jean Forette, to call you by your latest alias, you're under arrest, charged with the murder, by poison, of Horace Carwell, and I think we'll come pretty near convicting you by the testimony of Mazi. Ah, would you--not quite!"

He struck down the hand the prisoner had raised to his mouth, and there rolled over the floor a little capsule. The top came off and a white powder spilled out.

"Don't step on it!" warned the colonel as several other officers came in to assist in handling the prisoner, who was struggling violently. "It's probably the same poison, mixed with French dope, that killed Mr. Carwell. Jean had it hidden in the collar band of his shirt ready for emergencies. But you shan't cheat the chair, Jean of the many names!"

They led the Frenchman away, struggling and screaming that he was innocent, that it was all a mistake. By turns he prayed and blasphemed horribly.

"That's the way they usually do when they can't get a shot of their dope," said the jail physician, after he had visited the prisoner and given him a big dose of bromide. "He'll be a wreck from now on. He's rotten with some French drug, the like of which I've never seen used before."

The coroner's jury had been called together again. Once more the sordid evidence was gone over, but this time there was more of it, and it had to do with a story told weepingly on the stand by Mazi, and corroborated by Colonel Ashley.

And a little later, when the jury filed in, it was to report:

"We find that Horace Carwell came to his death through poison administered by Jean Carnot, alias Jean Forette, with intent to kill."

And a little later, when the grand jury had indicted him, the man's nerve failed him completely, because his supply of drug was kept from him and he babbled the truth like a child, weeping.

He had stolen two hundred dollars from the pocketbook of Mr. Carwell the day before the championship golf game, and, the crime having been detected by Viola's father, the chauffeur had been given twenty-four hours in which to return the money or be exposed. He was in financial straits, and, as developed later, had stolen elsewhere, so that he feared arrest and exposure and was at his wit's end. He had spent much of the money on Mazi, whom he induced to go through a secret marriage ceremony with him.

Then Jean, like a cornered rat, and crazy from the drug he had filled himself with, conceived the idea of poisoning Mr. Carwell. That would prevent arrest and exposure, he reasoned.

The chauffeur found his opportunity when he was ordered to stop the big red, white and blue car at a roadhouse just prior to the game. Mr. Carwell was thirsty, and in bad humor, and ordered the chauffeur to bring out some champagne. It was into this that Jean slipped the poison, mixed with some of his own drug which he knew would retard the action of the deadly stuff for some time. And it worked just as he had expected, dropping Mr. Carwell in his tracks about two hours later, as he made the stroke that won the game.

"But how did a chauffeur know so much about poison and dope as to be able to mix a dose that would fool the chemists?" asked Jack Young of his chief, a little later.

"Jean's father was a French chemist, and a clever one. It was there that Jean learned to mix the powder dope he took, and he learned much of other drugs. I suspect, though I can't prove it, that he poisoned his first wife. A devil all the way through," answered the colonel.

"But what did Bartlett and Mr. Carwell quarrel about so seriously that Bartlett wouldn't tell?"

"It was about Morocco Kate. Harry learned that she had sold Mr. Carwell a set of books, and, knowing her reputation, he feared she might have compromised Mr. Carwell because of his sporting instincts. So Harry begged Viola's father to come out plainly and repudiate the book contract. But Mr. Carwell was stiff about it, and told Harry to mind his own business. That was all. Naturally, after Harry found that Morocco Kate really was mixed up in the case--though innocently enough--he didn't want to tell what the quarrel was about for fear of bringing out a scandal. As a matter of fact there never was any shadow of one."

"And the mysterious notes to you about Viola having a poison book?"

"All sent by Jean, of course, to throw suspicion on her. I heard it rumored, in more than one quarter, that Viola strongly disapproved of her father's sporty life, and it was said she had stated that she would rather see him dead than disgraced. Which was natural enough. I've said that myself many a time about friends.

"Jean found Miss Carwell's library card, and took out the poison book in her name, afterward anonymously sending me word about it. I admit that, for a moment, I was staggered, but it was only for a moment. Here is what I found in his room."

Colonel Ashley held out a piece of paper. There was no writing on it, but it bore the indentations, identical with one of the penciled, printed notes.

"He wrote it on a pad," said the colonel, "and tore off the top sheet. But he used a hard pencil, and the impression went through. Just one of the few mistakes he made."

"Fine work on your part, Colonel."

"As for Captain Poland, the money transactions did look a bit queer, but we've since found the receipt and it's all right. A new clerk in Carwell's office had mislaid it. It wasn't Blossom's fault, either. He's a weak chap, but not morally bad. The worst thing he did was to fall for Morocco Kate. But better men than he have done the same thing. However, they won't again."

"Why, she hasn't--"

"Oh, no; nothing as rash as that. She's going to take a new route, that's all. She's a natural born saleswoman, and I've gotten her a place with a big firm that owes me some favors."

"And did Blossom come through 'clean' as he said he would?"

"He did, and he didn't. It seems that a year or so ago he inherited eleven thousand dollars. He invested half of the money in copper and made quite a little on the deal. Then, a short while before Carwell died, he got Blossom to lend him some money, which he was to pay back inside of a month or two. When Carwell's death occurred, Blossom was in financial difficulties on account of the demands of Morocco Kate. He could not get hold of the money he had invested, nor could he get hold of the money he had loaned Carwell. In his quandary he took certain securities belonging to Carwell and hypothecated them, expecting, later on, to make good as soon as he got some of his own money back. Of course the whole transaction was a rather shady one, and yet I still believe the young fellow wanted to be honest."

"How does he stand now?"

"Oh, he has managed to get hold of some of his money, and with that got back the Carwell securities. And, of course, the Carwell estate will have to settle with him later on, and Viola and Miss Mary Carwell are going to keep him in his present position.

"He and Minnie Webb are to be married very soon--which reminds me that I have an invitation for you."

"For me?"

"Yes. It's to the wedding of Viola and Harry Bartlett. The affair is going to be very quiet, so you can come without worrying about a dress-suit, which I know you hate as much as I do."

"I should say so!"

"And did Bartlett's uncle really mulct Mr. Carwell in that insurance deal?"

"Well, that's according to how you look at the ins and outs of modern high finance. It was a case of skin or be skinned, and I guess Harry's uncle skinned first and beat Mr. Carwell to it. It was six of one and a half dozen of the other. The deal would have been legitimate either way it swung, but it made Mr. Carwell sore for a time, and that, more than anything else, made him quarrel with Harry when Morocco Kate was mentioned."

The letters in the secret drawer, which had so worried Viola, proved to be very simple, after all. They referred to a certain local committee, organized for an international financial deal which Mr. Carwell was endeavoring to swing with Captain Poland. The latter thought, because of his intimate association with Viola's father, that the latter might use his influence in the captain's love affair. But that was not to be. So Viola's worry was for naught in this respect.

And so the golf course mystery was cleared up, though even to the end, when he had paid the penalty for his crime, the chauffeur would not reveal the nature of the poison he had mixed with the dope which had made him a wreck.

Beside the still water, that ran in a deep eddy where the stream curved under the trees, Colonel Ashley sat fishing. Beside him on the grass a little boy, with black, curling hair, and deep, brown eyes, sat clicking a spare reel. Off to one side, in the shade, a colored man snored.

"Hey, Unk Bob!" lisped the little boy. "Don't Shag make an awful funny noise?"

"He certainly does, Gerry! He certainly does!"

"Just 'ike a saw bitin' wood."

"That's it, Gerry! I'll have to speak to Shag about it. But now, Gerry, my boy, you must keep still while Unk Bob catches a big fish."

"Ess, I keep still. But you tell me a 'tory after?"

"Yes, I'll tell you a story."

"Will you tell me how you was a fissin', an' a big white ball comed an', zipp! knocked ze fiss off your hook? Will you tell me dat fiss 'tory?"

"Yes, Gerry, I'll tell you that if you'll be quiet now."

And Shag's snores mingled with the gentle whisper of the water and the sighing of the wind in the willows.

And then, when the creel had been emptied and Colonel Robert Lee Ashley sat on the porch with Gerry Ashley Bartlett snugly curled in his lap and told the story of the golf ball and the fish, while Shag cleaned the fish fresh from the brook, two figures stood in the door of the house.

"Look, Harry!" softly said the woman's voice. "Isn't that a picture?"

"It is, indeed, my dear. Gerry adores the colonel."

"No wonder. I do myself. Oh, by the way, Harry, I had a letter from Captain Poland today."

"Did you? Where is he now?" asked Harry Bartlett, as his eyes turned lovingly from the figure of his little son in the colonel's lap to that of his wife beside him.

"In the Philippines. He says he thinks he'll settle there. He was so pleased that we named the Boy after him."

"Was he?" and then, as his wife went over to steal up behind her little son and clasp her hands over his eyes, the man, standing alone on the porch, murmured:

"Poor Gerry!" And it was of the lonely man in the Philippines he was speaking.

In the silent shadows Colonel Robert Lee Ashley fished again. This time he was alone, save for the omnipresent Shag. And as the latter netted a fish, and slipped it into the grass-lined creel, he spoke and said:

"Mr. Young, he done ast me to-day when we gwine back t' de city. He done say dere's a big case waitin' fo' you, Colonel, sah. When is we-all gwine back?"

"Never, Shag!"

"Nevah, Colonel, sah?"

"No. I'm going to spend all the rest of my life fishing. I've resigned from the detective business! I'll never take another case Never!"

And Shag chuckled silently as he closed the creel.

The Codes Of Hammurabi And Moses
W. W. Davies

QTY

The discovery of the Hammurabi Code is one of the greatest achievements of archaeology, and is of paramount interest, not only to the student of the Bible, but also to all those interested in ancient history...

Religion **ISBN:** *1-59462-338-4*   **Pages:132**
MSRP $12.95

The Theory of Moral Sentiments
Adam Smith

QTY

This work from 1749. contains original theories of conscience amd moral judgment and it is the foundation for systemof morals.

Philosophy **ISBN:** *1-59462-777-0*   **Pages:536**
MSRP $19.95

Jessica's First Prayer
Hesba Stretton

QTY

In a screened and secluded corner of one of the many railway-bridges which span the streets of London there could be seen a few years ago, from five o'clock every morning until half past eight, a tidily set-out coffee-stall, consisting of a trestle and board, upon which stood two large tin cans, with a small fire of charcoal burning under each so as to keep the coffee boiling during the early hours of the morning when the work-people were thronging into the city on their way to their daily toil...

Childrens **ISBN:** *1-59462-373-2*

Pages:84
MSRP $9.95

My Life and Work
Henry Ford

QTY

Henry Ford revolutionized the world with his implementation of mass production for the Model T automobile. Gain valuable business insight into his life and work with his own auto-biography... "We have only started on our development of our country we have not as yet, with all our talk of wonderful progress, done more than scratch the surface. The progress has been wonderful enough but..."

Biographies/ **ISBN:** *1-59462-198-5*

Pages:300
MSRP $21.95

The Art of Cross-Examination
Francis Wellman

QTY

I presume it is the experience of every author, after his first book is published upon an important subject, to be almost overwhelmed with a wealth of ideas and illustrations which could readily have been included in his book, and which to his own mind, at least, seem to make a second edition inevitable. Such certainly was the case with me; and when the first edition had reached its sixth impression in five months, I rejoiced to learn that it seemed to my publishers that the book had met with a sufficiently favorable reception to justify a second and considerably enlarged edition. ..

Reference   ISBN: *1-59462-647-2*

Pages:412

MSRP $19.95

On the Duty of Civil Disobedience
Henry David Thoreau

QTY

Thoreau wrote his famous essay, On the Duty of Civil Disobedience, as a protest against an unjust but popular war and the immoral but popular institution of slave-owning. He did more than write—he declined to pay his taxes, and was hauled off to gaol in consequence. Who can say how much this refusal of his hastened the end of the war and of slavery ?

Law   ISBN: *1-59462-747-9*

Pages:48

MSRP $7.45

Dream Psychology Psychoanalysis for Beginners
Sigmund Freud

QTY

Sigmund Freud, born Sigismund Schlomo Freud (May 6, 1856 - September 23, 1939), was a Jewish-Austrian neurologist and psychiatrist who co-founded the psychoanalytic school of psychology. Freud is best known for his theories of the unconscious mind, especially involving the mechanism of repression; his redefinition of sexual desire as mobile and directed towards a wide variety of objects; and his therapeutic techniques, especially his understanding of transference in the therapeutic relationship and the presumed value of dreams as sources of insight into unconscious desires.

Dream Psychology
Psychoanalysis for Beginners

Sigmund Freud

Psychology   ISBN: *1-59462-905-6*

Pages:196

MSRP $15.45

The Miracle of Right Thought
Orison Swett Marden

QTY

Believe with all of your heart that you will do what you were made to do. When the mind has once formed the habit of holding cheerful, happy, prosperous pictures, it will not be easy to form the opposite habit. It does not matter how improbable or how far away this realization may see, or how dark the prospects may be, if we visualize them as best we can, as vividly as possible, hold tenaciously to them and vigorously struggle to attain them, they will gradually become actualized, realized in the life. But a desire, a longing without endeavor, a yearning abandoned or held indifferently will vanish without realization.

Self Help   ISBN: *1-59462-644-8*

Pages:360

MSRP $25.45

The Rosicrucian Cosmo-Conception Mystic Christianity *by Max Heindel* ISBN: *1-59462-188-8* **$38.95**
The Rosicrucian Cosmo-conception is not dogmatic, neither does it appeal to any other authority than the reason of the student. It is: not controversial, but is: sent forth in the, hope that it may help to clear... New Age/Religion Pages 646

Abandonment To Divine Providence *by Jean-Pierre de Caussade* ISBN: *1-59462-228-0* **$25.95**
"The Rev. Jean Pierre de Caussade was one of the most remarkable spiritual writers of the Society of Jesus in France in the 18th Century. His death took place at Toulouse in 1751. His works have gone through many editions and have been republished... Inspirational/Religion Pages 400

Mental Chemistry *by Charles Haanel* ISBN: *1-59462-192-6* **$23.95**
Mental Chemistry allows the change of material conditions by combining and appropriately utilizing the power of the mind. Much like applied chemistry creates something new and unique out of careful combinations of chemicals the mastery of mental chemistry... New Age Pages 354

The Letters of Robert Browning and Elizabeth Barret Barrett 1845-1846 vol II ISBN: *1-59462-193-4* **$35.95**
by Robert Browning and Elizabeth Barrett Biographies Pages 596

Gleanings In Genesis (volume I) *by Arthur W. Pink* ISBN: *1-59462-130-6* **$27.45**
Appropriately has Genesis been termed "the seed plot of the Bible" for in it we have, in germ form, almost all of the great doctrines which are afterwards fully developed in the books of Scripture which follow... Religion/Inspirational Pages 420

The Master Key *by L. W. de Laurence* ISBN: *1-59462-001-6* **$30.95**
In no branch of human knowledge has there been a more lively increase of the spirit of research during the past few years than in the study of Psychology, Concentration and Mental Discipline. The requests for authentic lessons in Thought Control, Mental Discipline and... New Age/Business Pages 422

The Lesser Key Of Solomon Goetia *by L. W. de Laurence* ISBN: *1-59462-092-X* **$9.95**
This translation of the first book of the "Lemegton" which is now for the first time made accessible to students of Talismanic Magic was done, after careful collation and edition, from numerous Ancient Manuscripts in Hebrew, Latin, and French... New Age/Occult Pages 92

Rubaiyat Of Omar Khayyam *by Edward Fitzgerald* ISBN:*1-59462-332-5* **$13.95**
Edward Fitzgerald, whom the world has already learned, in spite of his own efforts to remain within the shadow of anonymity, to look upon as one of the rarest poets of the century, was born at Bredfield, in Suffolk, on the 31st of March, 1809. He was the third son of John Purcell... Music Pages 172

Ancient Law *by Henry Maine* ISBN: *1-59462-128-4* **$29.95**
The chief object of the following pages is to indicate some of the earliest ideas of mankind, as they are reflected in Ancient Law, and to point out the relation of those ideas to modern thought. Religiom/History Pages 452

Far-Away Stories *by William J. Locke* ISBN: *1-59462-129-2* **$19.45**
"Good wine needs no bush, but a collection of mixed vintages does. And this book is just such a collection. Some of the stories I do not want to remain buried for ever in the museum files of dead magazine-numbers an author's not unpardonable vanity..." Fiction Pages 272

Life of David Crockett *by David Crockett* ISBN: *1-59462-250-7* **$27.45**
"Colonel David Crockett was one of the most remarkable men of the times in which he lived. Born in humble life, but gifted with a strong will, an indomitable courage, and unremitting perseverance... Biographies/New Age Pages 424

Lip-Reading *by Edward Nitchie* ISBN: *1-59462-206-X* **$25.95**
Edward B. Nitchie, founder of the New York School for the Hard of Hearing, now the Nitchie School of Lip-Reading, Inc, wrote "LIP-READING Principles and Practice". The development and perfecting of this meritorious work on lip-reading was an undertaking... How-to Pages 400

A Handbook of Suggestive Therapeutics, Applied Hypnotism, Psychic Science ISBN: *1-59462-214-0* **$24.95**
by Henry Munro Health/New Age/Health/Self-help Pages 376

A Doll's House: and Two Other Plays *by Henrik Ibsen* ISBN: *1-59462-112-8* **$19.95**
Henrik Ibsen created this classic when in revolutionary 1848 Rome. Introducing some striking concepts in playwriting for the realist genre, this play has been studied the world over. Fiction/Classics/Plays 308

The Light of Asia *by sir Edwin Arnold* ISBN: *1-59462-204-3* **$13.95**
In this poetic masterpiece, Edwin Arnold describes the life and teachings of Buddha. The man who was to become known as Buddha to the world was born as Prince Gautama of India but he rejected the worldly riches and abandoned the reigns of power when... Religion/History/Biographies Pages 170

The Complete Works of Guy de Maupassant *by Guy de Maupassant* ISBN: *1-59462-157-8* **$16.95**
"For days and days, nights and nights, I had dreamed of that first kiss which was to consecrate our engagement, and I knew not on what spot I should put my lips..." Fiction/Classics Pages 240

The Art of Cross-Examination *by Francis L. Wellman* ISBN: *1-59462-309-0* **$26.95**
Written by a renowned trial lawyer, Wellman imparts his experience and uses case studies to explain how to use psychology to extract desired information through questioning. How-to/Science/Reference Pages 408

Answered or Unanswered? *by Louisa Vaughan* ISBN: *1-59462-248-5* **$10.95**
Miracles of Faith in China Religion Pages 112

The Edinburgh Lectures on Mental Science (1909) *by Thomas* ISBN: *1-59462-008-3* **$11.95**
This book contains the substance of a course of lectures recently given by the writer in the Queen Street Hall, Edinburgh. Its purpose is to indicate the Natural Principles governing the relation between Mental Action and Material Conditions... New Age/Psychology Pages 148

Ayesha *by H. Rider Haggard* ISBN: *1-59462-301-5* **$24.95**
Verily and indeed it is the unexpected that happens! Probably if there was one person upon the earth from whom the Editor of this, and of a certain previous history, did not expect to hear again... Classics Pages 380

Ayala's Angel *by Anthony Trollope* ISBN: *1-59462-352-X* **$29.95**
The two girls were both pretty, but Lucy who was twenty-one who supposed to be simple and comparatively unattractive, whereas Ayala was credited, as her Bombwhat romantic name might show, with poetic charm and a taste for romance. Ayala when her father died was nineteen... Fiction Pages 484

The American Commonwealth *by James Bryce* ISBN: *1-59462-286-8* **$34.45**
An interpretation of American democratic political theory. It examines political mechanics and society from the perspective of Scotsman James Bryce Politics Pages 572

Stories of the Pilgrims *by Margaret P. Pumphrey* ISBN: *1-59462-116-0* **$17.95**
This book explores pilgrims religious oppression in England as well as their escape to Holland and eventual crossing to America on the Mayflower, and their early days in New England... History Pages 268

QTY

The Fasting Cure *by Sinclair Upton*   ISBN: *1-59462-222-1* **$13.95**
*In the Cosmopolitan Magazine for May, 1910, and in the Contemporary Review (London) for April, 1910, I published an article dealing with my experi-
ences in fasting. I have written a great many magazine articles, but never one which attracted so much attention...* New Age/Self Help/Health Pages 164

Hebrew Astrology *by Sepharial*   ISBN: *1-59462-308-2* **$13.45**
*In these days of advanced thinking it is a matter of common observation that we have left many of the old landmarks behind and that we are now pressing
forward to greater heights and to a wider horizon than that which represented the mind-content of our progenitors...* Astrology Pages 144

Thought Vibration or The Law of Attraction in the Thought World   ISBN: *1-59462-127-6* **$12.95**

by William Walker Atkinson   Psychology/Religion Pages 144

Optimism *by Helen Keller*   ISBN: *1-59462-108-X* **$15.95**
*Helen Keller was blind, deaf, and mute since 19 months old, yet famously learned how to overcome these handicaps, communicate with the world, and
spread her lectures promoting optimism. An inspiring read for everyone...* Biographies/Inspirational Pages 84

Sara Crewe *by Frances Burnett*   ISBN: *1-59462-360-0*   **$9.45**
*In the first place, Miss Minchin lived in London. Her home was a large, dull, tall one, in a large, dull square, where all the houses were alike, and all the
sparrows were alike, and where all the door-knockers made the same heavy sound...* Childrens/Classic Pages 88

The Autobiography of Benjamin Franklin *by Benjamin Franklin*   ISBN: *1-59462-135-7* **$24.95**
*The Autobiography of Benjamin Franklin has probably been more extensively read than any other American historical work, and no other book of its kind
has had such ups and downs of fortune. Franklin lived for many years in England, where he was agent...* Biographies/History Pages 332

Name	
Email	
Telephone	
Address	
City, State ZIP	

☐ **Credit Card**   ☐ **Check / Money Order**

Credit Card Number	
Expiration Date	
Signature	

Please Mail to: Book Jungle
PO Box 2226
Champaign, IL 61825
or Fax to: 630-214-0564

ORDERING INFORMATION

web*: www.bookjungle.com*
email*: sales@bookjungle.com*
fax*: 630-214-0564*
mail*: Book Jungle PO Box 2226 Champaign, IL 61825*
or PayPal *to sales@bookjungle.com*

Please contact us for bulk discounts

DIRECT-ORDER TERMS

**20% Discount if You Order
Two or More Books**
Free Domestic Shipping!
Accepted: Master Card, Visa,
Discover, American Express

www.ingramcontent.com/pod-product-compliance
Lightning Source LLC
Chambersburg PA
CBHW080729020726
47503CB00010B/2848